THE
PEKING
TARGET

By Elleston Trevor

CHORUS OF ECHOES

TIGER STREET

A BLAZE OF ROSES

THE PASSION AND THE PITY

GALE FORCE

THE FREEBOOTERS

THE BIG PICK-UP

A PLACE FOR THE WICKED

SQUADRON AIRBORNE

THE KILLING-GROUND

THE VIP

THE PILLARS OF MIDNIGHT

THE FLIGHT OF THE PHOENIX

THE BILLBOARD MADONNA

REDFERN'S MIRACLE

THE PARAGON

THE SHOOT

THE THETA SYNDROME

BLUE JAY SUMMER

THE BURNING SHORE

BURY HIM AMONG KINGS

THE SIBLING

By the same author writing as Adam Hall

THE VOLCANOES OF SAN DOMINGO

THE MANDARIN CYPHER

THE NINTH DIRECTIVE

THE STRIKER PORTFOLIO

THE KOBRA MANIFESTO

THE SINKIANG EXECUTIVE

THE WARSAW DOCUMENT

THE BERLIN MEMORANDUM

THE TANGO BRIEFING

THE SCORPION SIGNAL

⚙ THE ⚙
PEKING
TARGET
⚙

ADAM HALL

Playboy Press

NEW YORK

*The people and events described or depicted in this novel are fictitious and
any resemblance to actual incidents or individuals is unintended and coincidental.*

Manufactured in the United States of America.

First edition

Playboy Press/A Division of PEI Books, Inc.

Library of Congress Cataloging in Publication Data

Trevor, Elleston.
   The Peking target.

   I. Title.
PR6039.R51804 1982   823'.914   81-82460
ISBN 0-87223-755-9   AACR2

82000428

Designed by Tere LoPrete

To my *Sensei*
Shojiro Koyama

THE
PEKING
TARGET

I

LIMBO

✦

For a moment I thought I saw a face; then it was gone.

Chandler, standing beside me, hadn't spoken a word for ten minutes. No one had.

The smell of the river came on the night air, bland and rotten. We went on watching, and I glimpsed a black wet fin disturbing the surface not far from the bank. Bubbles popped in the soft light of the lamps, tracing a regular pattern.

The face came again and I kept my eyes on it, but it must have been a patch of rubbish or something, surfacing on the slow current; it vanished again, fading. From across the river, Big Ben started chiming the prelude to the hour. The air was sultry after the heat of the long summer day.

On our left the small boat was moving downstream, the two men in it paying out the lines to the long net. Someone on the bank swiveled the end floodlight, and we saw an oily black ripple as one of the divers neared the surface and rolled over, going down again. The eleventh chime of the clock faded to silence.

More people were walking down from the bridge, where

they'd left their cars. The police had a barrier halfway along Riverside Walk, to keep them back. The inspector in charge of the operation was standing somewhere on the other side of Chandler, not speaking, leaving it to his team to get on with the job: They obviously knew what they were doing.

I'd never met Chandler before; he was one of the new people, a pale thin man who kept his distance, afraid of questions until he felt more sure of his ground. I'd only asked him a couple of things and he'd stared at me for a long time, as if I were a bloody fool; it was just that he didn't know the answers. None of them knew for certain who it was in the river here.

Tilson had said it was Sinclair when I'd talked to him on the bridge earlier tonight.

The submersible lamps were swinging again, underwater; the divers moved like shadows across the diffused light, nearer the surface now. The men in the boat had started calling to the land crew along the bank.

I hoped to God it wasn't Sinclair. He was one of the best we had.

Higher along the embankment, at the end of the bridge, the police were still taking flash photos of the wrecked car. From the little Tilson had told me, Sinclair—or whoever it was—had been thrown from the car into the river when it had crashed, or had been dragged out of the wreck and dropped off the bridge.

The light was getting brighter now, and soon one of the divers rose like a shark, his black finned body breaking the surface not far downstream; then another came into view and a lamp swung clear of the water and flashed across our eyes before a man on the bank grabbed it and steadied it. We were all leaning forward now, and I heard someone say: "Right. They've got him."

Chandler moved at last, poking his thin face toward the river, where two more divers were surfacing, pulling at the draglines as the land crew took up the slack; then we saw the body as it floated clear of the long net, rolling in the turbulence with its white face showing and then darkening, showing again in the glare of the floods. They hauled him out and lowered him to the walkway, turning him onto his back and gently pulling his legs together. Chandler stooped over him.

An hour ago I'd been with a girl in the Gaslight Club, halfway through a late dinner and getting to know her, one of the Foreign Office staff, the only ones we were allowed to meet when we were on standby, for security reasons. A plainclothes man from the Yard had come in and told me I was wanted, and I didn't argue, because he'd mentioned the name Tilson.

I'd driven straight to the Thames with a police escort and found Tilson standing near the wrecked TR-4.

"Sinclair was coming in from Taiwan," he said plaintively, "with something to tell us, according to his signal from Calcutta. There was some trouble with the plane and he had to switch flights." He gazed unhappily through his horn-rimmed glasses at the diving crew along the river.

"When did he get in?"

"About an hour ago. We'd cleared Customs for him."

Some people from the Yard were taking measurements of the TR-4's position, and bringing flash equipment. We moved away a bit to give them room.

"What was he doing here, for God's sake?" I asked Tilson. I was getting worried. They don't often go for us on our home ground, any more than we go for them at the embassies. Sinclair would have driven straight from the airport to our place in Whitehall if he'd had something so important to say that he couldn't put it in a signal.

"We think he was got at," said Tilson.

"Pretty obvious. He knew how to drive, for Christ's sake." A flashlight popped, freezing the scene, and I noticed some blood on the seat of the crashed car. "Who met him at the airport?" I asked Tilson.

"He landed thirty minutes early. They missed him."

I went cold suddenly. Tilson was keeping an awful lot back, I knew that now, but this was quite bad enough. Someone had let this man fly into London with some vital information in his head and they'd left him without an escort and now he was down there somewhere among the dead cats and the weeds with his mouth shut forever.

Tilson shuffled his feet, and I noticed he'd come here in such a hurry that he was still wearing the plaid slippers he used at the office. "I suppose what happened," he said miserably, "is that he picked them up in his mirror on his way to our place and led them clear just in time. Led them as far as here." Glass crackled under the men's feet as they moved around the car with their cameras.

"Did anyone see him crash?"

"Oh, yes, a few people. They said another car ran smack into him and drove off without stopping. But someone said he thought he saw the car stop and two men go over to the wreck and pull the driver out. You know what witnesses are. We're doing what we can to spread the story of a drunk hit-and-run driver."

That was routine: This looked like a wet affair and the Bureau would try for an immediate blackout. The Bureau doesn't officially exist, and if anything awkward happens in public we go to ground. The police here wouldn't ask us any questions, because of our cards.

Tilson moved his feet again. "Sorry we had to break up your evening, old fruit. The thing is, we need to know for certain whether it's Sinclair, and you knew him better than most."

I'd left him keeping guard on the wreck, and come down here on foot along the embankment to report to Chandler, and now I looked into the dull blue stare of the man on the ground and said, "Yes, this is Sinclair."

People were still strolling along Grosvenor Road fifteen minutes later as I drove south beside the river, heading for Sloane Square.

I'd thought of ringing the girl at her place and trying to patch up the evening, but it wouldn't have been much use, even if she'd agreed. Tonight I was grieving, and scared. I'd known Sinclair for a long time and done some work with him in various parts of the world, tricky work that had taken him right to the edge of things, as it takes all of us when we're out there in the field; but they'd come for him and got him right on his home ground, and that hadn't happened before to any of us. In London they know where we are and we know where they are—mostly at the embassies—and there's no point in starting trouble, because it could escalate and end in a massacre and shake the whole of the diplomatic structure.

But they'd gone for Sinclair with a purpose and nailed him down, and the thing that scared me was the knowledge that there must be something awfully big going on in the background, and going wrong.

And grief, yes, mixed in with the fright. We're meant not to care what happens to anyone else and we try to play it like that, because there's a high mortality rate among the field executives and any kind of friendship would bring the whole thing too close to us and we'd start breaking up. But we can't avoid contact when there's a big mission going and the heat comes on and the thing starts running wild. Sinclair had been in the helicopter when they'd pulled me out of that awful mess in Mecklenburg after I'd gone in too close and no one could find me—no one except Sinclair. He'd turned the signals base inside out till he'd traced my last call and told them where I was: halfway across a minefield in the dark and with no support, my own bloody fault because I'd refused it, didn't want anyone getting in my way. The border guards had started firing and we put the chopper down three miles away on one skid and a rotor tip, smashing the whole thing up but getting out alive and with nothing to show for it except that Sinclair had started limping with his left—

Limping, but not anymore. Grief, yes, as I drove beside the Thames with his pale blue stare still on me, an unfamiliar sourness in the pit of my gut, some kind of emotion that was strictly disallowed by the faceless, nameless, dehumanized institution we worked for, and hated, and stayed with because it gave us what we craved: a clandestine but lawful place outside society where we could search endlessly in the shadows for our identities, sometimes unto the death. This Sinclair had been doing; but what had he found? The bastards had come for him too soon, cutting him down.

Grief, then, and anger, and persisting fright as I drove alongside the river in the warm summer night. They'd invaded our home ground for the first time, and made a killing.

The people walked slowly along the embankment, watching the lights across the Thames, not wanting to go home yet because it was too warm to sleep and the stars were out and the town stood shimmering in the night.

The blue light of a police launch was leaving a reflected path across the water as it came under Chelsea Bridge, followed by the white line of its wake. It was the last thing I remembered.

She was watching my eyes.

"I'm sorry," I told her.

"What?" She leaned closer.

"I'm sorry about the evening," I said. My voice sounded faint and not very distinct.

"Don't worry." She had calm brown eyes, with the reflection of lamps in them.

"What's going on?" I asked her, and tried to sit up, but my feet were too high; they'd raised them on something. She pushed me gently back.

"Don't worry. You're all right. But you've got to rest."

To hell with that. This wasn't the same girl at all.

"Listen," I said, "I want to know what's happening." But it didn't seem worth the effort. Drifting again. Drifting. Flash of a needle in the light as she drew it away from my arm.

"I want to know. . . ."

"Don't worry."

Chandler came.

"For God's sake," I asked him, "what's the time?"

He glanced up at the clock on the wall. "Nearly five."

"Five what?" I swung my head to look at the windows, but the blinds were down. "Five in the morning?"

"Yes." He pulled the metal-framed chair closer, narrowing his eyes as he stared at me. "How are you feeling?" He had the face of a watchful bird of prey.

"Bloody awful." My feet were still raised on pillows or something under the coverlet, and there was a saline drip plugged into my left arm, and my mouth tasted of gunpowder.

"He mustn't talk too much," the nurse said; she was on the other side of the bed; she was the one with the brown eyes I'd seen before.

"Is this Intensive Care?" I asked her, and tried to sit up, but my ribs hurt too much.

"Yes. But you're okay now. Just keep quiet."

I looked at Chandler. "What happened?"

"Someone crashed into your car in Grosvenor Road near Dolphin Square, and wrote it off."

I tried to get him in focus. They'd been plugging me with drugs, by the feel of things. "Was I driving?" It sounded an odd question. The thing was, I couldn't remember anything.

"Yes. But someone got an ambulance in time." He watched me with his bright black-eyed stare.

The room seemed to have gone very still; the nurse wasn't moving, nor was Chandler; he sat with his feet together and his pale hands on his knees, his face held slightly upward with its thin hooked nose sniffing the air. I looked away from him, wanting to think. So there was a memory gap of some sort. The crash had been wiped out. The second crash. Sinclair's, then mine. They were very much in earnest.

"Who are they?" I asked him, and then remembered the nurse, and wasn't surprised when he didn't answer. He looked up at her instead.

"It's really quite urgent that I put a few questions," he said. "Quite urgent."

She went out and came back with a doctor, who looked at me for a long time and then looked at the chart. Yes, he said, it was mainly shock, plus two broken ribs and one or two bruises and "a bit of retrogressive amnesia." The nurse must have told him I'd been asking Chandler what had happened.

The doctor was watching me critically. "What can you last remember?"

I shied from making the effort; it was like having to go back into a distant country where everyone was a stranger. "I remember some people," I said. "Some people walking on the embankment, by the river. And a man—" but I broke off. *A man floating on his back, staring up at me with his dead blue eyes.* But that had been before, beyond some kind of time shift. That had been Sinclair. "Some people," I said, "and a blue light."

"A blue light?" He was looking amused, as if I needed humoring.

"Listen," I told him, "I want Kimura here. Can you get him?"

"Who is he?"

I was getting bloody annoyed because tonight—*last* night— they'd killed Sinclair and tried to kill me and this idiot in the white coat was treating me as if I were a bit of flotsam washed up from the street. "Chandler, tell them to—"

"All right." He spoke to the doctor with a sudden and surprising note of authority. "This man is used to *shiatsu* massage and I think he'd respond well to it."

"Well, I don't know about that. What sort of massage—"

"For Christ's sake," I cut in on them, "get me Kimura, and I don't care what time it is: He'll come. And I don't want any more drugs, is that understood?"

Chandler took a few minutes sorting things out while I lay there with my rib cage throbbing and waves of dizziness coming and going as their voices faded and loudened again. Then there was only Chandler, pacing the room with short, accurate steps while his hook-nosed shadow kept pace with him along the wall.

"I can remember Sinclair," I told him, and managed to sit up without tugging at the saline-drip tube. "All I don't remember is the crash."

"I don't think it's important. Amnesia's pretty common after an accident. At least you know the facts. You're in a state of siege, of course, for the moment. There are two plainclothes men outside the door and we've got someone monitoring calls at the main switchboard in case anyone rings up to ask about your progress; the only people who know you're here are the people who tried to kill you, assuming they followed the ambulance. We sent—"

"They followed me from Riverside Walk, did they? I mean, that's how they got on to me?"

He stopped pacing and swung his narrow head to look at me, and I saw how relieved he was. Now that he was closer I could see the strain in him, and realized how much he had to handle. Maybe it was his neck on the block for having let Sinclair fly in with no escort to meet him.

"Yes," he said briefly, "we can assume that is how they got on to you. I'm glad you can still think straight. How do you feel generally?"

"I'll be all right when Kimura gets here."

"I've sent for him."

"I'm operational, if you've got anything for me."

He looked away in frustration. "You're not recovered yet. We sent some flowers to the young lady, incidentally, the one you were dining with. Your car's a total write-off and we're seeing to the insurance claim. Our chief concern for the moment is keeping you out of harm's way, and I suppose this is as good a place as any."

"You're expecting them to try again?"

"Of course."

"Who are they, Chandler?"

"We don't know."

"They're not the Soviets."

"No. This is quite out of character."

"Someone from the Far East, who followed Sinclair to London?"

"We've considered that. We've been in signals all night with Taiwan, Hong Kong, and Seoul. He was doing something for us in Seoul, you see, before he flew back via Taiwan and Calcutta."

"Was he on a specific mission?"

"It's not in my province to know. Mr. Croder was running him."

Then it was something big. I said: "They killed Sinclair to shut him up. But why did they try to kill me? They couldn't have—" then his thin, dark-suited body spun against the wall and the lights blacked out and all I could hear was a kind of buzzing, and after a very long time his voice fading in.

". . . the doctor here?"

"What?"

"Do you want me to get the doctor here?"

He was standing over me with his dark hollow eyes watching me closely. "How long was I out for?" I asked him.

"Only a few seconds."

I looked at the wall clock, but couldn't focus. "No. No doctor. Only Kimura."

"He's on his way here now. I'll stay with you till he arrives."

I hitched myself up again, feeling weak and furious and afraid. "Listen, they didn't go for you, or Tilson, or anyone else out there. Only me."

"They recognized you. They know you as one of our field executives. They might have thought you'd be replacing Sinclair."

My skin crawled. "Am I?"

Impatiently he said, "Someone's got to."

We don't like doing it. We don't like the feel of a dead man's shoes.

"Did you have me down," I asked him, "for this one?"

"That's academic now. You're not fit enough."

There was an edge to his tone and I knew he blamed me for what had happened. I shouldn't have let them get at me like that; I should have been more alert. But they hadn't come up on me from behind, because I always know what's in the mirror; they must have come at me at a right angle from Dolphin Square, because the other side was the river; they must have come at me on my blind side and very fast, but he was right: I should have heard them, and done something.

"Give me a couple of days," I told him.

If they had a mission lined up, I wanted it. I wanted to go back into that strange limbo and find out who they were, and hit them, and hit to kill. Then I'd be safe again.

"Time is too short," Chandler said.

The throbbing in my rib cage reached my skull, hammering there.

"One day, then. Give me one day, you bastard." But he and his shadow were tilting against the wall, dancing together weirdly into the dark.

II

CRODER

❖

"I'm not refusing the mission. I'm refusing Croder."

He didn't ask why.

We can refuse anything we like and we don't have to explain, because it's our life, or our death, and they know that.

"Then he might give you someone else," Tilson said gently, and went on checking the papers as our driver went through the red lights into Parliament Square. "In any case we might as well clear you, to save time." He held the papers up to the window at an angle to catch the light from the street. "No next of kin, sole bequest to Saint Dunstan's—you want any changes? And five hundred roses."

The man beside him was digging in his pocket, and held out a Walther P.38.

"He doesn't want anything like that," Tilson said. "Put it away."

They're always changing the staff in Firearms.

"Sign here, old horse, when you've read it."

"Cross out five hundred," I said, "and put one."

"One rose?"

"Yes."

"Right you are. One rose for Moira."

I'd had time to think about that in Moscow, when that bastard Ignatov was following me through the snow.

I signed the form and sat back, watching the rush of green leaves as we passed Victoria Tower Gardens. The driver went through the red again past Lambeth Bridge and we heard a siren start up but she didn't take any notice; they'd seen our plates now, and the siren died away.

"Croder's all right," Tilson said as he put the papers into his briefcase. "He looks after his people, you know that."

I let it go. The swinging of the streetlamps past the windows was beginning to sicken me and I didn't want to talk, least of all about Croder. Kimura had taken all morning to straighten me out, working on the nervous meridians and concentrating on the spinal column; but the lingering influence of the phenobarbital was still fogging the system and throwing me off-balance.

"Slow down a bit here, would you?" Tilson asked the driver, then turned to me again, talking quietly. We were going along Grosvenor Road now and I could see the flat expanse of the Thames. "The thing is to see how you feel when you arrive there, old fruit. You're not committed, after all; I mean, we all realize you're still a bit groggy."

I couldn't look at him. The scene through the windows was hypnotic, with the lights from across the river flowing in reflection beyond the dark swinging trunks of the trees.

"What's the area?" I asked him, not wanting to know.

"Peking." His voice had gone faint, but I still couldn't look at him. The sound of the engine had died away and we were moving in a kind of vacuum while the trunks of the trees went flickering past the flow of lights, just as I'd watched them before, somewhere before. "That's all I know."

"What?"

"That's all I know," Tilson said; and when I turned my

head at last, I saw he was watching me steadily. "That's all any of us knows. Don't worry, old horse, just relax."

"Those bloody drugs," I said, and looked through the windscreen past the driver's dark hair.

"Not entirely. That was the spot where you crashed last night." He told the driver to speed up again. "I just thought it might stir the old memory; we're a bit desperate for clues, because the witnesses said it was anything from a black Mercedes to a red Jaguar. Never mind."

I looked back through the rear window at the long perspective of the trees, at the area of limbo where memory had given way to shadows. "I'm getting nothing," I told Tilson.

"Maybe it'll come back to you later. No hurry."

"That Humber," I said, "was behind us when we left Whitehall."

"True. And there's another unmarked car ahead of us. We don't want any more larks."

This evening they'd smuggled me out of the hospital in a dry-cleaner's van.

"What happened to Chandler?" I asked him.

"He was going to run you. Then Croder moved in."

I had to make an effort to think, to try patching some sort of future together for myself. All I knew at this moment was that they needed me badly: With Sinclair dead less than twenty-four hours, they were dragging a half-doped executive through the night to try setting him up as a replacement.

"Where are we heading, Tilson?"

It was about time I began taking an interest: It might be dangerous not to.

"Battersea. The heliport."

"Are you going to fly me somewhere?"

"We're going to meet Mr. Croder." His tone became more gentle still, more amiable, and I was warned. "Just so that we all know what's going on, old horse, tell me one little thing: Do you really want this mission?"

"It depends on what's involved."

"I didn't mean that," he said carefully. "I mean do you want it *regardless?*"

I began waking up, because the driver was swinging left into the park. "You know bloody well I do."

"But of *course* you do." He nodded comfortably. His plump hands began moving again on the briefcase. "Those nasty people tried to smear you all over Grosvenor Road and you can't wait to find out who they are and rub their horrid little noses in the mustard, and quite right, too. Now you'd—"

"I've been out of action for three months and I'm fed up with refresher training and Sinclair's dead and if you bastards can't find me something to do I'm going to lose my grip. Put it that way."

"Now that sounds much more like my old friend. So you'd better finish clearance while there's time." He produced more papers and a wad of currency. "You heard about the death of Zhan Hongwen, the premier of the People's Republic of China, two days ago. The U.K. is sending the secretary of state to represent Her Majesty at the funeral, and you'll be joining his two official bodyguards."

"That's my cover?"

"Cover and access."

He gave me the papers and I looked at them in the half-light. *Detective-sergeant William Charles Gage of New Scotland Yard, seconded to the Foreign Office on temporary overseas duties.* The wad of notes was marked 1000 *yuan* and die-stamped by Lloyd's Bank. And now my hands were growing cold and a lightness was coming into my head because I'd been too groggy to realize how close I was to the new mission, after three months of debriefing and recuperating and trying to relax with the saunas and the girls and the long, bracing tramps across the downs at Brighton while the thought hovered in the back of the mind, the same thought we all have, in between missions—the thought that perhaps we ought to get out now before it's too late, before the luck runs out and we're cast up in a Gulag labor camp or lashed blindfolded

against a post in Beirut or by the grace of unknown gods
spread-eagled against the mountainside with a ripped parachute for a shroud and one last intimate friend plucking
strength from us with his bone-white beak.

Suddenly, this time, it was too late to get out: They were
already pitching me headlong into the dark and I was letting
them do it, because who the hell, after all, wants to die in a
pensioner's home with the veined hand limp on the plaid
rug and a torn bingo ticket for an epitaph?

But, Lord, I was afraid.

"I see we're on time," Tilson said, and we got out.

Five men were standing in a group below the rotor of the
RAF helicopter and one came a few paces to meet us, and I
recognized Croder.

"Has he been briefed?" he asked Tilson softly.

That was typical of the man. He'd spoken as if I weren't
there. Croder can get me to hate him instantly, the moment we
make contact.

"No, sir."

"Cleared?"

"Yes."

Croder turned to me, standing hunched in his dark blazer
with his thin head down and his eyes lifted to watch me in
the lamplight. "What have you decided?"

"I want the mission."

"With me as your Control?"

"No."

His thin mouth tightened; or perhaps I imagined it; Croder
isn't a man to give anything away, anything at all.

"You can't have it both ways," he said, and glanced down
at his watch. "And I can't give you very long." His dark, expressionless eyes were raised again to watch me.

I wanted to turn and walk away from him; I think I tried.
I sensed Tilson near me, and heard the four men talking together below the slanting rotor of the machine. I said: "Give
me someone else."

They wanted me for this mission, or they wouldn't have dragged me out of hospital with the shock still in my nerves and the drugs still clouding my brain. So it would have to be on my terms.

"I am already in control of this one," Croder said, his tight mouth nibbling at the words like a rat. "And I am inviting you to join me as the executive in the field. I believe you're the most appropriate man for the job, and so do my advisers."

"I'm not fit," I said. I was going to make him ask.

"There's no immediate action foreseen, in Peking. And you can rest on the flight out."

"The notice is too short." I was going to make him ask me outright.

"You don't like delays. They don't suit your temperament."

"But this is too rushed. I've had no London briefing."

Then he asked me. "Why won't you accept me as your Control?"

"Because of Moscow."

His hooded lids closed for an instant as he fought for patience. I knew how much patience he was having to use; he was extremely high in the London echelon, a controller who could pick his missions and his executives and his directors in the field without any competition, and any executive would work with him simply for the prestige. He wasn't used to refusal.

"You did well," he said, "in Moscow."

"I broke the rules."

With impatience coming into his tone for the first time, he said: "You showed compassion for Schrenk as a fellow executive, and as a result he nearly killed you. I would assume you've learned from it." He looked at his watch again. "I would also assume you'd want to do something about the people who wiped out Sinclair last night. It's the first time the opposition has broken right into our field and made a killing—tried, indeed, to do it twice. I'd expect someone of your caliber to—shall I say—react." He inclined his head slightly. "How-

ever, there's no more time left, and I must accept the fact that
you can no longer be counted on."

He was working on my weakest point: my professional
vanity. He knew that if I turned this mission down, I'd have
to face myself afterward.

As he turned away, I said: "Has anyone else been cleared?"

"Of course. We're pulling Fox out of Hong Kong. He'll be
in Peking by noon tomorrow, their time."

"Fox? You can't be serious."

"Unfortunately he's the only reserve."

He was lying, of course. Fox had done only five missions
and he'd run two of them into the ground. But I believed him,
because I had to, because I wanted to. I'd tried everything
else.

"Croder."

"Well?"

"Who would you give me, to direct me in the field?"

"Ferris. I wouldn't give you anyone less."

He was making it difficult.

"Where's Ferris now?"

"In Tokyo, waiting for a signal."

"Would he be directing Fox?"

Croder was silent for a moment, facing me with his shoulders hunched and his hooded eyes on me; then suddenly he
brought his guard down and I heard despair in his voice. "I
don't think it would matter who directed Fox, would it?" With
more urgency he said: "This is the first time we'll be operating in mainland China, liaising with the Chinese, and we
were rather hoping we could count on you to go in and break
new ground for us."

The last of my own defences came down, as he knew they
must. He was offering me a top controller, a top director in
the field, and virgin ground to break open for the Bureau.
And he was showing me his despair. I had the wry thought
that to go on refusing would amount to bad manners.

"If I took this on, I couldn't guarantee not to break any
rules, if I had to."

"I realize that. I'm prepared to take the risk."

My head seemed suddenly clear. "All right," I said.

"You accept the mission?"

"Yes. With you as my Control."

He turned quickly. "Mr. Toms, you can start up as soon as you like. Tilson, get the bag from the car, will you?"

"What about briefing?" I asked him.

He came to stand close. "You'll be briefed in the field. At this end we know nothing except that Sinclair was bringing us information of some kind—information so vital that he couldn't entrust it to signals or a courier; and so vital that he had to be silenced."

"Is there a specific objective, at this stage?"

He stood closer still as the helicopter's rotor began chopping rhythmically at the air. "We want you to find out what Sinclair was trying to tell us. That's a high-risk objective, I know."

Tilson was hurrying past us, giving my bag to the flight lieutenant to stow in the freight bay. The girl was turning the car and moving it clear of the downwash area.

"How do we fly?" I asked Croder.

"You'll go from here to Croydon and board an RAF personal transport with the rest of the delegation and three more security officers. Ferris will meet you in Peking."

"Understood."

He turned and led me across to the group of men, raising his voice above the noise of the rotor. "Let me present the Right Honorable George Bygreave, Secretary of State. These other gentlemen are Detective-inspector Stanfield of New Scotland Yard, and—I'm sorry, I—"

"Wiggins, sir."

"Oh, yes, Flight Lieutenant Wiggins, thank you. Your pilot is Squadron Leader Toms. Gentlemen, this is Detective-sergeant Gage, the reserve security officer."

We all nodded and Wiggins helped the secretary of state up the metal steps. The man from the Yard followed him on board and made room for me as the flight lieutenant squeezed between us and swung the door shut. Through the window I thought I saw Tilson out there lifting a hand—*good luck,* I suppose—and then the pilot gunned up and the last I saw of London was the thin, hunched figure of Croder standing with his feet together and his face tilted to watch us with the down-wash tugging at his clothes as we lifted off and swung toward the southeast across the lights of the city.

III

FUNERAL

❁

I had worked with Ferris before.

He'd been sitting on the stairs with the gun on his lap in the Hong Kong snake shop while I'd fought for a kill with the hit man they'd sent from Kowloon to wipe me out. He'd pulled me out of Morocco with the Coast Guard cutter's searchlight sweeping the sea as we lay prone on the afterdeck of the fishing boat and Sandra's jeweled revolver sank below the waves to the bottom, where no one would ever find it. He'd been with me when Alitalia flight 403 had hit the runway too short in Beirut and we'd lost two backup executives but saved the mission because the documents weren't on board.

And now he was walking with me from the Beijin Hotel along Wangfujing Street in Peking, a tall, thin, sandy-colored man with his body sloping forward and his wisps of pale hair all over the place in the light breeze coming off the rice fields to the north.

Dark suits, black ties. Someone from the Bureau had done my packing for me yesterday evening while Tilson had been getting me out of the hospital in the dry-cleaner's van; the other clothes they'd put in were much lighter: The July temperature here was already eighty degrees and it was only ten in the morning.

My ribs were still painful, but I'd slept off the lingering effects of the drugs on the long flight out and my head was clear enough to warn me that London must have been desperate, to have moved me into the field without warning and without a home briefing.

"They must have been desperate," I said.

Ferris turned his honey-colored eyes on me, watching me for a moment from behind his glasses. "I wouldn't disagree."

"Desperate to get me into Peking, or out of London?"

"You were a target there."

"I'll be a target here, once they pick up my trail."

We turned left toward the huge crowded square, edging past a group of uniformed schoolchildren carrying white posies for mourning. The street was roped off and all traffic had stopped.

"You didn't leave a trail," Ferris told me. "You came out here under RAF security." He noticed a cockroach at the edge of the pavement and moved to his left slightly, and I heard the faint cracking sound under his black polished shoe.

"Oh, for Christ's sake," I said.

"Another little soul saved for Jesus." He gave the soft dry laugh I remembered so well, the sound of a snake shedding its skin. "The thing is, London believes Sinclair had something rather important to tell us, and they don't want things to get cold. Logical, for London."

A squadron of military jets was passing overhead, in salute to the dead premier. When it was quieter, I asked Ferris: "Who was Sinclair's main source, do we know?"

"A man called Jason."

"One of ours?"

"A sleeper, yes, based in Seoul."

"He's there now?"

"No. He flew into Peking last night."

"To rendezvous with us?"

"That's right. He was told to meet you when you landed."

"Why didn't he?"

"I rather think," he said, "they got to him first."

I slowed, and he waited for me to come abreast again.

"Fill me in, will you?" He'd been letting me ask the questions, according to routine procedure. The director in the field tells the executive only what he specifically needs to know, but will answer most questions; the idea is to leave the executive's head clear of data that isn't essential, and data that could be dangerous.

"Jason checked into our hotel soon after ten o'clock last night," Ferris told me. "We had a secure rendezvous set up for thirty minutes later, so that he could tell me what kind of information Sinclair had been carrying, and hopefully where he'd found it." He combed back his pale wispy hair with his fingers. "So it's not really our day, is it?"

I didn't answer. The Sinclair information was my objective for the mission, and after two hours in the field I was being told that the only contact was lost. In a moment I asked: "You think Jason is dead?"

"I would think so, yes."

"They're working so *fast*."

He nodded. "These people are different."

"Who are they, Ferris?"

"I don't think they're political, and I don't think they're intelligence. But I think they might be a paid political *instrument*—a hit group—with *access* to intelligence sources. They seem too efficient for a government agency; they don't have to wait for orders before they move. As you say, they move very fast."

"Here and in London."

"Just so."

We passed a thin ragged boy kneeling on a newspaper, his head down in prayer. A lot of the people standing at the bases of the buildings were in the same attitude, all of them wearing black armbands. A huge military band was pushing its way through the crowd at the end of the square, with the police trying to help them.

"Is this a wildcat group we're up against?" I asked Ferris.
"You mean terrorists?"

"I suppose so." What worried me most was that the opposition was already hitting us without leaving a trace.

"I don't think they're terrorists, exactly. They're not trying to terrorize anyone. So far their action's been focused on the Sinclair information: They killed him to silence him; they tried to kill you because they realized you were connected with him; and they got at Jason because he, too, was a connection. There could be something they've got to protect, without counting the cost. Some sort of"—he waved a vague hand—"some sort of *project*."

"A big one."

"Certainly on an international scale. Otherwise Croder wouldn't have come in as Control."

It was getting more difficult to make our way through the crowd; at the hotel I'd been told that an estimated half-million people would gather in Tian'anmen Square.

"How long," I asked Ferris, "were you and this man Jason together at the hotel?"

In a moment he said: "The name's Ferris. Remember me?" He'd decided to make a joke of it, but I heard an edge to his tone.

"Sorry," I said.

"Don't mention it."

He was my director in the field and responsible for my safety and in the next few days or the next few weeks he was going to steer me through the mission and try to get me out alive, and he was telling me now that he hadn't been so careless as to make contact in public with Jason, who was the known source of the information that had led to Sinclair's death and nearly to mine.

The military band was now assembled opposite the Palace Museum and playing "The East Is Red," the Chinese-Communist anthem.

Ferris pitched his voice above the noise. "I made the rendezvous with Jason over the phone when he landed at the airport. I've never met either Sinclair or Jason, so at the moment I'm clean, and so are you; but we're only one step ahead of the action and I want to make high-security rendezvous and use contacts; there are quite a lot of Occidentals here for the funeral, but in a few days' time we'll be standing out in the crowd." He looked at his watch. "You've got five minutes to join your group before the cortege comes into the square from the other end. Make for the dais under the portrait of Jiang Wenyuan and do whatever the security man tells you—and don't forget you'll be under scrutiny."

The military band was now playing the "Internationale," and there was movement beginning in the crowd packing the far end of the square.

"I shall be standing behind the official mourners," Ferris told me, "and I'll meet you again after the ceremony. If for any reason we get separated and you need me, phone the embassy and ask for McFadden, second cultural attaché; he's the station officer for the Bureau and he's versed in speech code, so I want you to use it. Questions?"

"Yes. When is the English contingent flying back?"

"Sometime this afternoon, as soon as the secretary of state has offered his condolences to the vice-premier and his party. We then change your cover and papers."

"Understood."

I left him and pushed my way to the roped area below the immense portrait of the late premier and showed my credentials to an officer of the special police guard; he was almost casual in the way he let me through, and I remembered this was Peking, not Moscow.

" 'Morning, Gage."

Detective-inspector Stanfield took a couple of steps toward me and half-turned again to watch the secretary of state. "You want instructions, I understand."

"Just general procedure." All this man had been told was that I was Secret Service and working here as one of his team.

"We're expecting no trouble," he said quietly. "The main thing is to keep your eye on the body. There's no crush here, and everyone in this enclosure has had to show their papers, so he'll be all right. If anyone's got any ideas about lining up a potshot, the ANFU will spot him in the crowd—there's three hundred of them just at this end of the square. The thing is to relax—and as I say, keep your eye on the body."

"Fair enough."

The sun had climbed above the roof of the huge Palace Museum and the direct heat was stifling; the breeze from the rice fields was blocked here by the buildings. The secretary of state was talking quietly to Claudier and Veidt, the French and German delegates: I recognized a dozen people here from their press photographs.

"Three kings,"—Stanfield was speaking from the side of his mouth—"twenty-nine presidents and heads of state, twenty-one prime ministers, and sundry odds and sods. Quite a turn-out for someone who was only in office ten months."

I noticed Walter Mills, the U.S. vice president, surrounded by the ten members of his delegation, with the same number of security men positioned along the edge of the dais.

The crowds along the east side of the square were murmuring now, the sound of their voices trapped by the buildings; I looked twice in that direction and saw the cortege coming, the draped funeral carriage drawn by a white-painted jeep.

"Eye on the bod," Stanfield murmured, and I turned my head back to watch Bygreave. There were quite a few Europeans on the far side of him, but I couldn't see anything of Ferris.

At 10:15 the cortege reached this end of the square and Stanfield drew me along the dais as the first of the official mourners took their wreaths from the attendants and began laying them against the coffin, the premier's widow and two sons being the first to step down from the dais. The military band had stopped playing now and the square was quiet. Be-

yond the English delegates I could see hundreds of schoolchildren going onto their knees along the roped pavement, one
of them dropping her white bouquet of flowers and crawling
between two police guards to fetch it; from somewhere nearer
I could hear women sobbing, and wondered why. This wasn't
Mao, the Father of the Revolution, but a man without cha-
risma and less than a year in office; perhaps they always cried
at funerals because the flowers were so beautiful, or because,
unlike the men, their hearts could be moved beyond politics
to the thought that, whoever this was, here was a man dead.

It took twenty minutes for the Communist party and military delegates to lay their wreaths and bow three times in
front of the coffin. The first of the foreign delegates were the
Albanians, whose antirevisionist creed had been allied to
Mao's; they were followed by the North Koreans, Vietnamese,
and Cambodians, with the Japanese next in line.

The crying of the women was beginning to depress me; I
hoped someone would be there in London to cry for Sinclair.

Pigeons flew from the parapets along the facade of the museum, their wings black against the sun's glare until they
wheeled and caught the light; along the rooftops the flags were
at half-mast, some of them catching the breeze; down here the
air was still and stifling as the American vice president moved
forward and laid a wreath of tiger lilies against the catafalque,
leading the rest of the delegates past at a steady pace.

The British contingent followed; and as Detective-inspector
Stanfield moved to the edge of the dais, I went with him and
was close enough to read the name on the wreath of white
roses as Bygreave took it from an attendant—*Elizabeth R.*

The delegates formed a short line along the side of the
catafalque, watching as their leader placed the wreath carefully against it; then suddenly the sky was filled with flowers
and the bloodied body of the secretary of state was hurled
against me by the blast as the coffin exploded.

IV

ASSASSINATION

✺

"Then for God's sake," said the ambassador, "get him for me on another line."

The girl in green came through again with a file of papers, catching the toe of her lizard-skin shoe in the frayed silk rug but saving herself, dropping a loose paper and picking it up and going on into the ambassador's room. They'd left the door open; there was no point in shutting it with all these people wanting to see him.

"Then tell him to ring me back."

He dropped the phone and another one rang and he picked it up. "Metcalf here."

The chief of police came through again from the main entrance, a small man, hurrying, with an officer trying to catch up.

"Then tell him to hold the plane." The ambassador dropped the phone and looked up. "Who are you? Oh, yes, come in."

Another reporter tried to get through the main entrance and I saw the Chinese guard pushing him back with surprising strength for such a small man. The two people from the Xinhua News Agency were still talking to a girl in the room on our left and getting nowhere; she spoke rapid Cantonese with a lot of emphasis.

Night was falling outside the tall windows overlooking Kuang Hua Lu Street, and there was no sound of traffic. We'd been told that the Ministry of the Interior had ordered a curfew throughout the city beginning at ten o'clock; that was a few minutes ago. Checkpoints had been set up along the roads out of Peking, and there were long lines at the railway stations and the airport as passengers were put through an emergency screening. Half a dozen political agitators of high rank had been arrested, but their names hadn't been publicized.

I got up and started walking about again, feeling the draft of the slow ceiling fans. Ferris was aggravatingly calm, sitting at his ease on the wicker chair with one arm hooked over the back and his legs crossed, a foot dangling. But that was what he was for: to be calm, to keep his head while I went on fuming. "This isn't a mission," I'd told him when we'd come into the embassy, "it's just a mess they've got themselves into over here, and Croder's thrown me in to see what happens."

I was also worried because my face had appeared in two of the evening papers already and I knew that by this time tomorrow I'd get world coverage as the man standing behind the British secretary of state in the instant before he died. If that was Croder's idea of effective cover for an executive arriving in the field I didn't think it was all that funny, because it could cost me my life. The Bureau doesn't officially exist and we operate in strict hush, but after a certain number of missions we become known among the opposition networks and intelligence services—known, recognizable, and vulnerable.

I'd come out here under RAF security and the opposition didn't even know I'd left London; but all they had to do now was pick up a paper and when I went through those doors and down the steps and into the street I could walk straight into the cross hairs. They'd already tried once.

"You better get those chaps in here," I heard the ambassador telling someone. "And McFadden, too."

He'd been standing a few feet away from me when it had happened, though I couldn't remember much about it in any kind of order: It had seemed like a moving surrealist picture with sound effects—the heavy brutish grunt of the explosion and then the sudden blizzard of white flowers filling the sky as the shock wave came and the black-suited figure of the secretary of state was hurled against me, while slowly the flowers settled and the sky was filled again as hundreds of pigeons flocked from the buildings in fright and women began screaming. A moment of strange stillness, then the police began closing in, with press photographers racing in front of them and shooting wild. Then suddenly Ferris's voice right behind me: *"Come on—we're getting out."*

The secretary of state had died in the ambulance, they'd told me at the hotel; I'd gone straight there, smothered in blood from his injuries, to change my clothes and wash.

"H.E. would like to see you," the girl in green was saying, and Ferris got out of the wicker chair as McFadden joined us from the corridor, a compact man, freckled and ginger-haired and shut-faced: Ferris had introduced us in the signals room when we'd got here this evening.

"Sit down, gentlemen," Metcalf told us, "and someone please shut the door."

The room was crowded and the chief of police insisted on standing because there weren't enough chairs. The embassy interpreter, a young Eurasian girl, began translating for him without any preliminaries.

"The police guard on this building has been substantially reinforced, on instructions from the minister of the interior, and I hope this will not be found inconvenient for you; it is for your personal safety."

When the girl had stopped speaking, he gave a slight bow. "Inquiries are still proceeding at the place of embalmment, and all those who were involved in the construction of the coffin, in the security of the building, and in the preparation of the late Premier Jiang Wenyuan's earthly remains have come under our closest scrutiny." Another bow. He was facing the ambassador, standing directly in front of his desk, and didn't look at anyone else. "The findings of the five doctors who attended the late British secretary of state are that the pressure of air and debris from the explosion disrupted the heart and lungs, while at the same time the pressure invaded the cavities of the face and distended the sinuses, damaging the frontal lobes of the brain. As to the—"

He broke off as one of the telephones began ringing, and the girl in green reached over and picked up the receiver.

"No calls, Janet."

The chief of police waited punctiliously until she was sitting down again. "As to the explosive device itself, our skilled experts, who are members of the International Association of Bomb Technicians and Investigators, have collected material from the site and used electromagnets to probe the debris from the whole area. Analysis has been made and a considerable portion of the device reconstructed; we already know that it was of Japanese make, but do not regard this as necessarily significant, since terrorism is international and so are its weapons. We know also that the device was detonated by remote control, via a radio beam."

The ambassador lifted his head an inch. "They're absolutely certain of that?"

Ferris hadn't moved.

"Yes, Your Excellency."

Metcalf leaned forward. He was tanned and athletic-looking, but must have been close on sixty; this could be his last tour, and it hadn't been very pleasant, apart from the physical shock he'd received down there in Tian'anmen Square; he'd caught some of the blast and his left eye was still red from the effects of the flying debris.

"You mean," he asked carefully, "that the *timing* of the explosion was also controlled?"

"We cannot say that. We can say that the timing of the explosion was technically feasible." When the girl finished translating, he made to add something, but the ambassador cut in.

"You mean," he asked with even more care, "that if these—

if the perpetrators had wanted to explode the device at a precise and premeditated time, they could have done so? Is that right?"

"That is right, yes."

Ferris was gazing quietly at the wall, where there were yellowing photographs of Princess Ann taking a jump on a thoroughbred and Charles clouting a ball. We were pretty certain of one thing, and had talked about it this afternoon: This hadn't been an act of terrorism, a public and dramatic show to catch world attention; it had been an act of assassination, and, at the moment when the secretary of state had bent forward close to the coffin to place the wreath, there'd been someone in the crowd or on a rooftop with binoculars and a transmitter.

We also suspected something else, but hadn't wanted to talk about it: *This was the information that Sinclair had brought to London—that the secretary of state was marked for death. If Sinclair could have talked, we could have prevented it.*

Jason, too, might have known, and might have warned Ferris when he'd flown in last night, before the opposition had got at him. But why hadn't either of them sent a signal?

"Thank you," the ambassador told the chief of police. "I wanted to make sure of the facts, and of the implications."

"The implications we must divine later, when we have *all* the facts. I shall allow myself the honor of making further reports as the inquiry proceeds." He waited until the interpreter had finished speaking in her soft musical tones, then drew himself straight. "I wish to repeat, Your Excellency, that together with other city and government departments, the Metropolitan Police Department of Peking is shocked and distressed by the tragedy that has befallen your distinguished countryman, and will devote all its energies to bringing those responsible to justice."

A couple of straw mattresses had been brought in and a clerk sent to the Hotel Beijing for our toilet things: The last signal from London had ordered that Ferris and I should remain at the embassy until further notice. McFadden raked up an alarm clock and a small transistor radio to make us feel at home, which was civil of him.

The embassy cook knocked together a scratch meal and McFadden came along to share it with us in one of the offices, talking a bit, but not about the bombing; he missed England and wanted to know if *The Mousetrap* was still running and whether you could buy camel feed in Harrods these days. It was nearly midnight before Conyers came, and we moved into the main reception room because it was bigger.

Conyers was an American antiterrorist agent, but we didn't know his official background and he didn't explain. He was a quiet and slow-moving man with a weathered face and a bright blue stare and an artificial hand encased in a black leather glove.

"How are the other guys?" he asked no one in particular and lit a cigarette, flicking the match into the pot with the half-dead fern in it near where Ferris was sitting.

"Nothing serious," Ferris said.

Detective-inspector Stanfield had gone in the ambulance with the secretary of state, but had been released from the hospital an hour ago with minor injuries; he'd caught more of the blast than I had, because Bygreave had provided a shield. The three other security men hadn't been touched.

"I'm in Peking," Conyers said with a glance across the two doors, "because we had wind of something, but it wasn't anything to do with the British team. Your ambassador here has asked me if I have any ideas as to the motive involved in this thing. Frankly I haven't. Frankly I'm mystified. The Chinese have no motive for antagonizing the West at a time when they're looking for expanding trade and closer military ties. It doesn't escape your attention that I'm talking as if the British secretary of state had been assassinated. I believe he was. I believe that bomb was intended for him, and for nobody else. Some people are saying that this was an act of terrorism, designed simply to blow a dead body out of its box in front of a captive audience with instant media replay worldwide, courtesy of the international journalists present, a protest against the prevailing political constitution of the People's Republic of China. That's bullshit. There isn't any prevailing political constitution in this place, simply because they haven't had time to clear up the mess that Mao left all over the doorstep."

He took a drag on his cigarette. "This, gentlemen, isn't Lodd Airport and it isn't the Munich Olympics. Nobody has come forward to claim responsibility, even though the PLO and half a hundred other terrorist organizations would be sorely tempted to do just that, simply because this was a Hollywood spectacular and if there'd been any message for anyone it would've gotten an Oscar for Western Union. The only message I can see is that somebody wanted the British secretary of state to be dead. You boys will know a lot more than I do about that, but you have my deepest sympathies; it's a lousy way to go."

"You think it was a political assassination?" Ferris asked him.

"I think it was a political assassination." He flicked ash off his cigarette and I noticed his good hand was never quite still. He watched Ferris with his bright blue stare.

"Don't you think it's a bizarre way of doing things?"

"Sure. But hellish effective. Look, they didn't do it this way for fun. These are experts. Technically it took a lot of working out, and I know of what I speak." He glanced down briefly. "My left hand was last seen traveling at five hundred feet in a southwesterly direction, and although it was a mistake on my part, I'd been trixying around with these toys for ten years without so much as a broken fingernail. They decided this was the most effective way of working, that's all. Remember how the Basque activists terminated Admiral Luis Carrero Blanco, the president of Spain? They dug a tunnel thirty feet long underneath the street in Madrid where he used to pass every day on his way to morning mass, then they packed the place with a hundred seventy-five pounds of dyna-

mite and blew it up from a hundred yards away by remote
control. The president's car was lifted five stories high and it
wasn't found for several hours because no one thought of looking for it on the far side of the Church of San Francisco
de Borja, where it had landed. Bizarre? Sure. But effective?
Sure."

Ferris got up and began walking about and Conyers
watched him and waited to see if he wanted to say something,
but he didn't. He was just restless, and it didn't do my nerves
any good because Ferris walking up and down was like anyone else yelling the roof off.

"We also have to consider this," Conyers went on. "It might
seem that it would have been easier to pick up a telescopic
rifle and do it that way. But with an estimated crowd of half
a million people and the security services of fifty-three nations
plus the Peking contingent, can you imagine any way it could
have worked? They had to put the assassination instrument
right into the center of the target area, where it could be
guaranteed to do the job, and then they simply had to wait
for the target himself to approach the instrument—which,
again, he was guaranteed to do. How could they miss? They
didn't. And the man who pressed the button just went on
standing there. So let's forget the 'bizarre' angle, gentlemen.
It makes our teeth ache to say so, but this was a success story."

After what seemed a long time, Ferris stopped walking up
and down and said: "Does anyone feel a draft?"

"What?" McFadden took his chin out of his hands. He saw
Ferris was looking up at the two big fans overhead. "Oh," he
said, and went across to the scalloped brass switch on the
wall, and the fans began slowing down.

"You'd rule out the Chinese?" Ferris was looking at Conyers
now.

Conyers lit another cigarette and picked a strand of tobacco
off his lower lip and said: "The Chinese aren't a nation of
uniformed robots. I'd say that none of the Chinese in present
authority would want such a thing to happen, especially at a

time when, as I've said, they're looking forward to increased trade with the West, subscribing to the American presence in the Pacific, and entertaining—like they did just a month back—a U.S. Defense Department logistics delegation on their own ground here, for meetings with the Chinese armed forces chief of staff. I'd say that these people wouldn't want this kind of thing to happen to *any* Western government representative, and certainly not to a representative of Britain or the United States, with their close historic and military affiliations."

The big ceiling fans had come to a stop and a dying fly came down in spirals from one of the dusty motor housings, landing on the worn leather blotter of the escritoire and buzzing in mad circles until Ferris went over there and stabbed one finger down and wiped its tip on the blotter and came back and said: "Then who?"

Conyers blew out smoke. "Who? Holy cow. You're pointing at a broken window and looking around at a playground full of kids and asking who? Terrorist organizations aren't isolated units. They're Communist-inspired or -directed or -motivated, and all roads lead away from Moscow. They're all in touch with one another; they help one another; they lend one another hard cash and weapons and forged papers. The order for this coup might have originated anywhere on earth. But in the final analysis, like I said, I frankly don't see this thing as an act of terrorism anyway."

"Is terrorism criminal or political?" Ferris asked him.

"It's the criminal implementation of political ideals."

"Was Bygreave's assassination political?"

"Okay, I know what you're saying, but the fact that polar bears are animals, and white, doesn't mean that all animals are white. I'm going to put it on the line. I'm going to say that whoever assassinated the British secretary of state was a political but not a terrorist."

"Or somebody," Ferris said, "who was paid to do it?"

"Or somebody who was paid, sure, by a political group that is not a terrorist group, since terrorist groups do their own dirt without paying other people to do it for them."

I said: "A hit man?"

Conyers put his bright blue stare on me. "Or a hit group. This had to be the work of more than one operator."

"So we're not concerned with questions of nationality."

"Right. Not if this job was paid for. The Mafia will hit for the Church Army Zionists so long as the money's good."

Ferris was watching me, perhaps thinking I had someone in mind. I hadn't. Twenty-four hours into the mission we were still at ground zero, with a major objective already achieved by the opposition—*the* major objective, if it was Bygreave's death alone. Sinclair could have told us; Jason could have told us; but without the information they'd taken with them we couldn't make a move. If the Bygreave assassination had been the thing we'd been pushed into Peking to prevent, we might as well go home.

Except for London. London would have called us in by now.

"There's nothing on my mind," I told Ferris obliquely. "Nothing at all."

All I could think about was the way that man's arms had been flung out like a cross by the shock wave as his body was hurled against me in Tian'anmen Square this morning, knocking me down, while the flowers had clouded the sky. What would Sinclair have put in his signal? What would Jason have told us?

Don't let the secretary of state lay the wreath. Tell him to feign a sudden turn and ask the Chinese attendant to do it for him. Then get him back inside the RAF transport, fast.

No. They couldn't have known, or they would have sent a signal, in code. *Then what had they known?*

"The thing is," Conyers said, "the Chinese are working on it. They are the host country and it's their responsibility. And they're smart. They're also as conscience-stricken as hell over this thing, even though they didn't have any part of it—in my opinion. They want to get that son of a bitch that pressed the button, so they can prove to the world they didn't do it themselves. Look what they stand to lose if they can't: zillions of *yuan* in international trade; nuclear power equipment from the West; Japanese and American support against the Soviets. Who wants to support a country that can't even put on a funeral without a major international incident?" He dropped ash into the fern pot. "So maybe we should wait a few days and see what these guys can come up with. Maybe we—"

Then one of the embassy clerks came in and said that the man named Jason who'd been reported missing last night by Mr. Ferris had been found by the police with severe head injuries in a freight truck at Beijing Station and taken to the hospital, where they were trying to save his life.

V

DEATHTRAP

❁

I didn't know much about Jason. We work in a place where friends are dangerous; but we pick up gossip down there in the basement between missions, hunched over the tea-stained plastic tables in the café and always looking up when someone comes in, someone we didn't necessarily expect to see in here again; and I know that Jason stuck a limpet mine under the stern of a fishing boat out of Leningrad with so much electronic surveillance gear on board that there wasn't room for the fish. Then there was some trouble about a girl in Rio de Janeiro when he was there trying to bug a bordello and catch some pox-ridden generalissimo full of military secrets with his trousers down. And it was Jason who fell through the glass roof of the winter garden of the East German consulate in Budapest and the next day, on his way to the Austrian frontier with the target documents, cleared three security checks because his face was covered in bandages and his passport photograph was no better than anyone else's.

Now I was looking down at the closed eyes in the deathly face of the man in the bed, waiting for him to regain consciousness and trying to ignore the electrocardiograph on the wall, where the green dots of light had been bouncing lower during the last two hours, losing their rhythm.

"The signs are not good," the Frenchman said, "but you know what they say—while there's life, there's hope."

Ferris tried again. "Is there any chance of his talking to us, even though he's worsening?"

Dr. Restieux shrugged. "Nothing is impossible." He was the only one on the medical staff at this hour who spoke a European language, and Ferris had asked him to help us. "The trauma is quite massive, you must understand, and the suboccipital area of the skull is complex. There isn't an electroencephalograph available to us at the moment, so it's difficult to tell what's going on. This patient's brain could be dying and we wouldn't know. The human brain dies gradually, from the stem to the deeper regions, and that could be happening now. The blood-gas reports are showing signs of stability, but that doesn't tell us too much as to his chances. We have to wait." He hooked the chart back and turned away, but Ferris stopped him.

"Can anything be done to stimulate him?"

"Stimulate?"

"Can you bring him back to consciousness, even temporarily?"

Restieux looked puzzled. "You mean with drugs?"

"Drugs, electric shock, whatever would work."

"Not without harming the patient."

"But it could be done?"

In the bleak light of the intensive-care unit, the doctor's eyes widened slightly. "The question is academic. We're not prepared to harm the patient, whatever else is involved."

"I've discussed this with the chief of police," Ferris told him levelly. "This man might help us to find out quite a lot about the assassination of the British secretary of state, if he could talk to us even for a few minutes. He might help us to save lives in the future. It's extremely important for us to learn any information this man has in his possession, and if you're able to do anything at all, I'm asking you to consider it. The host country is responsible for the welfare of visiting delegates, and we're anxious to cooperate; my orders are direct from London."

Restieux went on watching him for a moment before he spoke. "And I am responsible for the welfare of my patients, and my orders are direct from Hippocrates."

When he'd gone, I looked at Ferris. "Have you been in signals?"

"Yes."

"London's pretty desperate."

He stared down at Jason's white face for a moment. "We were handed this one rather late, so we're having to make up time. No cause for concern."

He left me five minutes afterward, his crepe soles making a faint kissing sound along the linoleum. I sat on the paint-chipped metal chair, watching the slow dripping of the IV and the light patterns bouncing across the screen. It was now 3:30 in the morning and the building was quiet. There were two nurses on duty at the ward station, and one of them had been coming in here every few minutes, checking the IV bottle and taking Jason's temperature and noting it on the chart.

During the two hours I'd been here, Ferris had gone down to the telephone in the main hall at intervals, coming back and telling me nothing. There might have been nothing to tell: He'd obviously been signaling London via the embassy, reporting on Jason's condition and asking for orders; but unless Jason could tell us something, there wouldn't be any orders—we couldn't make a move. And I knew this: If Croder was so desperate for information that he was ready to risk Jason's life, the assassination in Tian'anmen Square hadn't been the end of things. Whatever operation the opposition had mounted, Bygreave's death hadn't been the objective; it could have been no more than the first step. Their operation was still running and there was nothing we could do, no direction we could take; it was like waiting in the dark for a blow that could come from anywhere, even from behind.

Just after 4:15 Jason opened his eyes.

I looked up at the screen and saw the green dot was bouncing slightly higher and with a steadier rhythm.

"Jason," I said softly.

He didn't move, but I thought he'd heard me; his eyes were turned to watch the ceiling above my head.

"Jason."

One of the nurses had come in five minutes ago and would be back again soon; I could call them both here if I needed to, just by raising my voice. Jason still didn't move.

"How do you feel?" I asked him quietly, and stood over the bed so that he could see my face. He looked at me for a long time, but there wasn't anything in his eyes; then they closed again as he murmured something.

"What?" I asked him. In a minute he said it again, but I couldn't make out any specific words; I had to put the sounds together and guess at a verbal pattern. *Two men.*

"Two men?" I asked him.

His lips moved. These were different sounds. *Killer.*

"Killer?"

I had to wait again. After a bit his lips moved again and I watched them; there seemed to be a W after the first K. KW something. KW ill?

"What did you say, Jason?"

Same sound. I watched his lips, and then got it.

"Yes. I'm Quiller. Don't rush it. Relax."

If I called the nurses, they might give him medication, do something to break this fragile thread of consciousness. One of them would be in here at any minute.

"You were attacked by two men?" I asked in a moment.

His eyes opened, and I think he tried to turn his head, because there was a spasm of pain and he grimaced and the sheen of sweat began covering his ash-white skin.

"Don't rush it, Jason. Take your time."

A minute went by.

Sounds came again. The only patterns I could guess at were *Elsie, I. Spur. Sool.*

"Say again," I told him softly, "when you're ready." I felt the sweat on my own face now because of the need to hurry, and to find the delicate balance between drawing some kind of information out of him and keeping him alive: The more we hurried, the more he might say but the sooner he might lose consciousness again, perhaps for the last time.

His eyes opened and looked up into mine. "Tell," he whispered, and this time it sounded perfectly distinct.

"Tell who?"

Then just sounds again, the same as before, or nearly. *Elsie I. Insool.* Ay eh? Not sense. Tell Elsie?

The pale lips moved, and I watched and listened. *See spur. C?* Elsie? Elsie spur? He was using all his strength on the syllables, slurring the consonants; I couldn't tell whether he was leaving out the beginnings and endings of words, or even whether he was rambling.

"Jason. Tell who? Elsie? Who is she?"

He was watching me back. *Tell see I eh. Tell see—*

"Tell the CIA?" I leaned closer.

"Ess. CIA."

"Tell them what?"

There were voices now in the distance, a man's and a woman's, someone talking to one of the nurses along the corridor. I tuned them out, concentrating on Jason.

"What do I tell the CIA?"

His eyes closed and I waited, flicking a glance at the screen on the wall where the green dot was bouncing lower again. In a moment he rallied, and sounds came again. *R spur.* Hasper? Ask her? After?

"Jason. Say again." I leaned closer still.

He opened his eyes. *Ask per.* Per? Spur?

"Ask Spur?"

"Ess."

"Who is Spur?"

Then there were footsteps and a young Chinese in a white coat came in, a stethoscope hanging from his neck. One of the nurses followed him, the small girl with plaits under her cap. He looked at me hard, saying nothing.

"Do you speak English?" I asked him.

"Mee-ye?"

"Parlez-vous français?"

He looked away without answering, and prepared a syringe while the nurse swabbed Jason's median vein. I tried him with German and Russian, desperate to stop him from doing anything to Jason now he'd begun talking. He didn't answer, and I had to move away to give him room as he lanced the tip of the needle into the vein and put slow pressure on the plunger.

The nurse made an entry on the chart and they both went out, leaving the air acrid with the smell of the ether she'd used on the swab.

"Jason," I said softly, and leaned over him.

His eyes opened slightly.

"I will ask Spur to tell the CIA. Is that right?"

His lips didn't move, and there was no understanding in his eyes.

"Jason."

But the pallor of his skin was now tinged with blue, and when I looked up at the screen on the wall I saw the dot of light leveling out and leaving a thin, featureless line.

"They've killed Jason," I said.

The line was silent for a bit; then Ferris asked: "How?"

"One of the doctors here injected cyanide, or someone posing as a doctor."

"I'll be right over," Ferris said.

"No. Keep away. This place is a deathtrap now."

VI

GRACE

✦

They wouldn't shoot. It would make too much noise. There were extra police patrols in the streets tonight and the curfew was in force until dawn. To shoot, in any case, was not their fashion; the creators of the martial arts preferred silence, and hidden strength.

I climbed higher and reached the top floor of the hospital. It was no good going down and into the street before I was informed. It was a four-story building with a flat roof, one of the new concrete additions to this ancient city, bare of tiles or balconies or arched outer walls that might have offered me exit. I would have to go out by a door.

Ferris had told me that he'd remain at the embassy, and had wished me luck; there was nothing else he could do. Once the executive is in hazard his director can only withdraw from the area and save himself, and remain available to receive the next man out if the executive is lost. Nor could Ferris send a squad of police into the hospital to bring me out under protection; the chief of police would have agreed to do that, to do anything, in fact, that would alleviate the guilt and embarrassment that he and the People's Republic security forces were still suffering; but the laws and edicts chiseled in the timeless rock of ages by that gaggle of demigods who lord it over us in London, world without end, didn't allow for that. In no circumstances will a director or an executive in the field call upon the police or any other service of whatever country is their host. It would lead to questions, and inquiries, and complications; it would place us under obligation to officials who might later decide to exert their power over us, bringing the risk of exposure. Ferris and I were in Peking as two security agents responsible for the safety of the visiting British delegation, and could call on the Chinese police for extensive help; but that was only our cover, and beneath our cover were two human ciphers with code names and nothing more, working in the dark of our own making for an organization that didn't officially exist; and we must make no sign, and leave no shadow.

Thus sayeth those tyrannical bloody red-tape artists in London who have never known what it's like to be trapped in a building with the fear of death creeping in the gut like a time fuse and not much chance of getting out.

I walked to the end of the concrete passage and found the trapdoor to the roof, and the iron ladder. The night was calm, with pale stars and a wash of light from the streetlamps four stories below. I began crawling when I neared the edge of the roof on the south side, to avoid presenting a silhouette against the skyline in case they chanced to look upward; but most of the time they'd be watching the doors.

They hadn't come into the building for me because the night staff was there, and they would have had to show themselves and use violence and make a noise. With Jason it had been easy, and they'd needed to silence him as soon as they could, cutting off the source of information. With me it would be more difficult and they could afford to take their time; I had no information; my death was required simply to protect their own security; they had an operation running and I mustn't get in their way.

One.

He was in the doorway almost directly opposite, his back flat against the wall and his head turned to watch the street; from there he could see the main entrance of the hospital and the windows along the whole of its length. He was in the loose blue cotton uniform of a factory worker, but in the low light I couldn't see his shoes. In terminal confrontation, shoes can be important; the hard edge of a heel can be lethal.

I crawled to the east parapet, straightening up in the cover of the elevator tower and feeling a tug of pain as the ribs opened out, a reminder that they hadn't yet healed. Body awareness was increasing, helping me to prepare for survival. I crouched low again, the sharpness of the loose flint burning against my palms as I dropped onto my hands and toes, reaching the parapet.

Two.

It took me five minutes to make him out, because he was deep in shadow and standing absolutely still; it was the blinking of his eyes that signaled his presence, covering and exposing the faint glow of the corneas. I couldn't see what he was wearing, but the color of his clothes was neutral, midway between dark and light. From his position he would be able to see the narrow flank of the building and the emergency entrance where the ambulance was parked.

I moved on, crossing the corners of the roof and once kicking a flattened tin can and dropping immediately into a crouch clear of the roofline. Sometimes I heard voices from below, the light fluting tones of women; the nurses had left many of the windows open along the north side above the park. It took me half an hour to locate the three other men: one at the end of a narrow street leading toward the embassy; one in the shadow of a bus shelter on the west side; one almost lost in the darkness of an alley where the lamp on the wall had gone out.

Total of five. At least five, possibly more.

I looked at my watch, its blue-green figures glowing among the stars reflected in the black glass panel. The time was 5:12 and I could wait until daylight and go down through the building and walk into the sunlit street and stay in the open where there were people; but they might not hold off; they might have instructions to make certain of a killing before I could reach the safety of the embassy; and that would bring the police, shouldering their way through the crowd of drawn faces watching the awkward-looking object spread-eagled on the pavement with the blood beginning to make a rivulet in the dust; and that would mean questions, inquiries, a full-scale investigation that would lead to the ambassador's office, and Ferris, and finally to London.

We must make no sign, and leave no shadow. Those are the rules set up by those bastards over there, planning their operations in the civilized comfort of their offices, unaware that this beleaguered little ferret would very much like to wait for daylight and try for the safety of the open street rather than crouch here with the sweat gathering and the knowledge that he must go down there now and in the half-dark make an end of it one way or the other.

Take no notice: This is only fear. They're right. The things we've pulled off, the really big operations that have blown the opposition networks or averted war or forced Moscow to rethink in the naked light of intelligence exposure, have been pulled off because the executives who got back home alive with the objective achieved were able to do it under total cover, picking their way through the shadows of their own anonymity, faceless and unseen. It works. It has always worked.

At 5:15 I moved away from the north parapet, straightening up and keeping close to the elevator tower and stepping over the low radio aerial that crisscrossed the roof, going down through the trapdoor and shutting it quietly.

There was no point in any case in waiting for the safety of daylight. They would trail me wherever I went, so that I'd have to keep away from the embassy, and Ferris; they'd trail me all day long through the city if they had to, waiting for a chance, then finishing me off on the street or forcing me to hole up somewhere like an animal and wait for them to come. Whatever I must do, I must do it now, because things would only get worse. They'd seen my photograph in the papers and they'd seen me with Jason and I was blown and must go to ground wherever I could. I didn't just have to get out of this building; I had to get out of Peking.

On my way down to the ground floor I passed three nurses and a boy mopping the floor; one of the girls asked me something and I made a gesture that could mean anything, going down the next flight of stairs before she could try to stop me. On the ground floor I turned left, because it was on the west side of the building that I might stand a chance. From the roof I'd seen that one man was posted on each side, with a fifth placed so that he could cover the main doors and the emergency entrance together. On the north side there was the small park, an open space with almost no cover; on the west there was only one man posted, and he was at the end of the alley where the lamp had gone out. He was the man I would have to go for, and try to put down; but he must be so sure of me that he wouldn't signal the others first. If he alerted them, I was finished; I might prevail over one man, possibly two, but not five.

At the end of the passage there was a narrow door, half-blocked by a pile of linen, and I stopped in front of it to loosen my tie and pull my shoelaces tight; then I opened it and went into the street.

The figure in the alley straightened up as he heard me, and faced this way. He was in silhouette now: From the roof I hadn't been able to see beyond him along the alley, but now there were three lamps visible and beyond them an open square in the dim light of the distance; it wasn't a cul-de-sac, and the way was open to me. If I turned to the left or right along the street I would move closer to a second man, with this one at my back. I must cross the street here and make straight for the one in the alley, and he must see me coming and feel confident, with the knowledge that time and strength and expertise were all on his side, together with the element of surprise—because I wouldn't look at him as I neared. Then he wouldn't call or whistle to the others; he'd want to take me alone, for his pride's sake. These would be trained men, trained in the dojo and the street to kill with finesse and with dispassion; they would be panther-quick with hands like knives, and they would enjoy executing the weaponless techniques they'd used a thousand times, a hundred thousand times, against each other with full control. Now the control could come off and they would experience the hot blood of a kill.

He mustn't signal them, this one in the alley. That was my only chance.

I walked across the street toward him, looking to the left and the right and then lowering my head a little as I picked my way through the light debris near the gutter, stepping onto the pavement, glancing to one side again as if distracted, moving straight toward him with no indication that I knew he was there, ten feet away from me, six feet, three.

Then he signaled the others with a quick call like a bird and came at me with a rising half-fist to the throat for an immediate kill, a strike that would have worked if I hadn't been ready for whatever he decided to do. I dropped and went inside and felt his fist rake along my shoulder as I struck for the celiac plexus and heard his breath catch before he swung clear and broke the power that was building up. Data was coming in as everything started to slow down in the way it does when the organism meets with crisis: I knew already that he was young and tiger-strong, a high dan in the arts with access to force sufficient to open my skull with a bare hand if I let him get in. If I tried to fight on his terms it would be lethal.

The others would have heard him, and would have started running by now. I supposed I had fifteen seconds, twenty, but no more than that, to do what I could to stay alive. A thought floated into my head and out again—*Ferris, you'll need a replacement*—before the man stopped withdrawing from the plexus strike and came in again, blocking my wrist and swinging one elbow in a curving blow for the chin and nearly connecting but losing the force that would have snapped my neck as I felt it whipping past my cheek before the momentum died. It left his body open, and it was here that I would have to work like a surgeon, remembering the charts and the wire-and-rubber-bag dummies and the long nights in Norfolk where Mashiro and Yamada and Dr. Dietrich had shown us that in dealing with a terminal confrontation one must try to move away from the kinetic action and concentrate on the body itself, feeling for its weak areas and worming one's way into the nerve centers and the major vessels and the vital organs where even a finger can stun or shock to death, given applied force.

His body was still open to me during the next few micro-seconds and I went for the seventh intercostal area to the left of the celiac plexus with a center-knuckle strike that connected and penetrated as far as the main fist profile before he doubled and broke its force; but I knew I must have reached the spleen and started internal bleeding because of the depth I'd achieved: He'd started to regurgitate and his breath was blocked off, and he had to come back at me without thinking, moving directly into Zen and using me as a reflection of his own body, hooking one foot into a sweep and bringing me down with one hand saving me and the outline of his bare foot filling my vision as he drove down with the force of a swinging ax against my face in the instant before I rolled and heard the air rush past my ear. He was now balanced on one foot and I wrenched at the knee, jackknifing it and bringing him down beside me.

Vision had been partially phased out by now; there was nothing to look at; we were fighting blind. I was aware of spinning shapes and colors in the background, that was all: the glint of a yellow eye, the angular silhouette of the roofline against the stars, the lintel of a doorway. Sound had closed in, to become intimate: the soft fierce inhalations as our breath was forced into our lungs, the rustling of his clothes as he spun sideways to break his fall, hooking a claw-hand across my face without preparation. Our sense of touch was heightened to an exquisite awareness, because the need for sight and sound had almost gone; we had to feel our way into the citadel and lay it waste in the silence and the dark, blindly and with deaf ears; but there was no sensation of pain, since pain works against the organism in hazard, distracting it from the effort needed to survive; blood from a wound somewhere was shining along his forearm, but I felt nothing.

Time had lost its meaning and I had no idea how soon the others would reach here, but it would be in a few seconds now. They'd have started running the moment they heard his call, and the distances involved were short. They didn't all need to get here at the same time: The first one here would finish me off, if I was still alive when he came.

I'd have to move faster, but my opponent was working for a hold now, knowing that it was all he had to do until the others arrived; he'd turned his body to lie across my legs while he flung one hand in a curve for my neck, aimed at the carotid sinus. I saw the strike in progress and jerked my head away, but not fast enough: The hand connected and colored light burst in my skull as the baroreceptors brought the blood pressure down, draining the brain and leaving me in a kind of twilight. Fear came into me at once and triggered a flow of adrenaline and the twilight brightened and I saw his hand again as it came toward my face and I knew that if I didn't stop this strike I was done for and the last thing I would see in my life would be the dirty-nailed hand of an unknown

Chinese boy in a darkened alley, and it seemed illogical and unnecessary.

Thoughts were shut off and I began working again, blocking the hand and catching the thumb and snapping it and hearing a hiss of breath. The stunning effect of his carotid strike was still slowing me, but I could hear footsteps now, someone running in the quietness of the street, and the adrenaline was forced into the bloodstream and I wrenched sideways and found his throat and put pressure there as he began using his knee in a reflex action, striking again and again at my groin but not connecting because he was too worried now by my hand on his thyroid cartilage: I was using my finger and thumb as a clamp and he began jerking his whole body to shake me off, but that was no good because I didn't want to die and I would do a great deal to prevent it, but so would he, and I rocked sideways as he went for the carotid artery again and the thought flickered in the shrinking mind, *Oh, Christ, it's no go, this time it's no go,* and I lay there at his mercy with the nerve light flashing through the numbing dark as the footsteps came closing in, their echoes hollow against the buildings, *this time no go and nothing left, only a rose for Moira. . . .*

I suppose if the boy could have done anything more to me, it would have ended there, but he was dead. The cartilage had been crushed in the clamp of my finger and thumb, and the soft tissue of the thyroid area had hemorrhaged, closing his windpipe; those were the sounds I'd heard in the last few seconds as he'd struggled for breath.

There was a transition period when my body had moved for itself, and memory started recording again only when I was flinging myself along the alley with my hands outstretched to fend off obstacles and my feet driving me forward with the sensation that the energy was coming from somewhere else, streaming into the organism and leaving it galvanized and frantic for life. Footsteps filled the alley, but the walls echoed and reechoed them in the narrow confines and they might only have been my own. The first of them had stopped, perhaps, to check the dead boy on the ground, giving me time to get clear, as if the boy had reached out from whatever cosmic field of consciousness sustained him now, and chosen to offer me grace.

VII

SPUR

✿

The monsoon was blowing in Seoul when I landed, and the evening sky was dark with rain over the mountains to the east: We could smell it, and the warm air was clammy against our faces as we crossed the tarmac at Kimpo and went into Customs and Immigration.

I was already noting the people around me. Ferris had booked me to Singapore by Cathay Pacific with a room at the Taipan Hotel and told the desk clerk at the Beijing Hotel to forward mail there, before using a pay phone and switching me to Seoul by Korean Airlines with a reservation at the Chonju and getting me aboard the late-afternoon flight without asking the Chinese for security; but the opposition would be watching for me now, and I could have been followed across.

"You have your smallpox-vaccination certificate?"

I gave it to the immigration officer.

After the incident in the alley I hadn't been near the embassy: I'd called Ferris from the clinic where they were patching me up and told him to get me out of Peking, and he'd done the rest, but I was nervous because those four hit men would be hunting for me and if they picked up my trail they wouldn't let me go free a second time.

"What is your business in Korea, please?"

"I'm a travel agent." I went through the details of the new cover Ferris had given me: Clive Thomas Ingram, a representative of Travelasia visiting Seoul to open up a tour program for Western Europe; references Barclay's Bank and British Airways.

Most of the passengers around me were Chinese, with one or two Japanese and Americans; others were still coming through the doors, letting the warm wind blow in and ruffle the papers on the desks.

"You have currency, please?"

I declared 100,000 *won* and asked where I could change pounds sterling, watching the young Korean in the dark blue jump suit leaning on the barrier by the exit; I thought I'd seen him on the tarmac outside.

"Enjoy your stay in Korea."

"Thank you."

Along the road into the town we fell into line with a dozen other taxis and kept station. Ferris hadn't said anything, but it was on my mind that if I got blown in this city, that would be it: He'd have to withdraw me to London. I could be expected to operate on the run, but only after we had a fix on the opposition and knew who they were and how to attack them; if they still kept us working in the dark we'd need a replacement out here, someone who hadn't been on the front page of the international press editions last night and this morning, someone who wasn't moving around inside a flexible man-trap that could reach across from the mainland and spring shut.

But if I could talk to Spur, I stood a chance.

Ferris said Spur might know.

I folded the map of the city and put it back into the holder on the front seat, watching the street names come up and telling the driver to drop me a block short of the Metro Hotel

because I wanted to look at the shops; then I walked to the
hotel and picked up a cab at the front of the line and told him
to take me to the main railway station; then I walked again,
going east for two blocks, changing my TWA overnight grip
from one hand to the other and using standard cover and
window reflections and seeing him again three times before
I decided to lose him in a street market and turn north.

It wasn't possible.

Ferris had laid a false trail to Singapore and taken me
straight to Peking Airport without going near the embassy and
seen me onto the plane after we'd both checked extensively
for tags, but the one I'd just shaken off was the young Korean
in the dark blue jump suit I'd noticed at Kimpo. He'd seen me
arrive and he'd followed me in and out of two taxis and held
onto me for a dozen blocks on foot. And he was a professional:
It had taken me a lot of selected cover and parallax movement
to lose him.

They couldn't be everywhere.

The streetlights were going on and the traffic along the
main streets was crowding the signals in the late rush hour.
I took three more blocks, rounding each of them and making
absolutely certain I was clean before I walked south and
found Changsin Street and saw the wine shop at the corner
of the small cluttered square. I went across to it.

"How now," Spur said.

He was standing behind the stacked counter, a short plump
man with horn-rimmed glasses and an open-necked shirt with
food down the front. It was a small place crowded with
bottles and crates, with two worn bamboo chairs and a round
table no bigger than a stool in one corner. I turned round once
and stood perfectly still, watching every open space in the
square outside. There weren't many; the place was like a
jungle lost in the middle of the city, with small trees and a
newspaper stand and bicycle racks and three fruit stalls
cluttering the view.

"It's all right," Spur said. "You lost him, as you know

perfectly well." He sounded mildly annoyed. I turned round and looked at him, feeling the pressure come off.

"He was *your* man?"

"He was."

"What was the point?"

"The point," he said with careful articulation, "is that I'm not a bloody idiot. When I'm told to expect someone, I try to make damned sure he gets here without fleas all over him. For your information, you weren't followed from the airport, except of course by my chap Kim, for at least part of the way."

"I know that." I dropped my bag and got out a handkerchief, wiping the sweat off my face; it was as humid in here as it was outside.

"Of course you do," he nodded, and reached for a bottle of wine. "I'd forgotten your reputation. One of the wild bunch, but not totally stupid. I'm Spur, but then you know that, too, don't you?"

"Ingram," I told him.

"Quite so, and spelled with a Q, if I've got my alphabet blocks in the right order." He gave a slight belch. "And you could do with a little drinkie-poo, I'm sure." He held out one of the glasses and I took it, but didn't drink. "Cheers, my dear fellow."

"Cheers. Doesn't that thing work?" There was an electric fan in the ceiling and I was running with sweat; but it was all right now, *they weren't everywhere* and I'd got here clean.

"Fuse blown," Spur said. "What happened to your face?"

"There was a bit of action."

"Ah. And why aren't you drinking? This is a Côtes du Rhône."

"I'm on a diet."

"How bloody depressing." He came round the end of the counter and sat down in one of the wicker chairs, gesturing to the other and putting his glass of wine carefully on the small rickety table.

I was catching a lot of vibrations now. I could trust anyone Ferris sent me to, but trust wasn't enough; this man was my

only link with the nameless and faceless opposition and I
wanted to know if he'd stand up to pressure and what he'd
behave like if the action got out of hand. One or two things
in the environment had caught my attention: a faded sepia
photograph of Funakoshi on the wall over the cash register,
and the way the bottles of wine were stacked in the window.
The photograph was probably there for half-forgotten sentimental reasons: If Spur had ever achieved second or third
dan, he'd let himself go to seed and I doubted if his reactions
were any faster now than an ordinary man's. But the bottles
in the window were more interesting; they were stacked in a
certain pattern, and from my chair I could sight through gaps
at three different angles that revealed strategic points in the
square outside: the corners of two streets and the neck of an
alley in the far distance.

"I suppose you've heard," Spur said, "the news from Peking,
have you?"

"What news?"

He looked slightly surprised. "Someone shot the American
ambassador dead, not long after you left there. It's been on
the radio."

"The *American* ambassador?"

"Seem to pick on anyone," he said, "don't they? But I
don't think it's like that really. There must be a definite
policy, wouldn't you say?"

"For Christ's sake, Spur, were we meant to stop that one?"

He sipped some more of his wine. "Something you ought to
know, dear boy. I'm not Bureau. I was once, but not anymore.
So there's no question of 'we,' you understand."

I took a breath and a minute to think. "How well did you
know Jason?"

"How well do we know anybody, in this trade?"

I didn't think he was blocking me for any purpose; I thought
it was the way he worked. I said: "I was with Jason when he
died. He only told me two things. One was to see you. The
other was to tell the CIA. He didn't say what." I waited.

"Tell them, perhaps, to warn their ambassador?"

"That's what I mean. From what you knew of Jason, do you think he'd got wind of this? And wanted me to tell the CIA in time?"

He considered this carefully. The last of the daylight had gone from the patch of sky through the window, and the yellow light of the lamps out there in the square threw shadows under the trees. Two or three children were playing near the newspaper stand with some kind of toy that looked like Diablo; a lean dog was scavenging among the shadowed doorways.

"I like your expression," Spur said, "had Jason 'got wind of.' Rather apt, for the monsoon season. And it sums up what's going on at the moment. We're not getting any signals that mean anything. We're not getting any real information. We're just, when we're lucky, getting wind of things."

I got out of the chair, going to the open doorway and looking out, coming back, sweating in the heat of the evening and wishing to God that Ferris hadn't sent me to someone whose joy in life was to stonewall. "Look," I told him, "Ferris sent me here because he thinks you know something. Do you?"

"Oh, yes," he said sleepily, "I know a lot of things." A faint spark had lit his pale acorn-brown eyes behind their glasses, and gone again. "But I don't owe Ferris anything, you see, or London. They are both desperate, or they wouldn't ask for my help. London doesn't like me, because I walked out of their stinking little sweatshop right in the middle of a mission, when signals had broken down and my director in the field was holed up in a Hilton Hotel and shit-scared to make a run for the embassy, and I was stuck on the wrong side of the enemy lines with half the Turkish police force hunting for me with tracker dogs and orders to shoot me on sight. There wasn't, you see, a hope of surviving unless I chose to walk out, and that is precisely what I did, because I'd had enough of those murderous bastards in London. They'll set you up and shove you out there, and if you don't come back with the loot, then you can fry, haven't you ever noticed?"

There was a new note in his voice now and I listened to it and after a time recognized it for what it was: a smothered cry of rage that covered something deeper, something darker in what London had left of his soul. They'd burned him out, but there was more than that; and I didn't want to know what it was, for his sake, because he was trying to live with it and not doing very well.

"How long," I asked him, "were you in the field?"

"Too long." He drained his glass and got up and looked at me with his eyes naked for an instant. "Too long. You know the signs, don't you?" He reached for the bottle across the counter and came back with his glass half-full again. "Just look at that bloody wind out there. Brings a few more tiles off every time it blows. You want to watch that, old boy, when you're walking in the street. This can be a dangerous city."

I'd caught enough vibrations now to know there was only one way in.

"But the going was good," I said, "once."

"What?" His pale brown eyes flickered again. "It was good, yes, once. What was that thing? *Whatever else may come to me, let fear be never a stranger; let me walk unguarded ways that breed the instant stroke and the flaming deed; let me thrill to the call of a desperate need, and the trumpet tones of danger.* But that was for us, my boy, not them. All they could think about was how to screw you out of a pension if you ever got back with your skin. I work for the Yanks now, and I'll say one thing about them, they don't mind paying a man for his honest labors."

So he couldn't have saved the ambassador. He hadn't known.

"You're giving me ideas," I said easily.

"What? Oh, balls, you don't do it for the money." He gave a slight burp. "You ever walk out on a mission, did you?"

I'd been waiting for that. "One day I will."

He lowered his eyes. "Wise man. You'll learn. I learned."

The tension had gone out of him but I waited, because if

I rushed him now he'd close up and there'd be no information
and the next time it'd be the British ambassador or someone
else on the U.S. team: Whoever the opposition were, their
target was the West, and somewhere in Peking there was a
third marked man and this time we'd have to stop them if we
could. London was waiting for Ferris, and Ferris was waiting
for me, and for the next few minutes I'd have to go on waiting
for Spur; it was the only hope.

"Who's running you," he asked me after a time, "for this
one?"

I think if I'd hesitated I'd have blown it, because he needed
my trust.

"Croder."

"*Croder?*" He lifted his glass. "And the best of luck. But
of course that's your style, isn't it? You want them to flay you
alive. Don't give yourself a chance, do you? Not exactly your
own best friend."

Quickly I said: "Is anyone?"

"What?" He watched me for a while, trying to see if I
meant it, and I knew how close I was to losing the mission.
I was certain now that he could give us enough information
to lead us to the opposition and show us how to go in there
and destroy them before they could destroy anyone else in
Peking. He wasn't just playing hard-to-get; he was suddenly in
a position where he could make them beg, in London, make
them crawl to him, so that he could face himself again and,
with this much power over them, get rid of the guilt that was
giving him no peace. *You ever walk out on a mission, did you?*

They'd never forgiven him; but now they were in his hands.

"You mean," he said in a moment and still watching me,
"I'm not my own best friend?"

"Not if you're like me. What is it, Spur? Standards too high?
Why do we have to expect more of ourselves than we expect
of anyone else?" In the dim light of the shop, I went close to
him. "You know something? One day I'm going to walk out
on a mission just to see what it feels like. You know? Just to

make those bastards in London know they're not God Almighty *every* time."

The reflection of the lamps in the square was on his glasses and I couldn't see his eyes; all I knew was that he was watching me in the silence, going over what I'd said and testing it for flaws. But that was all right; I didn't like London either, and he knew it; we all know it; we're all the same. I went on waiting, looking into his pale and shadowed face while the children out there went on laughing in the game they were playing, and somewhere a horse and cart went rattling through the square. Then Spur turned slowly away from me and drained his glass of wine, putting it on the stained counter so carefully that it didn't make a sound.

"There is only one man in Asia," he said softly, "who would have ordered the assassination of the British secretary of state in that particular way. His name is Tung Kuo-feng, and I'd better tell you about him."

At the top of the wide staircase there was a metal grille in the doorway and Spur opened it, ushering me into the room and closing it after him. The place was large and cavernous, the result of knocking down a couple of interior walls to make one room. Three bamboo chaise-longues with Thai silk coverings; two enormous tapestries on the walls showing a lion hunt with Burmese riders and mounts caparisoned in gold brocade; a whole series of carved teakwood tables crowded with jade and ivory; and the thick brown coils in the corner where a stick of incense was burning.

"Don't sit there," Spur said with his silent laugh, "he doesn't like it. Name's Alexander, but he doesn't answer to it; he's deaf, of course."

I went in the other direction: I hate anything without legs, and this bloody thing was fully grown by the look of it, strong enough to strangle an ox.

"This is the only house in the whole square without any rats, you see. Besides, he'd be lonely without me. Tung Kuo-feng, yes, a Chinese, scion of a family traceable to the early Ch'ing dynasty. You can sit here, if you like. Kim's bringing us some tea."

Kim was the boy he'd summoned from nowhere, clapping his hands, telling him to look after the shop below. "It's a pity we haven't got Youngquist here with us—I could have briefed you both." He was lighting a couple of arabesque lanterns, and they began throwing mottled patterns across the rugs.

"Who's he?" I asked him, and he looked round at me with a sudden jerk of his head.

"Youngquist? Oh, chap in Peking, useful as a contact." He turned away again to adjust the lantern flames. "I picked up the scent of Tung Kuo-feng on the frontier, in the demilitarized zone at Panmunjon. There's rather a lot of spook traffic between there and Seoul, as I'm sure you know, and that's why the CIA finds me so useful."

Youngquist? I'd never heard of him, and I didn't like the way Spur had closed up. I would ask Ferris.

"Tung isn't a young man anymore," he said reflectively. "I'd put him at sixty or more. But extremely fit. Lots of *ki*, you know, the real thing. Lots of meditation. He was running one of the very exclusive tongs in Shanghai in the good old days, not totally disconnected from the opium trade. My information on him is rather on the thin side, but up-to-date. Not many people like talking about him, you see; it's not healthy. Put it down there," he said as Kim brought in a black lacquer tray with tea things on it. That bloody thing in the corner had started moving, its shadow creeping along the wall. "Have you fed Alexander yet?"

"No," the boy said in English.

"Well, we won't do it in front of our visitor. Just leave him alone for the moment." He turned to me again. "It's absurd— we have to buy him frozen rats, when in fact he's here to clean up the real thing. There's a lesson there, my dear fellow: If you're too bloody efficient, you risk losing your job. Tung," he said as he poured the tea into the rice-grain china, "has got some very superior people working for him, twelve at the latest count. He's—"

"Eleven," I said.

"What?"

"I ran across some of them in Peking."

"Ah." His pale eyes studied me for a second or two. "And one of them wasn't quick enough, yes. But they wouldn't have been Tung's people; they would have been hired for the rough work, you see. If you'd run across Tung's people, you wouldn't be here now. You ought to watch that. If those bastards in London are putting you solo into the field with Tung Kuo-feng, you don't stand a chance. And I know a good deal about you. Not a chance in hell. Lemon?"

"Yes."

He cut a slice for me. "Lapsang souchong. They dry the leaves on wooden racks, and to protect the wood they soak it in tar. That's where a lot of the flavor comes from. Tung's people, you see, comprise a hit team, for the most part; but they're used for special operations, like the one in Peking. And when they hit, they don't miss. They're utterly loyal to him, and regard him as a living Buddha. They began in the usual way: He trained them as terrorists; and once they'd made their first kill they couldn't go back to their normal lives as students. One was a computer technician, and three had got their Ph.D. in social science at Peking University; but as you know, the creature man is not driven by his brain but by his emotions, which aren't all that different from those of a well-educated baboon."

He was maddeningly slow, but I couldn't hurry him. The information I wanted was coming on stream now, and nothing must interrupt. He wasn't doing this for London; he was doing it for a fellow slave of the Sacred Bull, which is the name we have for the Bureau, the dispenser of so much sacred bullshit. A wrong word from me and I could lose everything.

"Rumor has it," he said as he sipped his tea, "that Tung is

peddling snow, though I rather doubt that. But I know he runs a Triad, and that it's very powerful. I'm sure you know that Triad societies were first organized in the seventeenth century, to combat by secret means the tyranny of the Manchus, who overthrew the Ming dynasty. Their original aims were therefore legitimate, but like the Mafia they deteriorated over the passage of time to become illegal gangs." With sudden emphasis he went on: "But don't misunderstand me. The people of the Triads are rather more sophisticated than our Sicilian friends; they are secretive, subtle, and infinitely more dangerous. Such a man, then, is Tung Kuo-feng. Whether or not he's engaged in exporting heroin out of the Golden Triangle I don't know, as I say, but that bombing in Peking carries his signature: It was decorative, ironic, and effective. Tung to a T, if you'll forgive the expression."

I waited until I was sure he'd finished.

"Where is he now?"

"Don't move," he said softly. "Just keep absolutely still. It's all right."

I tensed, and felt slight pressure along my left leg as the bloody thing came gliding past me, its scales making a whispering across my shoe as it turned and came back, its head lifting and sensing me.

"He just wants to know who you are," I heard Spur murmuring, "and if you moved too suddenly you'd frighten him and he'd bite. Just keep still."

I could smell the thing now: a faint acrid scent like something rotten. That was why Spur burned the incense in the corner there. The narrow head was lowering now, and the sinuous ten-foot body went gliding toward the bamboo basket by the wall, where it formed coils again.

"Everyone loves old Alexander," Spur said with his silent laugh. "He was the gift of a grateful Armenian whom I got off a murder charge in Calcutta. Of course I told him it was just what I wanted. And where, you were asking, is Tung Kuo-feng now? He's in South Korea, that much I know. I'll put out a few feelers and give you a buzz if I get any warmer." He put down his teacup gently. "Or perhaps you'd rather do the buzzing, would you?"

"Yes."

"And you don't want me to have you followed about anymore, I quite understand. I hope you'll forgive my saying so, but the less we see of each other, the more I'd like it. If you're going to be so foolhardy as to tackle a chap like Tung Kuofeng on his home ground, I'd rather stay in the clear. Sudden death has never appealed to me as a way of avoiding taxes."

The Chonju Hotel was halfway down a narrow street of small shops that sold jewelry, silk, lacquerwork, and porcelain, one or two of them still open despite the moist wind that was rattling at the shutters and singing through the spokes of the bicycles that leaned everywhere against the walls.

I went into the lobby of the hotel and checked in, fetching the desk clerk away from his game of Jang-gi with an ancient Chinese under the leaves of a big potted palm.

No messages, either from Ferris in Peking or the British Embassy here in Seoul; and suddenly I felt cut off and helpless to make a move. It was hard to believe that in London they'd opened up a plot board for this mission in Signals, with a man sitting there at the console waiting for Ferris or our contact at the embassy to feed in information and request instructions, while Croder stood by with his mouth tight and his black eyes hooded and that brilliant and complex brain of his keyed to the work of sending me through the dangerous intricacies of a mission that was blocked at the start by the will-o'-the-wisp elusiveness of the opposition.

Four men dead, within four days—Sinclair, Jason, the secretary of state, and the U.S. ambassador to Peking—and I was holed up in a back street of Seoul with the monsoon fretting at the shutters and the lamplight flickering and no messages in the key box, nothing to work on, while somewhere

Tung Kuo-feng was planning his next move, playing his own game of Jang-gi with a fifth man on the board and ready for sacrifice.

Nerves. Discount. Nerves and the faint putrid smell of that bloody thing still in my senses, and the haunting memory of the death I'd brought to the boy in the alley, his tigerish fierceness stilled by my own hands as he lay under me with the blood filling his throat.

I went up the stairs, past grilled windows and a huge brass gong hanging from the wall; the corridor of the second floor was deserted as I walked to my room at the far end and opened the door.

Instant impressions: the sheen of dark silk and the scent of sandalwood; the glow of an emerald bracelet on a slender wrist; and in the ivory fingers with their lacquered nails, the blue metal of a gun.

VIII

LI-FEI

✳

A gun at close quarters is always dangerous because of the
unpredictable factors involved: the state of the opponent's
nerves and the degree of his fear and the position of the safety
catch and the distances and angles that will govern the tra-
jectory of the shot if the gun is fired. Timing, above all, will
decide the difference between success or failure.

She was only just inside the door and well within my reach,
so I hit for the wrist and the gun spun across the floor as she
cried out in pain and came at me with her lacquered claws,
hooking for my eyes with the soft ferocity of a cat as her
scent wafted over me and her face was held close to mine, the
faint light from the street glowing in her eyes as she fought
me, her breath hissing in fury.

She was hardly bigger than a child, but it took a moment
to subdue her; and even with both slender arms locked behind
her back she still went on trying to struggle. I left things like
that for a couple of minutes, giving her time to think. The
Astra Cub .22 was lying on the numdah rug between the
window and the bed, and her dark head was turned in its

direction; her breath came painfully in the quiet of the room as she began whispering to me in Chinese—to me or to herself or her gods, I couldn't tell.

I said in English: "I'm going to hand you over to the police." I was Clive Ingram, an innocent travel agent, and it was outrageous to find myself attacked like this in my own hotel room.

She didn't answer, but stood quivering with her head still angled to watch the gun. I was aware of warm silk against me, and of the fury that was still in her as I kept the lock on her arms; I could feel blood creeping on my face where her nails had torn the skin close to my eyes, and I knew that if I let her go she'd fly to the gun or spin round and try to blind me.

I told her again that I was going to call the police, this time speaking in French, and her small head jerked upward as she tried to look at me.

In the same language she said: *"I shall kill you."* Her breath shuddered out of her with the force of what she was saying.

"Why?"

"One day I shall kill you, however long it takes. Do you understand?"

"Not really." She knew I could snap her fragile arms and finish with it, but she also knew that a civilized male of the species wouldn't want to do that. If I let her trade on it, she wouldn't give me a second's chance. "My name is Ingram," I told her wearily, "and I'm an English travel agent on a visit to Seoul. You're mistaking me for someone else." I waited, feeling the small vibration of her heartbeat as her fury went on forcing its rhythm; but her breath was slowing now, and I was encouraged. I wanted to get her out of here, and sleep; I hadn't slept since the flight out from London two nights ago, and the death struggle in Peking had left me bruised and drained.

It occurred to me that this woman hadn't seen me very clearly in the gloom of the unlit room, so I pulled her backward and felt for the light switch with my shoulder, moving it down; then I walked her across to the mirror on the dressing table and for a moment we stared at each other: She was a pure Chinese, her delicate bone structure lit and shadowed by the lamps on the wall and her amber eyes glistening; I looked less elegant, with streaks of blood on my face.

"You see," I told her, "I'm no one you know."

She stared at me for another few moments and then broke, her head going down and the tears coming and her slight body shaking under my hands; and when I released her she covered her face and sank slowly to the floor, the gold embroidery of her long silk *hanbok* glowing in the light as her black hair fell forward and revealed the pale ivory of her neck. I left her there, going to pick up the gun. She'd come close to killing me and by mistake, and now the reaction was setting in.

For a long time she didn't move, and when the worst of the sobbing was over I asked her gently: "What is your name?"

She turned her tear-wet face. "Soong Li-fei."

"What were you doing in my room?"

I was holding the gun, its trigger guard hanging from one finger; but she didn't even glance at it.

"It was a mistake," she said, so softly that I only just heard; her French was cultured, with the accent of Touraine.

"What kind of mistake, Li-fei?"

Slowly she straightened up, wiping at her face with the backs of her small hands. "It was for my brother. They killed my brother."

The wind was rattling one of the shutters, and I went across to the windows and secured the stay. Her handbag was on the floor near the door, where she'd dropped it; it was of the same dark eau-de-nile silk as her dress. I took it over to her and she found a handkerchief and blew her nose a few times, turning away from me.

When she was quiet again, I said: "They killed your brother?" I went over to the handbasin and washed the blood off my face. "Who did?"

"This is the wrong room," she said, "or you are the wrong person. Please let me go now."

"Someone told you I killed your brother?"

"No." She put away her handkerchief and clicked the bag shut. "It was a mistake, m'sieur. I apologize."

"Then someone must have told you that the man who killed your brother would be coming to this room tonight."

"No."

"It's got to be one way or the other, Li-fei."

She watched me with reddened eyes, the last of the tears still glistening on their lids. "I had the room number wrong."

That was possible, but I had to make sure. In the initial phase of a mission I like my privacy.

"Who gave you the room number?"

"I forget." She was lying with a child's simplicity now, embarrassed, wanting to go. Her lip was trembling and she was making an effort to keep control; it occurred to me that she'd cried tonight from disappointment because I'd been the wrong man and she hadn't been able to avenge her brother.

"When did they kill your brother?" I asked her.

On a sudden sob that she couldn't stop—"Yesterday."

I went across to her quickly and held her small cold hands, and she looked up at me in surprise. "Was this in Seoul?" I asked her.

"No. In Peking."

My nape crept; but she'd said yesterday, not this morning.

"How did they do it?"

She opened the little silk bag quickly, showing me a news clipping folded many times. It was in Korean.

"I can't read it," I said.

"It says—" but there was another sob, and she gripped my hands tightly, refusing to break down again. "It says it was a ritual murder, on the steps of a temple." She thrust the small wad of paper back into her bag and closed it.

I felt the tension leaving me. "What was his name?"

"Soong Yongshen."

"I'm sorry. Do you live with your parents?"

"I have no parents."

And no brother now. "I'll see you home," I told her. "Where do you live?"

"No. Just let me go, please."

The monsoon sang through the street outside, banging at the shutters and swinging signs on their rusty hinges. It would blow her away, scattering her like fragments of porcelain.

"I'll get a taxi for you downstairs."

"No. I don't live very far."

I took out the gun and put it into her hands, and her ivory fingers closed round it clumsily, as if she'd forgotten what it was, and what it was for.

"Thank you."

"I'd throw it away, Li-fei."

"No," she said at once. "I will find him, and kill him."

"Where did you get it?"

"From a friend."

I went with her to the door. "What do you do?"

"I'm an official interpreter for the airline."

"French and Chinese. No English?"

"No. Japanese. There are so many who speak English."

We were by the door now, but I didn't open it yet; I'd been giving her time to recover. "What did your brother do?"

She caught her breath but steadied. "He worked for—for some kind of organization. I'm not sure."

"Why would anyone want to kill him?"

"He did something wrong. It was something to do with the dreadful thing in Peking."

"What dreadful thing?"

"The bombing at the funeral."

Blown.

As if from somewhere outside myself I noted that my voice didn't change in the slightest, but my skin was creeping along the whole length of my spine as the nerves reacted.

"What did your brother do wrong, would you think?"

"I don't know."

I'd been in this city three hours and no one had followed me in from the Chinese mainland and only Ferris knew where I was staying and already I was blown and I didn't even know how to start believing it.

She wanted to go, but I kept her.

"How do you know he did something wrong?"

"I was told." My voice hadn't changed and my face hadn't changed but her eyes were wider now as she watched me, her own nerves picking up the alarm in mine. There was nothing I could do about that.

"Who told you?"

"It would be dangerous for me to say."

"That doesn't worry me."

She was frightened now, underneath the perfection of the pale porcelain skin, underneath the elegance of the softly articulated French. There was nothing I could do about that either: It wasn't my fault that I'd walked in here at gunpoint tonight.

"It would be dangerous for me," she said, "to tell you anything."

"I think you're running with the wrong set, Li-fei." I chose the Parisian idiom of the *milieu* and she looked suddenly bitter, her head going down.

"Yes. There are things happening that I don't—that I don't understand. But I understand that my brother is dead."

I listened to every word and the way she said it; I watched her cinnamon eyes and the way they changed when she spoke of her brother and when she spoke of other things, the ones she didn't understand; I listened and watched for the slightest sign that she wasn't in point of fact Soong Li-fei, an official interpreter for Korean Airlines, but an exquisite and deadly emissary of the Tung Triad who'd been sent here to trap me with the performance of an accomplished actress. There was no sign; but my mind was clouded with fatigue and the dizzying certainty of the impossible; that I was blown and within the next hour would have to go to ground and somehow stay alive.

I'd tested her, but it had been crude: When I'd put the loaded gun back into her hands the safety catch had been on and the whole of my body's musculature had been tensed and prepared to hit the thing away again if she changed her mind and tried for a second time. I'd have to test her again when the chance came, before I could be sure.

I asked her now: "Did someone tell you I'd killed your brother? I mean, did they give me a name?"

"No."

"What did they say? How did they put it?" I gave an edge to my tone and she heard it, and looked trapped.

"You have nothing to do with this," she said in sudden despair. "It was a mistake—you are not the man I'm looking for. Please let me go, and I promise you'll never see me again."

Choice: Threaten her or make use of her. I could threaten to get the police here and accuse her of attempted murder if she didn't tell me what I wanted to know; but she might still decide it was safer to keep silent, whatever I chose to do: I had no means of knowing how unyielding she might be, how enduring, at the dictates of the torment that was driving her; the shock of her brother's death would have unbalanced her for a time.

"All right," I told her, "it was a mistake. Go home and give that gun back to your friend, and forget about vengeance; it could get you life imprisonment."

She closed her eyes for a moment in relief and then stood back as I opened the door for her, giving me a formal little bow and saying something softly in Chinese and then in French. "I thank you for your great kindness. May good fortune always be with you."

I went down the stairs with her, past the great brass gong, and left her at the entrance doors, which were still open to the warmth of the night. She walked down the steps into the windy street, and didn't turn her head.

Here in the old quarter of the city the streets were narrow, sometimes no wider than alleyways, and Soong Li-fei slipped through them as if carried along on the warm rain-smelling gusts of the monsoon, the dark silk of her dress shimmering in the lamplight as she vanished at a corner and reappeared as I turned after her. She had looked over her shoulder twice since I'd begun following her, but she couldn't have seen me; I'd been working my way from cover to cover through the shadows of the fluttering fan palms and past bicycles knocked over by the wind. The few people I passed walked with their heads down against the gusts, hurrying, some of them dodging into the small restaurants that were scenting the night air with the smell of *kimchi* and *sinsollo*.

"Hey, mister—you wanna girl?"

"No."

"You wanna boy?"

"No."

The wind sent another bicycle over with a clang from its bell. She had told me at least this much truth: She didn't live far from my hotel; she was already slowing her pace at the end of a narrow street of shop-houses and turning to go into a doorway; then a man came from the shadows and stopped her.

Contact.

He was asking her something and she was replying, explaining, shaking her head. He didn't think she was a prostitute—in this quarter she was too pretty and too elegant. I watched them from the distance of a stone's throw, keeping in the cover of shadow.

This was a contact, the first I'd made in security since I'd left London, the end of a thread that could lead me through the night and the wind to Tung Kuo-feng. But it wasn't going to be easy: There was the length of the street between the contact and me, and he was close to a turning; there would have to be some luck.

Soong Li-fei was already going into the doorway, leaving the man standing there alone; then he moved, and so did I, at first walking fast and keeping to cover and then breaking into a soft run as he vanished beyond the corner. I ran hard now, taking the risk that he'd hear me above the noise of the wind's rattling among the shutters and along the tiled roofs, but there was no sign of him as I swung into the alley at the intersection; it ran for fifty yards and opened into a small square filled with trees and parked horseless carts and a few benches. There was limitless cover for him here but I didn't think he'd used it; I didn't think he'd seen or heard me; I thought he'd simply moved into a doorway and gone inside, into one of a dozen buildings, and with no clue as to which.

I walked twice from the square to the intersection and back, desperate for the sign of a half-open doorway, a silhouette against a light, the sound of a voice; but he'd gone. There was no point in my staying; if I saw him now I wouldn't recognize him for certain as the man I'd seen talking to Li-fei; in the distance and the lamplight I'd seen nothing more of him than that he was a young bareheaded Asian in dark slacks and a white open-necked shirt.

I went back to the hotel the way I'd come, checking now and then to make sure I was alone. The big carved entrance doors at the top of the steps were still wide open, but there was no clerk at the desk. I looked for a copy of the *Korea Herald* in English behind the counter, but found nothing. I'd get one tomorrow; I wanted to see the report of Soong Yongshen's death on the steps of the temple in Peking before I signaled Ferris with information.

The time by the American Express clock on the wall was just gone eleven as I went up the stairs, my shoes quiet on the marble. Rock music was coming faintly from somewhere, and a woman's liquid laughter; a door banged in the street outside, or it was the wind shaking something; a sound was coming from the big brass gong on the wall, so low that it was hardly more than a vibration as it trapped the other sounds and held them like an unceasing echo.

Sleep. It was all I wanted now. She'd been going to kill me but it hadn't happened, and I was still here. Someone had made contact with her, someone who could have led me to Tung, but I'd lost him; so be it. Tomorrow was another day, and with luck I'd outlive this one. But I'd get no sleep until I'd gone to ground; it was just the thought of it that slowed me a little as I climbed to the second floor, my senses lulled by the strange murmuration of the gong. The fatigue curve is not constant; it dips faster as time goes on. But I wasn't totally relaxed; one must never be totally relaxed in a red sector, if life is still held to be sweet.

Light was filtering through the grilled windows of the stairwell, throwing the restless shadows of the fan palms in the square outside; faintly through the colored glass I could hear them rustling; my own shadow came for a moment against the wall as I turned on the curving stairs.

The woman had stopped laughing. There was still within me the degree of alertness necessary for the memory to remain aware that she had been laughing before, and now had stopped. I was also noting other things, as the impressions of light and sound and touch went shuttling secretly across and across the undefined borderline between the conscious and the subconscious, arousing the interplay between the primitive and the modern brain that would turn incoming data into decision when the need came.

I reached the second-floor passage, my shadow moving again on the wall, this time with the other shadow as if we were dancing. But we were not dancing; this was more serious, and as time slowed down I was aware only of the primitive animal-brain impressions: the flare of alarm along the nerves and their response; the swift rushing of adrenaline and the contraction of muscle; the locking of the breath as the strength of the organism gathered with the force of a storm and then broke loose. Nothing was thought out; everything was done in the light of ancient wisdom, tapping the store of racial memory wherein it is recorded, for all of us, what must be done to survive when there is no time to think.

Something snapped, possibly his arm. I remember very little about it, but that first sound was sharp. For an instant I felt his breath fanning against my face before the force in me, which was in essence the force of the living creature refusing to be killed, reached its peak and he spun slowly with his back curving against the low balustrade and his arms flying upward, the hands set in the shape of hooks; then he was flung away from me and began going down as I watched, down the lamplit stairwell, his body turning slowly until one of his shoulders hit the huge brass gong and broke it away from the wall, so that it fell with him like a giant discus, striking the marble floor below and sounding his death knell with a clangor that shook the night.

IX
RAIN

❁

"You mean you don't wanna lay me, honey?"

The rain thundered on the roof.

"No. I just want to stay here for a day or two."

She gazed at me from beneath her heavy black eyelashes. "But not like a love nest?"

I'd found her in a doorway, sheltering from the torrential rain the monsoon had brought to the city half an hour ago. She was all I had, but I'd better not tell her that, because those bloody penny-pinching secretary birds perched at their desks in the Accounts Department in London would go into instant molt when they saw my expense sheet.

"Not like a love nest," I told her.

There was a kind of eldritch laughter somewhere in the remnants of my soul and trying to get out, because this was an ultrapriority mission with a crack London controller and a first-class director in the field with instructions to give me all necessary facilities from Signals through embassy to shields and support, and here I was in a Seoul back street, soaked to the skin and trying to get a fifty-year-old whore with green eyelids to take me in from the rain.

"Are you stoned, honey?"

We were standing in the passage between the front door and the stairs and the door was still open and I could hear the sirens in the distance as more patrol cars zeroed in on the Chonju Hotel a few streets away, where a man was lying with his back broken under the weight of a brass gong. They wouldn't be looking for me yet: Clive Ingram, travel agent, was still ostensibly staying at the hotel, and his overnight bag was still in his locked room; he might easily be dining out or seeing a film or holed up at the Pacific Club with friends, and wouldn't be reported absent until the morning. No one had seen me leave; the lobby had been full of people with white faces looking down at the body under the gong, and I'd gone out through a fourth-floor window and across the rooftops.

"No," I told the woman, "I'm not stoned." I got out my wallet and peeled off some notes. "What about a hundred thousand a day, minimum three days?"

She looked at me hard. "Don't fool around, do you?" She took the notes and led me upstairs. "You running drugs, are you?"

"There are two conditions," I said, watching the calves of her stout veined legs as we climbed the stairs. "One is that as far as anyone else is concerned I'm not here. And while I'm here, you don't see any clients."

"That's no sweat. But what did you do out there, buster? You in some kinda trouble?"

"Not if you don't talk."

She was panting as we reached the big low room at the top of the stairs. Stained cotton rugs, two sagging divans, a cheap bead curtain over a door in the corner, a big Japanese lantern and a dead palm in a chipped reproduction Ming container. The wall was papered with old posters: *Sadie Nackenberg's in Town . . . Sadie Be Good. . . If You Knew Sadie Like I Know Sadie* . . . New York, Chicago, Los Angeles, New Orleans. And hundreds of photographs.

"Show biz," she said with an echo of desperate pride, "that

was me. Those were the good days, like Streisand says. Where are you from?"

"London. My name's Clive Ingram."

"Hi. I'm Sadie. Born in Memphis, U.S. of A. Been in a fight?"

"There was an accident." There were still scratches on my face from Li-fei's nails, and I'd fallen nine or ten feet onto a pile of stacked crates at the back of the Chonju Hotel when the creeper had given way.

"You on the run, mister?"

"My wife doesn't understand me."

"Uh-huh. She throw you out the window?"

"Something like that."

"Goddam women's lib, it takes the joy out of everything." But she was watching me critically, wondering how far 100,000 *won* would go if one day she had to bribe the police. "Listen, I don't want no trouble here. This is a respectable place. I mean, I don't want your wife here. Or whoever. I have a businesslike understanding with the cops, you know what I mean?"

Water was dripping from my clothes as I stood checking the usual things: exits, windows, telephone, visual security from the street and other buildings. Tonight it wasn't easy; all I could see from the windows was the rain through the flimsy curtains.

"If you don't talk to anyone," I told her, "you won't have any trouble." But I'd have to be careful when I went into the street; by morning the Homicide Bureau would be pushing the street patrols for results. "Is there a shower?"

"You bet. You don't have any dry clothes?"

"I want to go straight to bed. They'll dry overnight."

"I got some hangers. Bathroom's through that curtain and turn left. Careful with the faucet, it needs fixing, you can get yourself drenched." She looked at my clothes and gave a husky laugh. "What am I saying?"

The telephone rang twice while I was in the bathroom and

I listened to the soft rasp of her voice through the thin white-plaster wall: *That's okay, honey, I didn't expect you a night like this, I'll miss you too, so forth.* I dried myself on a towel marked Seoul-Hyatt and wrapped myself in the blanket she'd given me. The phone rang again and I listened again, in case. I wasn't safe here but I wouldn't be any safer anywhere else. Spur might have put me up, but I wouldn't have been able to sleep with that bloody thing crawling all over the floor. As soon as they found my room still empty at the Chonju in the morning the police would be checking every hotel in the city. The embassy would give me a bed but you don't go to ground in your embassy when you're blown; London is terribly fussy about abuse of diplomatic hospitality overseas, and in any case the opposition would expect me to go there for refuge and I'd never get out again without walking into a trap.

"You can see the kinda clients I got," Sadie told me the third time the telephone rang. "They call me up when they can't make it. Most of them are in the U.S. forces out here, some of them lieutenants and upwards, fresh outa West Point, but underneath the war paint they're just boys from back home, and you know something? They miss their mothers; half the guys that come here don't even ask me for sex, they just wanna talk to someone who can speak the queen's goddam English. Gee, honey, you look real cute in that poncho."

The rain was still drumming on the roof and sending cascades into the street below. Five minutes away from here the girl with the cinnamon eyes would be listening to it, the girl with the Astra Cub .22. *What had the Asian said to her when he'd stopped her outside her apartment?*

He hadn't followed me back to the hotel: I'd checked to make sure I was alone. He'd taken a different route through the maze of alleys and reached there before me, not knowing at that time that I wasn't still in my room.

Did you kill him? he'd asked her outside her apartment.

No. He's not the man, she'd said.

It was possible. Anything was possible, but I had to look for a likelihood, a logical scenario. It could have been someone else who stalked me in the corridors of the Chonju, but I didn't think so; it would have been too much of a coincidence. The man who had turned slowly in the air as he went down the marble stairwell had been Asian and he'd worn dark slacks and a white open-necked shirt. Soong Li-fei wasn't just an official interpreter for the airline: She'd had a brother who was in Peking at the time of the funeral bomb—"It was something to do with that dreadful thing in Peking"—and they'd killed him because he'd "done something wrong." She had a friend who had lent her a gun, and someone had told her that the man who'd killed her brother would be checking into the Chonju Hotel tonight, room 29. She had Tung connections, strong ones, close ones, whether she knew it or not; and they'd tried to use her as a killing instrument, and when she'd failed to kill me, the young Asian had gone there to do it himself.

"I had one young guy," Sadie said, "who spent the whole time just showing me the photographs of his mom and dad and his kid sister, telling me about them. Then you know what he did? He tried to lay me, but there was no spring in his step and he said, 'Shit, man, when am I goin' to grow up?' We both of us ended up crying in each other's arms—at least that's what I tried to make it sound like, but you know what I mean. People think this job don't carry any responsibilities, can you believe it?"

"*La vie est pleine de surprises,*" I told her.

She squinted at me over a cigarette. "How's that again?"

"An old Chinese proverb." I asked if I could use her phone and she said okay and I rang the British Embassy and spoke only in French, asking them to get the cipher clerk out of bed. He came on the line after ten minutes and I gave him *Jade One,* the code word for the mission, and put the whole thing across in routine speech code because it was all I could do without a one-time pad and he wouldn't have one: *taken ill* for "blown" and *confined to his room for* "gone to ground,"

and so forth. Ferris would have a bloody fit when he got this
one: There'd now been a total of four attempts on my life and
I'd had to kill twice and now I was blown for the second time
since I'd reached the field and we still hadn't got any access
to the opposition. It was like a two-way mirror that only they
could see through. I'd worked only once before in the Orient
but I was beginning to remember how it felt: Nothing is what
it seems; your feet are on shifting sands and the images you
see are only reflections and the sounds you hear are only
echoes and the logical process of Western linear thinking
takes you through shadows and leads you into the ethereal
haunts of illusion until you start losing your grip, and then
you're done.

Fatigue, of course. Have to brace up, you know. Spot of
Horlicks and a sound night's sleep, that's all you need.

Not quite. I need some magic.

"Attendez, ce n'est pas tout." I asked for information on
Soong Li-fei, spelling her name out in French, saying she was
allegedly an interpreter for Korean Airlines. I asked for information on Soong Yongshen, allegedly her brother and dead
by ritual murder in Peking. I asked who Youngquist was.

*I also reported that although Ferris couldn't have told
anyone that my new cover was Clive Ingram and that I was
booked into the Chonju Hotel in Seoul tonight, the opposition
had sent a woman there to meet me, with a gun.*

Some kind of magic, yes, was needed here, to arm me
against theirs.

The rain beat on the tiles overhead and I gazed into the
watchful eyes of Sadie, the whore from Memphis, her thick
black lashes narrowed against the cigarette smoke that drifted
between us on the sultry air of the room.

Who is Sadie?

She's just a whore from—

Are you sure?

Fatigue, yes, ignore.

"Bien, c'est tout maintenant. Je repète: Ji—à—dé—eu, un."

I rang off.

"She no speaka da English?" Sadie asked me.

"That's right."

I asked her where I was to sleep and she took me to a small room at the back of the building with a single bed in it already made up and an electronic alarm clock on the bedside table showing the correct time and a plastic baseball trophy on the dressing table underneath an array of faded silk flags and pennants—ASU Sun Devils, Cincinnati Reds, Dodgers—and a tin-framed photograph of a young man with a crew cut and a winning smile, with fly spots clouding the glass.

"This is Danny's room," she said, a warmth touching her voice and lingering. "That's him up there. He's my son. I keep everything ready for him, when he comes to see me."

"A handsome boy. When d'you expect him here next?"

She turned away. "Oh, not yet awhile, I guess. Hasn't been here for a year or two—he keeps pretty busy, see, works for the Hertz people in Hong Kong, but he always calls me up at Christmastime, never misses. You be okay in here?"

"Yes." I asked her if she had an English-language newspaper and she found one for me from the kitchen, the *Korea Herald* of today's date. Front-page headline: WORLD SHOCK AT SECOND ASSASSINATION IN PEKING.

I said goodnight to Sadie and shut the door and opened the small window at the foot of the bed and did a quick survey as the rain cascaded from the clogged gutters into the street below. This was the second floor and there was a narrow balcony directly underneath; it looked as if it might collapse if I hit it too hard, but that would be all right: It would break the fall. Telephone wires, drainpipe (out of reach and dilapidated), a rope of dead creeper, four windows overlooking this one, two of them curtained.

I shut the window against the din of the rain and got into bed and looked again at the paper. Picture of Omer J. Rice, U.S. Ambassador to the People's Republic of China, shot to death yesterday by an unknown assailant as he was leaving the embassy. Vice President Liu Faxian orders ceaseless and untiring efforts to find and bring to justice those responsible for these monstrous crimes; photograph of Faxian. U.S. Embassy placed under massive day and night police guard as CIA investigators are flown in from Seoul, Tokyo, Taiwan, and the United States to assist ANFU, the Chinese security service, in their inquiries. Report from the Tass agency in Moscow declares China a country where the diplomats of other nations are no longer safe. The body of the late Ambassador Rice to be flown by special plane to his home-town of Springfield, Massachusetts. Chinese government placed in difficult and precarious position by these mystifying acts of violence against the West.

And on page three a grainy picture of a young Chinese national, Soong Yongshen, who was the apparent victim of ritual murder on the steps of Huang Chiung Yu, the Temple of the God of Paradise. Police were said to be following certain leads indicating a possible connection between Soong Yongshen and the funeral bombing of yesterday morning that had killed the British secretary of state. Picture: British secretary of state.

I looked for a long time at the photograph, aware of a memory stirring. This man's face was like another I'd seen yesterday in Peking, somewhere in the crowd at the funeral. But sleep was coming down on me like a dead weight and I folded the paper and dropped it onto the bedside table and switched off the lamp, listening to Sadie's husky and muted voice in the outer room saying, sure, honey, it was a hell of a night to be out, and in any case she'd be out of town for the next few days visiting a sick friend on the coast, so they'd have to take a rain check, and, Jesus, they could say that again and no kidding.

I lay in the dark with one or two last thoughts circling, trying to form an equation in my mind. I remembered now whose the other face was, the one that was rather like the British secretary of state's: It was the American vice president's; I'd seen him among the mourners in Tian'anmen Square. To an Asian they would look identical. The lilting voice of Soong Li-fei was in these last thoughts, telling me something again, that her brother had "done something wrong, something to do with the dreadful thing in Peking," where the police were said to be following leads indicating a possible connection . . . between Soong Yongshen . . . and the funeral bombing of yesterday morning. . . .

Thoughts circling in the dark, nothing very coherent, long time no sleep. Perhaps Soong Yongshen had made . . . a mistake . . . of some kind . . . yesterday in the square where the flowers had gone whirling into the dark sky and come drifting down in waves of sleep . . . sleep . . .

I woke at first light and heard Sadie doing something in the kitchen and went out there to see her, giving her a shopping list: some clothes, shoes, toilet stuff, a map of Seoul and a map of Korea. The rain had stopped and we could hear shutters banging along the street as people opened up their shops.

When Sadie had gone out I rang Spur.

"Do you know speech code?"

He tried some but it was out-of-date and I didn't want any confusion. I asked him if he spoke Russian.

"*Niet.*" His speech was slow: I'd woken him up. "Chinese, bit of Japanese, bit of French."

I tried out his French but it wasn't good enough.

"There isn't a chance in hell," he told me in English, "that this line is bugged. Or have you got someone with you?"

It was mission paranoia and he'd spotted it. I said: "So far they've tried to get me four times—do you want me to spell that?"

There was a silence; I suppose he was giving that soundless laugh of his. Then he said: "Time you retired, old boy, like I did. Make some money."

"Have you got any information?" I asked him.

"Yes. Are you ready?"

"No," I said quickly. "I'll come over."

"Just as you like. But not before tonight. I'm still working for you. Say about nine, all right?"

It crossed my mind to take the risk and ask him for it now, but I remembered how strong their magic was, the way they knew where I was moving, the way they'd been making one move ahead. Paranoia isn't all negative: It can keep you from getting too careless or too bold. By this time the police working over the Chonju Hotel would be asking the desk clerk for my description; last night they would have gone the rounds, knocking on every door and questioning the guests, getting their alibis and asking what they'd seen, what they'd heard. I'd left my things in room 29 as a matter of routine procedure for a skip, to let them assume I was simply out for the evening, giving me time to use if I needed it. That time was now up, because I hadn't returned, and by now there'd be an all-points bulletin posted for me throughout the city: Clive Thomas Ingram, British nationality, full description, wanted for questioning.

"All right," I told Spur, "nine tonight."

Then I rang off. It had been tempting to ask him to come and talk to me here, but that, too, would have been a risk: I didn't know how clean he was; he could be under constant or intermittent surveillance without knowing it, in spite of the care he'd taken to arrange the bottles like that in the window; he was tapping the spy rings in this city for the CIA and he was in place and without support; he'd once been in the field for the Bureau, but that was over now, and it doesn't take long before you lose your cunning. If he came here to see me, he could bring my death.

Nor could I go to see him before I was ready to break cover: Going to ground means exactly that, and I couldn't leave here until Ferris had produced new papers for me and a change of identity; and even then I'd have to move by night and cross the street every time I saw a policeman. The longer I was missing from the Chonju Hotel the more they'd suspect me, and before this day's end I would become the subject of a manhunt.

While Sadie was still shopping for me I rang the embassy and asked for the cipher clerk and we spoke in speech code. He told me that Ferris had signaled three times during the night to ask for my present location and an urgent rendezvous when he arrived in Seoul at noon today; and such is the loneliness of the ferret in the labyrinth, and such is his need for the support and comfort of his director in the field, that the tension in me broke as I put the phone down and thought, *Christ, I've still got a chance.*

X

ARABESQUE

✦

"You American?"

This table was against the wall between the entrance and the door to the toilet on the opposite side. From here I could watch the entrance and if necessary get up and turn my back on it and reach the toilet before anyone coming in could get to me across the crowded room. I'd checked the windows in there: They were narrow but low down and opened onto an alley; also, anyone coming in here from the street would be half-blinded by the near-darkness after the sunshine outside. But I would have to recognize them.

"No," I said.

I'd walked here from Sadie's through the steaming streets, where the sun was heating the puddles and the choked gutters after the rain; this place was more than a mile from where I was staying; it was a long, low building half-lost among the derelict houses between the railway and the Han River, and to look for me here would be to look for one fly on a flypaper. The room was nearly full, two-thirds customers and one-third working them over. Hard rock came from the cobwebbed gratings along the wall.

"You want hashish? Coke?"

Technically I was safe here, a good distance from the main entrance and the corners of the room; but there would be nothing I could do if they came for me: I was watching the entrance but if anyone came in here to kill me I wouldn't recognize them; I didn't know them, as they knew me.

"No," I said.

This was what it was like, and going to be like, fighting Tung Kuo-feng. It was like, and going to be like, fighting the unknown.

I hadn't told Sadie where I was going: I hadn't even known myself. I'd walked for an hour, double-tracking and making absolutely certain that I wasn't followed, until I'd found this place, the type of bar the police left alone because it would be a waste of time to do anything about it. The moment I'd got here I telephoned the embassy.

A dozen small emeralds hit the table in a shower from a black velvet bag, and the man watched my eyes.

"Direct from the mine," he said, but I went on watching the entrance, and in a moment he swept the stones back into the little bag and moved on to the huge sailor sitting with a girl at the next table.

The entrance was a bright gold oblong, a cave mouth with the black silhouettes of people passing through. I went on watching it.

Sadie had done well for me: a good shirt, Manila suit, tan shoes, Thai silk handkerchiefs to match. "You look real sharp, honey. I sure hope I don't go an' lose you to another woman."

A man came in and stopped, his thin stooping figure outlined against the hot bright street, his glasses throwing a spark of reflected light. I didn't move. But now I was ready to buy emeralds, or hashish, or anything they wanted to sell me. You wouldn't believe what it feels like, when your operation has been immobilized and you've been blown and gone to ground, to see your director in the field show up at the rendezvous.

By the time he'd seen me and made his way through the crowd my mood had swung in the opposite direction to something like anger; it happens like that when things are chancy: You suddenly wonder where your nerves have gone, and there they are all the time on the roller coaster.

"Did he *know* about this?" I asked Ferris the moment he sat down. I meant Croder, and he knew that.

"About what?"

"Those assassinations. Did he know the targets?"

"Not till it happened."

"For Christ's sake, he knew it was something big. Why—"

"How's everything?" he asked me cheerfully, and I shut up and just sat there while he ordered a beer and watched me for a minute with his narrow head tilted, his pale eyes hidden by the reflection on his glasses. "Been rough, has it?"

I didn't like the way he was having to play it so very cool, to cover his own gooseflesh.

"Does London want me called in?" I asked him.

He made me wait, simply because it was good for discipline. He had to get me back to where I'd started out, with lots of reserve control.

"Not so far," he said.

I felt myself slacken off a little; it had been one of the fears that had run with me through the dark of the last four days: that when they saw that the opposition was closing in on me and certain to kill, London would call me in.

"Then who's Youngquist?" I asked him. It was a name Spur had dropped, and failed to cover convincingly.

The boy brought the beer for Ferris, and he sat for a moment with his thin, sensitive hand round the glass, moving it in small precise circles on the teakwood table.

"He's your replacement," he told me.

Ice along the spine.

I didn't forgive him for a long time, for using both barrels at point-blank range.

"When's he replacing me?"

He looked surprised. "As soon as you're ready."

I tried to think back to the signal I'd sent to the embassy. Something was wrong. I said: "I'm not ready."

"Part of your signal read: *Where is Youngquist?* I assumed you wanted him to take over."

This time I made him wait, and when I was ready I leaned over the table and spoke very quietly. "In the six missions we've done together, have I ever asked for a replacement?"

He didn't have to think. "No."

"What makes you think I'm asking for one now?"

He moved his head and the reflection left his glasses and I could see his eyes, and they were surprised. "You're staying in?"

"Yes. I always have."

"I must say I'm rather glad." He drank some beer.

I sat back again. "I think this is a good time to get one thing straight. If you ever get a signal from me asking for a replacement, discount it. Okay?"

"That's what I did this time," he said. "Then I began thinking."

"You want girl?"

"Fuck off," I said.

Ferris gave his soft, sinister laugh. "Of course I didn't tell London. I wanted to see you first."

"I should bloody well hope so. What did you begin thinking?"

"Well, they tried to smash you up in London, and you flew out here full of dope; then there was that thing in Peking, which left you a bit washed out; and according to your signal they tried again twice. I don't know the details, but it struck me that you might not be physically operational anymore. Sorry."

"I would have said so."

"Point taken."

"What happened," I told him, "is that I had to send that signal in speech code and in French. I asked who Youngquist was, not where."

He thought that over. "We'll have to do better, won't we?"

"I don't want any cutouts or contacts, Ferris. The police are looking for me, as well as the opposition. They can pick up my trail at any time. Any kind of contact could be fatal."

"Agreed. I'll try setting up a radio."

"Do that. And one other thing: When was Youngquist sent out here?"

He'd been hoping I wouldn't ask him.

"After they tried to finish you off, in Peking. I told Croder you were still operational, but he makes his own rules."

I was going to have to work on him. "What else has he done?"

Reluctantly Ferris said: "There's now quite a bit of support in the field."

"Oh really."

"I told him you prefer working solo."

"Good of you."

He said: "There's no point in your going through the roof. This is Croder, and we'll both have to live with it."

"Just keep the support away from me," I said slowly. "Tell Croder that's what I want. Tell him that if he's not prepared to let me have it, then he can have Youngquist. Tell him he's decided to send this particular executive into the field, and if he wants me to do the job, then I'm going to do it my way. Tell him that, Ferris, or, by Christ, I'm leaving the mission."

In the oblique light from the colored lanterns I could see the slight movement of his jaw muscle, and noted it. When Ferris gave that much away it was like someone else smashing tables.

"It really would be rather nice," he said in his thinnest tone, "if one day some kind soul would give me a mission to field-direct where Control and the executive aren't mortal enemies."

He was in a rage, but I couldn't help that. I said: "It's my life on the line, not his."

I didn't have to spell anything out for him. Contacts and cutouts can be a lot of help in an operation when signals have broken down or we have to pass papers or a code or documents back to base; but when the executive is on the run and trying to stay alive until he can find access to the opposition, then a contact with less than executive-level training and experience can trip him or expose him and bring him down.

"I'll do what I can," Ferris said.

"Tell him those are my terms. No contacts, cutouts, shields, or supports. No one else in the field with me. Unless I ask."

He sipped at his beer and put the glass down without a sound. "Understood. Now I need a report."

It took me ten minutes: Soong Li-fei; the man on the staircase; and the information I'd got from Spur.

"We've heard of Tung." Ferris nodded.

"Oh really." I waited.

"You'd better finish your report first."

"Fair enough. There's a leak somewhere."

His head moved slightly. "Oh?"

"You put me on that flight to Seoul with total security, but when I checked into the Chonju Hotel there was this woman Soong Li-fei waiting for me."

"But you said she told you she'd made a mistake—you were the wrong man."

"They told her I was the right one. They told her I'd killed her brother, and she went there to square the account."

"Do you think she's in the opposition?"

I thought about it, aware of the dangers of the halo effect: the exquisite features and the cinnamon eyes, the delicate poise of her head, the soft lilting accents, the grace of her walk. Discount all that and remember there'd been a gun in her hand and a bullet ready to rip through the rib cage and bury in the heart.

"I gave her the chance of using the gun on me again, and she didn't take it; it didn't even occur to her. She said she had a brother, Yongshen, who was murdered in Peking; and that was true. And I think if she'd been putting on an act while I was with her, she'd have made a name by now on the stage, and a big one. I don't think she's in the opposition, but I think they tried to use her to kill me. So there was in fact a leak."

"At the embassy," Ferris said at once.

"The cipher clerk?"

"No. He's Bureau. But he must have been overheard when I signaled him to tell him where you'd be in Seoul. Or there's a bug."

"For God's sake," I said quietly, "get it out."

"Yes indeed."

I finished my report, telling him about Sadie.

"Is she safe?"

"No one," I told him, "is safe. All she's got to do is make a slip of the tongue in the wrong quarter. That whole area is a red sector now: the Chonju Hotel, Li-fei's house, and Sadie's place are all in the same network of streets and alleyways, and Spur's wine shop isn't far off."

"You need a new base."

"And a new name."

"I've got your papers with me."

"They'll have to be good. I can't avoid a police check forever."

He passed me a fat envelope and I put it away at once.

"A good one," he said. "Made in London."

"There wasn't time."

"They sent me five, the day you arrived. That, too, is Croder. He obviously knows you've got staying power."

I didn't want to talk about Croder and I didn't want to think about needing three more changes of cover: The statistics are that if an executive gets blown more than twice he's either dead or back in London with the psychiatrists trying to stop him jumping out of windows.

"Have you got a safe-house for me?" I asked Ferris.

"Spur says you can stay with him."

"Civil of him, but he happens to keep a full-grown boa constrictor as a pet. You'll have to find somewhere else."

"Surely it's harmless?"

"Till it wants someone to play with."

"It's going to take time to find somewhere else."

"Then hurry."

"How long," he asked with a shut face, "can you stay at Sadie's?"

"I'm not going back there. These people are only one step behind me and one fine day she's going to have to call in the cleaners to get the blood off the rug, and you know how fussy London is about involving the public at large in our operations. Until you can find me somewhere I'll hire a car and use it as base. I can sleep in it if I've got to. That whole area's a distinct red sector now and I'm going to stay clear of it after I've seen Spur tonight."

Ferris stopped his beer for an instant in midair. "He's got something for you?"

"So he told me, on the phone. I'm seeing him at nine o'clock."

Silhouette.

"Then I'll be at the embassy from nine onward. Phone me when you've talked to Spur."

"Will do." I watched the silhouette in the entrance, against the glare of the sunlight.

Ferris said: "Until London can dig up something from Signals Analysis, Spur's our only hope of finding a way in."

The silhouette was wearing a peaked cap and a holstered revolver. I told Ferris: "Give me everything you've got for me. I might have to leave."

His eyes flicked to the entrance and back to me. "There's been a major break in Peking. The police there suspect Soong Yongshen."

I began listening carefully. "Suspect him of what?"

"The funeral bombing."

"He worked the remote detonator?"

"So they believe. They're keeping us informed."

The man with the peaked cap and the holstered revolver came into the room and the lanterns showed up his uniform and I relaxed; he was a U.S. Navy officer, not a policeman.

"Let me know," I told Ferris, "what progress they make with the Soong Yongshen angle."

"Of course. We checked on his sister for you. She's on the records as a bona fide interpreter for Korean Airlines."

"All right." In a moment he was going to ask me where she was located, and I wasn't going to tell him, and he probably knew that.

"The reason," he said a fraction too casually, "why Control has put all that support into the field is that this thing is a lot bigger than anyone thought."

"I see," I said.

He tried again. "No one will get in your way. You've got my word."

I was getting fed up. "I can't take your word for anything, you know that. Croder's making the rules and if he wants you to do something then you do it. Without telling me, if those are your instructions."

In a moment he said: "You're being difficult."

"That's a shame."

The thing was that after six missions together we knew each other quite well, because a mission is like a lifetime; and he knew that if the Peking police found hard evidence that Soong Yongshen had blown up that coffin we'd have a way into the opposition: through his sister. I didn't think she was in the Tung Triad, but she knew who they were: possibly her dead brother and certainly the "friend" who'd lent her a gun and sent her to room 29 of the Chonju Hotel to kill me with it. But if I went to see Soong Li-fei, I'd go alone, without Ferris covering the area with support in case I needed it.

To move closer to Li-fei would be to move closer to Tung, and into danger. *But I won't have Control pushing me across the field like a pawn across a chessboard and I won't work for any local director, even Ferris, who isn't given total discretion and total authority to act independently of London if he decides it's necessary.*

Croder was sitting at the center of a signals network in

London and getting instant replay of what was happening in
Peking and Seoul, but at a distance of three and a half thousand miles he couldn't sense danger in a glance from cinnamon eyes or feel the hands at the throat on a hotel stairway.
The epicenter of *Jade One* was the shadow executive and it
moved with him through the eye of the storm, and that was
the way it must be.

"Any other business?" Ferris asked me. His voice was like
a stone.

"Look," I told him, "if Croder wanted to send in an executive who could work best with a flock of bloody nursemaids to
look after him he should have done that. But he didn't. He
sent me. That's simple enough, surely? Any other business?
Yes, I think they meant to kill the American vice president,
not our chap at all."

I like getting a reaction from Ferris because he hates showing any. Not that he shot down the chandeliers or anything on
this occasion; he just murmured: *"Holy God."*

"Amen."

"Tell me."

"It didn't add up," I told him, "until you said the Peking
police suspect Soong Yongshen of doing that bang over there.
But now it does. The woman, Li-fei, told me her brother had
done something wrong, and that it was something to do with
'that dreadful thing over there'—she meant the bombing. Her
brother died by ritual murder, from all reports, with his head
off. From what Spur told me about Tung Kuo-feng I'd say
he's the kind of man who would punish any member of his
Triad who made a serious mistake, and probably with death.
I think Soong Yongshen might have made a mistake of that
order when he pressed the beam transmitter in Tien'anmen
Square while our secretary of state was placing his wreath. If
you look at the photos of both those men—Bygreave and the
American vice president—you'll notice they look rather alike;
and to the Asians, one round-eye looks just like the next."

Ferris was quiet for a time, and I waited, watching the oblong of sunlight. The huge sailor at the next table had started singing; it sounded like Greek, and he had quite a good voice; it sounded much better than the hard rock coming out of the wall.

"You mean the original target," Ferris said as he leaned toward me across the table, "was the American vice president?"

"And they shot the American ambassador to compensate for Soong Yongshen's little mistake."

"This wasn't a random attack on the Western delegates, or some kind of terrorist action with no specific target?"

"It was an attack," I nodded, "specifically directed against the United States."

"If you're right."

"If I'm right."

Four Koreans came through the crowd and stood in a circle round the big sailor, and for a moment I thought they were going to form a chorus, but they were asking him to leave. He didn't make any fuss; he embraced two of them heartily enough to leave bruises, knocked over the chair, and hit his head on one of the lanterns before he blocked the entrance on his way out and put the whole place into eclipse.

It was easier to talk now, but there wasn't much else to say.

"Haven't you got *any* way in for me?" I asked Ferris.

"We're working on it. We're working on it very hard."

"I never knew Croder was so slow."

"Couldn't resist it, could you?" His smile had a chill factor of sixty below.

"No."

He said: "I'm hoping Spur can set you running. We all are."

"Good old Spur."

I paid the bill and asked him to send someone round to Sadie's place with 200,000 *won* and a bunch of flowers, and he said he'd do that. He told me to maintain signals by phone through Spur until he'd trod on the bug in the embassy, and I told him I would. We didn't mention Li-fei. A few minutes later he got up and I watched him walk through the bright doorway into the street, with the thought in my mind—one of those thoughts that cling to the psyche like a limpet mine when the mission goes badly—that I might never see him again.

8:51

John Victor Miles, journalist, the Far East representative of *Political Scene,* a left-wing independent quarterly published in London. Passport; entry visa; WHO smallpox certificate; four letters of reference; photographs of wife, two children; international driver's license; ticket for the violin recital at the National Theater in two days' time; various credit cards; other material.

Datsun ZX, dark blue, hired from the Korean Tourist Bureau's Arirang service. The passenger's seat tilted back flat for reclining and the speedometer dial showed a top speed of 220 kph.

I parked it off Toegye Street and walked four blocks through the alleyways to the wine shop in the square, doubling twice and using random cover as a routine exercise and halting for a moment to look around, uncertain of my way, as I reached one of the sightlines through the wine shop window display, giving Spur a chance to recognize me and to note, during the next half-minute as I approached, that I wasn't bringing anyone with me.

The air was perfectly still after the monsoon and last night's deluge; gutters still ran glittering in the lamplight as water from higher ground found its way into the square; in the far corner two dogs fought over scraps in a blocked drain.

The door of the wine shop was open and I went inside, but Spur wasn't there. I called out twice but he didn't answer, and there was no sign of Kim. A boy ran past the open doorway hauling a handcart full of what looked like papayas, the wheels rattling over the stones; then the silence came down again.

"Spur?"

I'd told him nine o'clock and he'd said all right. It was nine now.

"Spur?"

No one answered, so I went up the wide staircase and looked through the grille at the top. Two of the arabesque lanterns were burning, their light throwing a mottled pattern across the rugs where Spur was lying, his body half-hidden by the strong dark coils that had formed a spiral around it.

XI

SHOCK WAVE

※

I hadn't made a mistake.

The digital clock on the instrument panel of the ZX flicked to 9:14 as I drove south, perhaps instinctively drawn to the place where I'd talked to Ferris earlier today.

But I hadn't made a mistake. What was starting to happen now was unavoidable.

I hadn't telephoned Ferris. He said he'd be standing by at the embassy from nine onward, waiting to hear whether Spur had given me information we could use as a way into the opposition, to Tung Kuo-feng. To have telephoned Ferris would have been a mistake, and tonight a mistake could be fatal. I had stayed long enough at the top of the stairs, looking through the grille at the shapes lit by the arabesque lamps, to be sure.

The man and the snake were both dead. Spur's face didn't leave any doubt; his lungs had been crushed. It took longer to be sure that the creature was also dead; it had still been coiled round the man's body, but no longer tightly: I could see narrow areas of lamplight between the coils and the man's body, and the thing's head was lying flat along the floor, upside down, with the jaws open and flecked with foam.

I wasn't going to open the grilled gate and go in there to look closer; it would have made me sick. Instead I threw a 100-*won* coin and landed it an inch from the snake's head, and got no reaction, trying again and thinking they should perhaps put a notice on the gate here: *Do Not Throw Coins at the Boa Constrictor*. The mind is irrational, and finds little jokes for you in the midst of horror.

Then I came away.

I walked the four blocks through the alleys and side streets with due care and attention, and knew by the time I reached the Datsun that I hadn't been followed. It would have been a mistake not to check this carefully, and, as I say, I hadn't made a mistake. What was happening now was unavoidable.

He'd be lonely without me.

Well then, he wasn't lonely now; they were cuddled up together.

What kind of man had Spur been?

Everyone loves old Alexander.

Not really.

I had been driving south for three minutes and was now going round Namsan Park. The car went very well, though the gearbox was a fraction tight because there were only 3476 miles on the clock. Traffic wasn't too bad because most people were eating at this hour or watching the prime-time shows.

I'd wanted to drive for a while before phoning Ferris at the embassy, because I was safer in the car than on foot: You can see at once if there's a tag on you.

There was one on me now.

It had occurred to me during the last few minutes that Spur had been killed because he'd got too close to the Triad. I didn't know how it was possible for that bloody thing to have been incited to kill, but I didn't have any doubts. Spur must have had it for some time, because the screws in the hinges of the grilled gate were dulled over and one of them had started to rust, presumably because of the humidity here in the summer rains; and it must have been born in captivity, because that Armenian in Calcutta hadn't just pulled the thing out of the jungle and wrapped it up for Spur: It'd be like giving someone a live lion. Old Alexander, whom everybody loved, had been a domesticated pet until by some potent magic its primitive brain had been goaded into the area of racial memory and inherited characteristics and it thought it was back in the rotting dark of the jungle, where this other creature that walked in jerks on its hind legs was an enemy, and food.

But what had made it die, up there in the light of the arabesque lamps? Spur couldn't have done anything to it; the thing was a huge galvanic spring that could strike and coil with the speed of a tension trap. What made me so sure that it had been incited to kill was that the Tung Triad always chose indirect means when it could.

Spur's death had conformed to the pattern. Sinclair had either been killed in his car or thrown into the Thames half-dead, to drown. They'd tried to smash me up in a hit-and-run and they'd killed the secretary of state with a remote-controlled bomb and then they'd sent Li-fei to shoot me instead of doing it themselves. The U.S. ambassador had been shot dead but it might not have been done directly by a Tung agent; they might have used someone like Li-fei.

I take note of patterns in the shifting sands of a mission: You can read from them a great deal about the opposition. This man Tung enjoyed high drama: a cloud of flowers exploding against the sun; a headless man on the temple steps; a woman's grief in the shape of a gun; and a jungle death in downtown Seoul.

Also, he was a man of some magic, though it was not magic that had brought the black Porsche into my rearview mirror; it was the result of expert planning. I had made sure that no one was shadowing me from the wine shop to the Datsun, but that was the most I could do, and I'd known that.

They'd used chain surveillance, which is impossible to detect unless you can recognize your opponents. In any given network of streets there are always men standing still, waiting for a bus or buying a paper or looking into a shop window, and there'd been men like that in the streets I'd walked through a few minutes ago.

Four of them—at least four, because there was that number of exits from the square—had been positioned within sight of the wine shop, either in the street or at the windows of a teahouse or a restaurant. They had seen me go into the wine shop and they'd seen me come out and they'd started their routine looping action, one of them staying where he was and keeping me in sight while the others moved off to make quick detours round the streets where I walked, so that at all times there was one man watching me, standing still, as each of the others went ahead of me along a parallel street and took up his station.

I had used checks and cover all the way from the wine shop to the car to make certain I wasn't followed. But I was followed. The Datsun had been delivered to me, left parked outside the Jang Chung Gymnasium by a runner from the embassy at Ferris's request, and when I'd taken it over I was unsurveilled; and when I'd driven it to Toegye Street the mirror had been clean all the way. They'd picked me up at the wine shop and let me lead them far enough from the area for Spur's death and mine to seem unconnected, and now the black Porsche was turning left when I turned left, and right when I turned right, because chain surveillance isn't possible when there are vehicles involved.

A flashy car, the Porsche, for an intelligence agency. But then, we weren't up against an intelligence agency of any prescribed type; we were up against something more mystical than that, more exotic, more deadly. The two men whose faces made a blur behind the windscreen of the Porsche weren't concerned that I knew they were tailing me; wherever I went, they would go, until they were ready to make the kill.

Left, right, right again, and left. The low curved snout of the Porsche heeled on the turns in the mirror, sharklike under the lights.

9:17

I took the street going west along the south boundary of Namsan Park and used the smaller streets through the blocks where the embassies were—Thai, Belgian, Indonesian—and twice hit the floor and changed down and got wheelspin and swung out past a taxi and a small truck, just as an essay. It was no go: They were professionals and they had a machine to beat mine if they tried hard enough. But already the pattern was changing ahead of me, and at first I didn't believe it because they'd had so little time; then it became perfectly clear because every time I tried to pass the Chevrolet pickup in front of me it pulled nearer the middle of the street to block me.

This was the pincer, and a classic.

The elements of the evening fell into shape in my mind as I drove a dozen yards behind the pickup truck, a dozen yards in front of the Porsche. Spur had infiltrated the Triad to get information for the Bureau and he'd been discovered, and the information was now locked safely in the cold relic of his brain. Tung's agents had learned—from Spur himself or via a tapped signal—that the information was to have been passed on to me this evening; and they had moved in to follow me to a convenient place for the kill.

They would try very hard tonight. They'd been losing face: I'd defeated their attempts in London, Peking, and this city on four occasions, but now they had me in their sights and this time they wouldn't let me go.

The Porsche and the pickup must have been using short-wave radio with concealed antennae, and there would be other vehicles in the area, called in to strengthen the trap. But in these short city streets with traffic lights prohibiting a long fast run, two vehicles were enough if they went for the pincer technique.

The pincer technique is terribly simple: The leading car jams its brakes on and you hit the rear while the trailing car rams your tail hard enough to force the doors open before you can do anything about it, and when they come running you've got the choice of getting out of the car and moving into their gunfire or sitting still behind the wheel and waiting for them to come and pour shot into you there. Better than the constrictor trick but very sticky, a study in red.

It was a classic because it seldom failed. Two Americans, McDonald and Buchelli, had been taken as hostages in Salvador in 1979 by this method, and their chauffeur killed. The technique had been used in Beirut, Mexico City, Stuttgart, and Budapest, and the defensive-driving course in Norfolk attempts to train us in defeating it; but there's not really much you can do. You can't speed up because the vehicle ahead will block you; you can't slow down because the one behind will keep you going; you'll be allowed to stop when they are ready, and then it's too late.

Tonight I tried playing the lights and took one on the yellow and led the Porsche through on the red in the hope that a police patrol would see it and give chase, but I was out of luck. Soon after turning south toward the Han River I hit the gearshift and put the ZX into a drift through the neck of a side street and made headway and drifted again at right angles into the next street and gunned up and pulled out to pass a Toyota and had to brake hard as it blocked me. Mirror: a dark blue Mercedes coming up fast and settling down as my own speed steadied.

Four vehicles. At least four, possibly six: I could have turned right instead of left and they knew that and would have been prepared. I suppose it was a compliment, but now I was afraid. There's something about a trap that works quickly on the nerves, perhaps because it's claustrophobic.

I tried again, bringing a thin howl from the gears and using controlled drifts that had the treads whimpering as I turned right and traversed the block and turned left and took up station immediately behind the Chevrolet pickup again:

They'd been sighting along the intersections and keeping pace.

Mirror: Porsche.

Sweat on the wheel rim. Normal psychological reactions now: not afraid anymore, but angry. Felt good, drowning in adrenaline; breathing deeper, faster; vision very clear as the pupils expanded.

Fight the good fight, so forth.

Whatever else may come to me, let fear be never a stranger.

Bloody Spur, got what he wanted, died with the fear of Christ in him as that thing started contracting. I'd rather smash this banger straight into a wall than go the way he went.

All right, try it again: a side street to the right and then left again, clouting the curb and skinning past a taxi and pushing the lights through the red, but it was no go: The Ford station wagon blocked me at once and the black Porsche came up on full gun in the mirror; it had done as I had done, making the same turns one intersection behind and keeping station.

Very well. Force my way out.

Lights.

We waited on the red with the station wagon immediately in front of me. I couldn't see anything through the rear window because it was tinted. My foot was on the clutch and the gearshift was in first and I was ready to hit the gun if anyone got out of the wagon, smear them across the road if they came for me.

Watching all three mirrors, listening for the click of a door from the Porsche behind me: Shoot the red if they came for me from behind.

Green.

We drove three more blocks due south and the pace was slow because there was more traffic here, approaching the Third Han Bridge. Then the station wagon began slowing, making me brake. There was nothing ahead of it at this point: It had a clear run but it was still slowing, forcing me to slow with it. In the central mirror the Porsche was closing up.

So they were going to do it here.

Light traffic. There has to be a steady traffic stream for the pincer to work; otherwise you can wrench into a U-turn and lose them if they're not quick enough. Tonight it wasn't possible.

The wagon hit the brakes but I was in first gear and used my right foot immediately. There was too much wheelspin but it left enough traction to bring the weight down at the back as the power began piling up, and I had the wheel hard over in case there was a chance; the treads were screaming a lot and I could smell rubber burning as the acceleration got us over the inertia and took the ZX in a short sharp swing to clear the rear end of the station wagon with glass from my nearside headlamp flying up like snow: The wagon gave a shudder and shifted across a few inches as the ZX pulled away from the impact and I used the curb in the neck of the side street to kick the car straight before I could change up and get some real speed going.

Shots or a tire blown somewhere.

It was a short street with vehicles parked along one side and no traffic moving. The Porsche came into the mirrors almost at once because I hadn't been able to do anything difficult to follow and he didn't have to knock the station wagon out of the way in the acceleration phase. Headlights came full on, half-blinding me in the mirrors as I drifted the ZX into a left turn at the intersection and saw the narrow perspective of the street opening up in front of me with the dark blue Mercedes and the pickup truck standing at right angles to the street and blocking it.

They'd tracked us from the left side of the trap and got far enough ahead to set up the ambush, and I knew now that the station wagon had jammed its brakes on to try for the pincer but reserved the option of pushing me into the side street if I got clear. They'd decided not to waste any more time: The pincer depends on mobility but now they wanted to make sure I stopped, and the ambush would do that for them.

The speed felt like a rising 50 and I slowed at once. The

Mercedes and the pickup truck didn't leave any room on
either side for me to get through; I couldn't see anyone moving anywhere but the Mercedes had still been rocking on its
springs when I'd swung into this street, so there hadn't been
time for them to get out: They were crouched below window
level and waiting for me to stop; then they would come out
with their guns and leave me with precisely the same option
as with the pincer: I could move into their gunfire or sit behind
the wheel and wait for them to come to me.

Beyond the two vehicles I could see the flat sheen of the
Han River, quite close, with a street running parallel to it on
this bank. If I could do anything at all I'd have to reach the
bridge, but the chances were thin.

I was sitting in my own sweat now with the full headlights
of the Porsche closing on me from behind and throwing the
shadow of the ZX against the flat gray sides of the pickup
ahead of me.

Feelings of intense anger again, but there were compensa-
tions: This was a better way to go than most, and what you
find yourself hoping for is an effective shot into the brain so
that you can simply phase out, with no final thoughts of
guilt—*I shouldn't have let them snare me into anything so
simple*—and shame—*mission unaccomplished, executive deceased.*

Still slowing, as they would expect me to. Slowing, with
the shapes of the Mercedes and the pickup looming quite
close now.

A sudden blizzard inside the ZX as they blew out the rear
window with a silenced shot: glass snow everywhere, flying
at the back of my head and the inside of the windscreen. I
slumped lower in the seat and turned my own headlights full
on so that I could work out the options better. There were
only two: I could let them proceed with the kill or I could
try ramming.

Slowing to something like 20, to let them think I wouldn't
be giving them any trouble.

Then I hit the brakes hard and we were into the storm as the Porsche rammed into the rear of the ZX and they began shunting. An awful lot of noise now from the final drive couplings and metal hitting metal but they were still using the silencer and a shot ploughed into the windscreen frame above my head as if they'd simply thrown a stone. I thought the glare was less now from their lights; it had been quite an effective impact when I'd braked, and one of their lamps must have gone. I didn't know what the speed was now but it didn't matter very much: Linear thinking was phasing out as the organism realized the need to survive. Linear thought: The idea is to ram the stationary obstacle, and the best place to go for is the rear wheel because that end is lighter in a front-engined vehicle; you don't rely on your momentum to create the necessary force, you've got to do it on an acceleration curve with the power building up as you go. First gear, foot hard down, take aim at the target.

Then I stopped thinking, because the conscious doesn't stand a chance against the powers of the subconscious when the living creature reaches the edge of life and makes its decisions according to the laws of survival; all the conscious mind has to do is feed the data in and keep clear and shut up.

Shunting still going on. Metal tearing as we hit and parted and hit again, the flight of a bullet somewhere very close and then the bang of its impact against the door pillar. The street full of noise and light: the travail of the two machines as they worked together in collision and recoil, the acid glare of the headlamps as I left them full on, bringing reflections from the windows of the two motionless vehicles.

I tugged the seat belt tighter and pushed the gearshift into first and hit the floor with my right foot and centered the ZX at the rear wheel of the stationary Mercedes while the power built up and took us through the final few yards to the impact. Fierce deceleration and pain burning against the ribs and shoulder as the weight of my body strained against the seat belt; secondary impact from the rear as the Porsche smashed into me and rebounded with both lamps dark and nothing but a blur in the mirrors. A glimpse of a face at the window of the Mercedes before the whole vehicle began shifting on its tires, heeling against the shock and swinging wider, letting the ZX through with the nearside door panels shrieking as they grazed past the dark blue tail with the outside mirror snapping at the stem and falling away.

We were through, and I dragged the gearshift into second and kept the power on and saw the bright surface of the river dead ahead as the Porsche followed me through and a shot ripped fabric from the roof lining and buried into the frame of the windscreen. There wasn't room to do anything now except try making the turn into the road alongside the river, and I started the drift, but a front tire burst and the steering went wild and the ZX went almost straight on with its wheels ploughing across grass and a footpath and some kind of boating deck before the front end sailed clear and began going down in a curve. Final impression: my own headlight beams striking the surface of the river and reflecting against the buildings on the other side in the few seconds before the front of the car hit the water and was buried in a white shock wave.

XII
CAT

Peace.

Peace, and the sense of another place.

My body weightless and at ease. So this is what it is like, and it will go on forever.

Night and silence, who is here?

My eyes open, watching the dark; my ears lulled by the soundless water; one hand drifting and touching but feeling nothing that has definition. So death, after all, is nothing spectacular; it is isolation, and the slow running on of the mind.

But there was something there.

Ignore it; there's nothing here.

The weight of my body shifting in a slow dance, touching and coming away. Night, and easeful silence.

Pressure of some kind, a sudden huge rising of the dark under my face, *and then no breathing.*

Ignore it; the dead don't breathe.

Listen, you've got to—

Be quiet, I'm resting. Go away.

My ears covered and uncovered by the slow rising and falling of the water; my eyes filled with dark, and nothing to—

Water, yes. Do you want to drown, you bloody fool?

Leave me alone and shut up. I'm not interested in panic.

For Christ's sake, you've got to—

Leave me alone and—

Got to wake up, wake up, wake up.

The huge rising of the dark again *and no breathing.*

Pressure in the lungs. Water, did you say?

Don't you know what drowning is? Don't you—

Shuddup.

But the night rose and slammed against my face and blocked off the breathing and I moved suddenly, throwing out one arm and feeling the soft resistance of the water.

Push yourself up. Push up.

Air, yes, and breathing.

A long time choking. This isn't death. This is dying.

Then nightmare: Where am I and can I make it and I don't want to die, so forth. A kind of consciousness returning, flying back into me and finding me embattled against the force of a primitive element. A time of uncertainty, until the black water rose again and I moved my head, tilting it back so that I could breathe, taking the first step toward the light.

For God's sake, get out of here.

Where?

Car in the river.

Then shock and the spreading illumination of thought through the shadows of my mind. I began moving, feeling, thinking.

You've got to try—

Shuddup. I know what's happening now.

But orientation wasn't easy. I was faceup, bobbing against the inside of a dome. Something, yes, had shattered the rear window so the water had come in when we'd sunk into the river.

How much air is there?

Not much. My hands clawing around me now, desperate

to identify objects, shapes that would help me navigate from
death to life: the steering wheel, the seat squabs, the gearshift
lever; they were below me—the car was right side up. I had
hit the seat belt release when I'd seen we were going in, and
I was floating just below the roof with my face in a bubble of
air that was trapped there by the rearward angle.

It won't last long.

Leave me to think. Something's wrong.

Something was wrong because I wasn't floating as high as
I should be: My head didn't touch the roof when the black
water rose against my face and blocked breathing; something
was keeping me down.

Sensation in the legs, the feet; something was tugging. It
was the seat belt. I'd been turning slowly inside the car and
the seat belt had wound round my feet.

Turning which way?

Choking, a long paroxysm this time, bringing disorientation
and the touch of panic. When I put my hands out to feel what
was happening I found they were closer to the smooth arc of
the steering wheel: I was still turning, and with each revolution I was being dragged down. For a long time the organism
took over and fought like a cat, kicking at the seat belt's
twisted webbing but doing no good, my hands frantic for a
grip on something that would pull me higher and let me
breathe, while the conscious mind knew there was nothing
there to grip.

Black water smothered me and blocked my breath.

Turn. Turn.

But which way?

Then the water rose again and blocked my breath and this
time it didn't recede because the air was escaping from the
bubble: The car must be tilting forward in the mud. I struck
out with my hands, pulling at the steering wheel and spinning,
feeling the padded seat squabs and using them as levers,
spinning again, feeling the water rising to the point where
I had to hold my breath because there was no more air.

Turning the wrong way.

Hands frantic now because I wasn't breathing anymore:
The water was at eye level and it didn't go down. The seat belt
was tugging all the time, providing an anchor, securing my
body to the huge mass of the car while the water lapped
across and across my eyes and the pressure began building up
in my lungs and there came the terrible temptation to suck in
whatever was there, even water.

Turning, turning the other way now, my hands in a frenzy
as my body spun, *my head bumping against the roof for the
first time* and my face lifting to find the last of the air—but it
wasn't there anymore: The bubble had rolled along the under-
side of the roof toward the smashed rear window. My feet were
still trapped, but as I went on spinning in a vortex of my own
making I felt them release and I jackknifed and turned
half-round and dived and felt the scraping of the rear window
frame against my back as I cleared it and rose, using my
hands as fins to turn me face upward so that when I reached
the surface I could breathe.

Light burst against my eyes and my lungs exploded and
dragged in air and water and I choked and then breathed
again with my whole body shaking to the thudding of my
heart, while the black river water lapped at my face and
covered my eyes as I kept my head tilted back to let the
breathing go on, following the rhythm of its own biocosmic
tide as the life came back into me and the thought process
started again, arousing imagination.

They would look for me.

I brought my head forward a little and opened my eyes and
waited for them to clear. The men up there on the riverbank
would be watching for movement, so I let myself drift; the
river was swollen after the rains and the current was fast;
the streetlamps were moving steadily past me against the dark
sky. I was quite close to the bank, where flotsam was caught
and gathered for a moment before it was tugged clear again;
the lights of a car were moving along the road that ran
parallel with the river: It looked like the dark blue Mercedes.

A pickup truck had stopped near the bridge and I could see two figures moving across to the bank; when I turned my head I could see the black Porsche standing at the spot where I must have gone in, with several figures ranged along the bank and watching the river. They were covering the situation thoroughly, watching for me to surface from the car, and watching for a glimpse of my drifting body further downstream.

The water lapped and tugged, turning me round in the eddies, blocking my ears and receding as the sound of traffic came intermittently from the streets. There was a man standing a hundred yards downstream, where the Mercedes had now pulled up and doused its lights; with the current moving at this speed I would be floating past him within a minute and at a distance of thirty feet or so.

I could dive and swim underwater for as long as my breath held out, but it wouldn't be for more than half a minute because there was still a severe degree of oxygen loss and my lungs were already working hard to replace it; in half a minute I wouldn't move far from the bank with the current this strong, and when I broke surface I'd present a sure target with the light pattern disturbed. The only chance was to go closer to him and use camouflage.

I turned slowly over, facedown, and veered toward the bank, feeling the gentle bobbing of flotsam against my neck; then I lifted my face enough for my eyes to make a selection, and chose a cardboard box that was drifting at an angle low on the surface, with scum and smaller flotsam clinging to it; then I turned slowly onto my back with my face under the box, and moved my hands behind me where their paleness wouldn't show. And then I did nothing. I drifted.

When you have done everything you can, you can only wait, and hope that karma will decide in your favor; but it isn't easy; you don't become, suddenly, a fatalist, uncaring as to whether you are going to live or die.

Ignore, and let go, and drift.

The cardboard box was perfectly empty, with no shavings

or paper left inside; it had been ripped open to get at the contents and there was a split along one corner, giving me a glimpse of a streetlamp and then the gleam of a star; it was the only way I was aware of movement, because my body was drifting at the same speed as the current and the water around me was still. Sometimes, much closer, right against my face, I caught sight of other flotsam through the split: some eggshells and a cylinder of straw from a wine bottle, something unidentifiable and covered with slime, and the sheen of wet black fur on a drowned cat.

I went on drifting, watching through the split, slowing my breathing and letting my lungs fill only tidally to keep my body's mass low in the water with the legs angled downward. It wasn't easy to judge how close I would be to the man on the bank when I passed him, but it wouldn't be more than twenty feet. That was very close.

The flotsam was restless around the box, and once I thought I could feel the fur of the dead cat caressing my face: It was a sensation only slightly stronger than the feel of the lapping water, and infinitely delicate; perhaps it was its tail.

I would have liked to raise my head enough to get my ears clear of the surface so that I could listen; but if the men along the bank called to each other it would probably be in an Asian tongue I wouldn't understand, and if one of them shouted *there he is,* it wouldn't mean anything to me, or give me time to draw the last quick breath and wait for the bullet's spinning force to sting and pucker the flesh; it was better to keep my head low, and hear nothing, and drift.

Poor kitty. How did you get here? How long has it been since our paths began meeting? Since the day you were born, I suppose.

I could see a streetlamp. The man on the bank had been standing between two of the lamps, so this would be the first of them; it wasn't far now. If I could drift past him without being seen, I would survive the night; the other vehicles had stopped upstream, closer to where I'd gone in. But twenty feet was close, mortally close. On the other hand there were the shifting reflections of the city's lights across the surface, blinding him a little to my dark shape underwater; all he might see, if I kept still, would be the cardboard box and the eggshells and the dead cat.

What did the lettering say on the box? Condensed milk? Condoms? Sardines? You used to like sardines, kitty, whenever you could get them off the kitchen table before they caught you at it. I used to like sardines. I would have given you some of mine.

The thin, needling glare of the streetlamp faded out as I went on drifting, and for a time I could see nothing at all; then the pupils expanded and I saw one of the eggshells bobbing in the scum.

Tidal breathing, while the split in the box winked suddenly to the passage of a star. *Night and silence, who is here?* No one. No one at all, only a box and a dead cat, so you can put away your gun.

I watched for him now; we were close.

Ignore the slow creeping of fear, the instinctive tensing of the nerves as the live body becomes gradually exposed to the death-dealing weapon in the enemy's hand like a floating sacrifice on sacred water; ignore and think of other things.

How did you go, kitty? Was it a car that slung you across the road with a smashed skull and no hope of getting even, or did they get fed up with your favorite sardine trick and shove you into a sack on the way to the river? Did you have time to fight them, with your sinews threshing and your bright claws flashing, your ears flattened and your sharp teeth bared? I hope so, but we can't always choose how we go, can we? You know that now.

Movement against my face.

The current was strong here and eddying, because of some kind of obstruction in the bank. The cardboard box was drifting away from my face.

Don't move.

Fatal to move. Fatal, perhaps, to lie still and let the box go. Without the box, what would he see? The cat, and not much else.

The cold wet touch of its fur against my face.

Don't leave me, kitty. Don't leave me now.

The current went on tugging, swinging my legs away from the bank. I opened one eye, allowing a thin band of vision across the pupil, and saw the silhouette of the nearest buildings against the sky, also a distant streetlamp, and a parked car, much closer, and the short figure of the man on the bank.

He was standing right at the water's edge, his body leaning to watch the surface, his right hand holding the gun. I would be drifting past him in a few seconds now.

The box had gone; I could see one corner of it as it drifted away. The cat was curled against my face, its fetid stench half-choking me, its tail moving across and across my eyes in the eddying water. There was nothing to do now but wait, and watch my enemy.

It was dangerous to leave my one eye open, even so little, but I wanted to see what was happening. He might catch the glint of my conjunctiva, and loose a shot to see if there was any reaction; but the cat's body was still half-smothering my face, vouchsafing me the security of camouflage: It was too heavy for the current to drag away, as it had done with the box.

I watched the man on the bank.

I watched his gun hand.

If his hand moved I would turn and dive, not with any hope of being in time but as a last gesture in the name of survival. At twenty feet he could place six shots effectively grouped in my body before I could reach any depth, but that would be preferable to lying here on the water and watching the flash of powder against the dark.

Drifting. Far away, the sound of the city's traffic.

A short man, his body leaning forward, his eyes looking into my eye but not as yet identifying it for what it was, since it was out of context; he was for the moment unaware that somewhere among the eggshells and the scummy flotsam and the dead cat there was shape possessed of intelligence. When he became aware, he would lift his right hand.

Can you see him, kitty? Of course not; all you can see now are your heavenly hosts, their pink tails frisking as you chase them among the stars.

Drifting.

He watched me, keeping perfectly still. His head was turning to follow me as I passed the place where he stood. A shadow, moving insubstantially across him as the river's reflections shifted, made it seem that he was starting to lift his gun hand; and within the period of time required for the nerves to hit muscle I reached the decision to dive, before the brain made its urgent analysis and in the next microsecond countermanded the impulse, leaving the organism to float onward without motion.

The man's head was still turned to watch me as he made his own more careful analysis of these abstract shapes in the water here; then he looked suddenly in the other direction, attracted by flotsam further upstream; and we went drifting away and away, kitty and I, in the silence of the night-running river.

XIII

RDV

One hour later, at 11:06, I invoked an extreme-urgency rule and telephoned London direct, asking for the *Jade One* console and using the established code phrasing to warn Control not to signal through the embassy because communications there were compromised. I also requested a rendezvous with the director in the field at 09:00 tomorrow at the currency-exchange office at Kimpo Airport. I gave the number of the telephone I was using and rang off.

I'd recognized Croder himself on the line—he has the voice of a dispassionate hangman—but he couldn't ask any questions because my code prefix had warned him that it was a shut-ended signal: The taxi driver was still in the room with me and he understood English. The first two drivers had turned me down when I'd stopped them, but this one—a small bearded Hindu with permanently surprised eyes—had been ready to agree that I wouldn't get into a hotel in this state and that for 50,000 *won* I could stay the night at his place if I didn't make any noise. I'd explained the fact that I was soaking wet and smothered in weeds by mentioning a drunken brawl over a woman.

There was a call at three in the morning and he got me out of my low narrow bed to take it. Phrase-coded instructions were that a rendezvous would take place with a contact instead of my director in the field, and on the subway station at Jongro and Waryong Streets at 09:00 tomorrow. The names were spelled out in letter code and so were the brief specifics, *broken glasses* being the main identification key.

He'd repaired them with a piece of white adhesive tape, and I took him through a four-step introduction check before I felt happy with him, not because he was doubtful in any way but because I was now ready to think that every other man-in-the-street of this city was working with the Triad.

"All I want," I told him, "is an rdv with my director. That's what I asked London for."

He was a bland, shut-faced character with dirty nails and a terrible haircut and he gazed at me sideways most of the time while he sucked on a toothpick.

"They asked me for info," he said.

"I haven't got any. Christ, if I'd got any info, I would have given it to London, wouldn't I?"

"Orders," he shrugged, but I had the feeling he was rather less crass than he sounded: When he wasn't looking at me he was looking everywhere else and without letting it show; and underneath the crumpled tourist's clothes there was a certain strength in his stance, a certain weight.

"Spur is dead," I told him, and saw a spark come and go in his colorless eyes. "The opposition did a chain job on me and set up a street ambush and I went into the river with the car. They tried hard this time, really hard, but if you call that information, I'm happy for you. Tell them I want Ferris and a new cover before the police pick me up and ask for papers."

He hadn't looked away from me now for the last ten seconds, and the toothpick had stopped moving. "How did they do Spur?"

"They put a snake round his neck."

"That thing," he said softly.

"That thing. Who gave you the instructions to meet me?"

"I clean forget." He gazed at me obliquely for a moment and added: "It wasn't through the embassy."

"Fair enough." It was all I needed to know. In any given operation the executive in the field has communications access to the embassy and to whatever other facilities are assigned to him (they gave me Spur); but there are always others that he never knows about, because it would endanger them. The executive is something like a leper: Nobody wants to go near him, because if the opposition can trap him and put him under that bright white light before he can get to his capsule he's liable to break and expose people and they won't know it until they switch on the ignition and come down in fragments. Two years ago a stamp dealer in Dresden was put into direct touch with the executive making his final run at the end of a sticky mission and the whole thing happened: The executive was tripped and grilled before he could cyanose and two weeks later the stamp dealer lost his footing on a crowded underground platform in the rush hour and the train didn't have time to stop. And that man had been a Bureau sleeper in Dresden for twelve years before someone in London panicked and told him to make direct contact with an executive.

What had happened now was that Croder had signaled a facility unknown to me in Seoul, and that facility had passed on the instructions to the man who was watching me now, his eyes narrowed against the flying dust as a train came in from the tunnel.

"Are you dead or alive?" he asked me.

"What?"

"After the river."

"I don't know. I heard some sirens when I was climbing out of the water, so they've probably sent divers down or pulled the car out by now; all we can say is that I'll be down as missing, officially."

His bland eyes were watching people getting off the train:
I could see some of their reflections—a girl in red, a man with
a cap. "Dead would be good," he murmured. "I mean convenient."

"I'm going to stay dead until they pick up my tracks again."

"If that doesn't sound," he said gently, "like a contradiction
in terms." His wide mouth smiled over the toothpick.

He wasn't just a contact, I knew that now. A contact is a
teaboy and he doesn't cheek the executive. I said: "Are you
Youngquist?"

He stopped watching the people getting off the train and
looked at me instead. "We vary," he said, "don't we?"

So this was why.

"Tell Ferris I want to see him at South Gate in two hours,"
I told him. "I'll be at the north curb. And do something about
communications, for Christ's sake; the embassy's out and I
haven't got anywhere else. Give me a number to phone."

This was why Croder had sent a contact to meet me instead
of Ferris: This man wasn't just a contact; this was Youngquist, my potential replacement, and London thought it was a
good idea for us to meet and get to know each other, by way
of easing the transition. As we stood together with the drone
of the train filling the station as it pulled away, its lights throwing a chain of yellow oblongs across the walls, it occurred to
me that I couldn't find any rage to help me through this moment of truth; all I can remember thinking was that I'd got
away from the opposition five times now but I couldn't get
away from Croder.

Youngquist gave me a number. "Ferris wants to see you,
too. He left the specifics to you, so I'll tell him it's South Gate,
the north curb, eleven hundred hours. Look out for a light
green Toyota with CDs on it. Anything else?"

"Yes. In future, keep out of my bloody way."

"They told me," he said, "you were like that."

* * *

I got in and slammed the door and we drove five blocks to the elevated car park and went up to the seventh floor and found it deserted.

Ferris switched off the ignition and said: "They've told me to call you in."

"They can't do that."

The rage came now and I got out and hit the door shut and sent echoes among the concrete pillars. Ferris followed me out and paced in a tight circle with his hands in his pockets and his eyes down, looking for something to crush: I'd never seen him like this before.

"Those are my instructions," he said thinly.

"When did you get them?"

"Half an hour ago."

After I'd seen Youngquist. After Youngquist had passed on the information that I'd been got at for the fifth time and survived. Not his fault: He'd been there to pass on whatever I told him. But London was panicking now.

"They didn't like the bit about Spur, did they?"

I saw his eyes flicker. "It's a setback, you ought to know that. He was our main source."

"He'd got something for me. That's why he told me to go and see him. What he can get, we can get."

"I don't think I follow," he said. I could feel the chill.

"There's a source. He had access to it. All we've got to do is find it."

He looked at me for a moment and then turned away, pacing again in his tight little circle; I suppose he knew that was the worst thing he could do as an answer: to ignore what I was trying to tell him; but then, he knew that what I was really trying to tell him was that I'd never been called in from a mission before and I didn't know how to handle it.

"If you could give me any reason," he said, "why they should leave you in the field . . ."

"I'll give you a dozen reasons. I've taken on jobs that no one else would touch; I've let those bastards use me as a sacri-

fice when it was the only way we could get through to the
objective, and simply because I've got the alley-cat savvy to
survive I've done that, and no thanks to them; I let Croder
pull me out of hospital and kick me into the pitch-dark with
no background information and no specific objective and now
he's breaking out in a rash because I'm not getting anywhere.
Doesn't he know I've only been in the field three days?"

Ferris stopped pacing and watched me for a moment as if
something I'd said had got through to him. But it hadn't.

"I didn't mean personal reasons."

"They're all I've got."

"They won't do. Croder didn't have to con you into this
operation. You'd been out of action for three months and you
were burning to hit back for Sinclair. You wanted this job
badly. All you didn't want was Croder, because he told you
to eliminate Schrenk in Moscow and you wouldn't do it, and
it nearly blew up the mission. It would be rather cozy," he
said, and took a short step toward me, "if you'd regard Croder
as the most efficient Control that anyone could hope for, instead of the kicking boy for your own guilt feelings."

"For Christ's sake leave Freud out of it. What sort of reasons do you want me to give you?"

"Technical."

"I haven't got any. You know that. We couldn't get anything out of Jason in time. We couldn't get anything out of
Spur before they went for him. They're always one step ahead
of us. But give me a bit of time, can't you?"

He looked down. "I'd leave you in, if it were my decision.
It's not."

"You'd leave me in?"

He considered this, as if he had to make sure. "Yes."

"Then tell that bastard—"

"All I can tell Croder is that we're not making any progress
here in the field. We've never been up against anything so
difficult as the Triad—and this is Croder's thinking: We need
more support out here; the mission's changing shape—it's not

the kind of operation we thought it was; London thought they could get you some kind of access when the action started, but they can't; we're losing ground, day after day, and all you've been able to do is stay alive. Croder thought he was sending an executive into the field through planned routes and with extensive communications, but now he knows that all he did was to push one lone man against a battalion. We don't know how many people Tung Kuo-feng has working for him; it could be hundreds."

"That doesn't make any difference. The way to kill an octopus is to put a spear into the brain."

In a moment he said: "If you could do that . . ."

"I can't do it if they call me in."

He began pacing again and I didn't say anything more; there wasn't anything more I could say that would do any good. London wanted technical reasons for leaving me in the field and I hadn't any. If they—

"Stand still," I said.

He stopped at once and looked up, and we listened to the sound of the car. There was nothing but a waste of concrete here with pillars breaking up the sound into echoes and it was difficult to get an aural fix; but the engine was loudening all the time.

The sixth level had been less than half-full when we'd driven through it ten minutes ago, but this car wasn't stopping.

Ferris didn't move. He watched me.

I turned slightly until I was facing the long perspective of concrete, waiting for the front end of the car to come into sight, then realizing that we wouldn't have a chance if we didn't go now.

"Come on," I said, and moved, pulling the door of the Toyota open. Ferris worked very fast, starting up before his door had slammed shut, kicking the thing into reverse and heeling it into a tight arc and hitting the brakes and the gear-shift and giving it the gun. We couldn't go upward: This was the highest level; we could only go down. Tires screaming a lot as Ferris got wheelspin, place like a torture chamber with all the echoes. We passed the other car halfway through the first turn and I crouched low and sighted across the bottom edge of the windscreen: camouflage-green Chrysler station wagon with U.S. Army plates, a young GI and an Asian girl, both of them looking the other way, up here for a bit of snatched privacy and glad we were going.

On the level below I told Ferris to shove the bloody thing in a slot for a minute, and then I just sat there in my own sweat and for the first time wondered how far gone I was, sitting here still crouched in the instinctive low-profile target position while the signals flashed through my mind from Ferris to Croder: *They've tried five times now and I don't think he can stand the pace.* . . . From Croder to Ferris: *There's no point in leaving him out there if he's losing his nerve.* . . . Sitting hunched up with my eyes screwed shut, wondering how to face the man beside me when I opened them, because there had been no chance, no chance at all, that anyone of the Triad knew where we were.

After a long time I heard Ferris saying quietly, "Why don't you go home, Q? Anyone else would."

I opened my eyes and straightened up in the seat and took a breath and held it and took another one, wanting to get some steadiness in my voice.

"This is home."

"Where the brink is?"

"That's right."

After a while he said: "The most I can probably get for you is another twenty-four hours out here."

"Then get me that."

XIV

SHADOWS

❁

Decapitation produces almost total blood loss from the facial area within a few seconds, but the embalmers had injected their resins skillfully and the face of Soong Yongshen was recognizable as the face of the young man in the photograph above the open coffin as I stood looking down at him. The white death robe had been drawn all the way to the chin so that nothing remained visible of the manner of his passing.

The room was still and airless, and sickly with the smells of formaldehyde and the incense burning in the sconces; the shutters had been closed against the noonday sun, and in the light of the many candles the massed bouquets of flowers bloomed with unearthly color.

Soong Li-fei had not been here when I arrived a few minutes ago, but she came in now, wearing a white *chongsam* and with her eyes red from crying. The instant she saw me she stopped dead and glanced quickly at the faces of the three men who were waiting for her patiently with their flowers and paired silk scrolls; she greeted them hastily, listening to their

half-whispered condolences and then making a sign for me
to follow her through the screened doorway.

"Why did you come here?" she asked quickly in French.

"To talk to you."

"They're looking for you, and there's nothing to say."

"Who are 'they'?"

We were in a narrow hallway, darkened by the closed
shutters, and her cinnamon eyes were in shadow: I had to
learn what I could from her voice alone.

"You must leave. You're in great danger here."

I could feel her aura of tension as we stood close together;
I meant nothing to her, except that perhaps she was grateful
for my not having brought in the police and accused her of
attempted murder the night I'd arrived in Seoul; also she was
sick enough of death, and didn't want to see murder done in
a house of mourning.

"Who is it that's looking for me?" I asked her.

She said impatiently: "Any of them might come here at
any moment, to offer condolences. Please go—I'll show you
the back way."

I held her arm lightly; it was the arm of a china doll, ice-
cold under the silk sleeve though the hallway was stifling.
"What did the man say, outside the house here, two nights
ago? What did you say to him?"

She sounded confused. "What man?"

"You were walking home from my hotel, the night of the
wind, and a man spoke to you outside the door." I was watching her eyes, but there was too much shadow for me to read
them.

In a moment she said hesitantly: "He asked me if I had
killed you, at the hotel."

"And what did you tell him?"

"I said you were the wrong man, and that they'd been mis-
taken."

She was trying to pull away, to lead me along the hall to the
back of the house; I didn't let her. "What else did you say to

each other, Li-fei? The quicker you tell me these things, the sooner I'll leave."

She moved again. "I've nothing to tell you. It's all finished with."

I let her go, because I knew how to stop her. "I know who killed your brother."

She caught her breath, and I waited; but she said nothing. I could hear quiet footsteps now in the room through the screened doorway as someone came in from the street; or perhaps it was one of the three mourners going out: It was impossible to tell from their sound. I watched the doorway, and the play of shadows on the ceiling, cast by the candlelight.

It had been dangerous to come here, I'd known that; but Ferris had told me he'd try to get me another twenty-four hours and I'd have to hurry. I'd phoned the airport as soon as I'd left him, and they'd told me that Li-fei was at her house; her brother's body had been flown in late last night. I'd had to come here; there was no choice.

"It was Tung Kuo-feng," I told her, "who ordered your brother's execution. Your brother made a serious mistake."

A vertical band of candlelight was falling across the hall from the doorway, and she had moved into it when she'd drawn away from me; it lay half across her body, so that one of her eyes was lit by it, watching me without blinking.

"How do you know these things?"

"I know them."

The shadows on the ceiling were changing, as a man's head moved past the candles in the room of the dead; I listened to their feet shuffling, but still couldn't tell whether anyone else had come in. If one of the Triad was here, he might come through the doorway: Soong Yongshen had been an important figure among them, and entrusted to carry out the assassination in Peking; the fact that he had made an unpardonable mistake, and had died for it, didn't mean the Triad wouldn't officially mourn him, for fear of his outraged spirit.

Li-fei turned her delicate head a degree, so that she could

watch the narrow gap between the screen and the doorway; I could only watch the shadows.

"Yes," she whispered, "it was Tung Kuo-feng who ordered my brother's death." She watched the doorway. "Tung Kuo-feng," she whispered again, as if her tongue could be a dagger.

"Tell me where to find him."

She swung her head. "You want to find him?"

"Yes."

"What would you do?"

"Kill him."

The eye lit by the candlelight widened. "Why?"

"I've got my reasons."

"Who are you?"

"His enemy."

She watched me. I waited.

"I must know who you are."

"What difference does it make who I am?"

With sudden impatience she said: "Because of trust. There are those who trust me."

I would have to go the long way round, and go carefully.

"Did you know your brother was going to Peking to carry out an assassination?"

She closed her eyes and in a moment said with a soft fierceness: *"No.* I would have stopped him." Her slender body had begun swaying slightly in the band of light, and she spoke in a kind of rhythm. "He said he was going to Peking to do something very important. He said he'd been chosen as the one to do it; he said it was an honor for him; he said it with pride." I watched tears glistening at her eyelids now, and her voice had soft anger in it. "I knew he was with one of the Triads; but he was young; many young men like my brother go into the Triads, for the adventure of it; many are taken to prison when they're caught; the lucky ones lose their taste for crime and come away, and find jobs. My brother didn't come away in time."

"Do you think Tung Kuo-feng should have killed him?"

"What for? Why should he want him killed?"

"He made a grave mistake. Your brother killed a man, too: the British secretary of state, a diplomat trying to make peace in the world, a man with a wife and two daughters."

She half-turned away from me, closing her eyes for a moment. "Yes," she whispered. "My brother killed a man for Tung Kuo-feng. There is no excuse for that. But he was my brother, and Tung Kuo-feng took his life away. I cannot forgive that."

"Tell me where to find him," I said.

The shadows were moving on the ceiling. I was standing within six feet of the doorway, close enough to make lethal contact if a man came through and recognized me and reacted; but he might not come alone.

"I don't know where he is," Li-fei said, her tone tormented. "You must go, or they'll—"

"Someone must know where he is. Think."

"There is no time. I—"

"You must have heard your brother talking about Tung."

"No. The people in the Triads never talk about themselves to those outside."

"Who were your brother's friends?"

"I don't know which of them are in the Triad. They—"

"Think, Li-fei. I want to know where I can find Tung."

The shadows on the ceiling moved, one of them flickering as a man passed close to a candle. I watched them, waiting for a shadow to grow enormous, filling the doorway as the man came through.

"There is a priest," Li-fei whispered, "who might know."

"Here in Seoul?"

"No. But not far away. In Karibong-ni."

"What languages does he speak?"

"He speaks only Korean and Cantonese."

"Take me to see him."

She was silent for a while, and then said: "Very well."

*　*　*

The priest was at evening prayer and we waited for him outside the temple in the gathering dusk, while at intervals a small bell tolled, sending echoes among the walls of the garden.

"He tried to save my brother," Li-fei told me, "to stop him from joining the Triad. It was no good; nothing would have stopped him, and I shall never know why." Her light voice trembled; the ashes had been placed in the urn only an hour ago.

"How old was your brother when you lost your parents?"

"He was five."

"It would have left him bereft. Perhaps he saw a father in Tung Kuo-feng."

"Perhaps."

We saw the priest coming, a thin and ancient man in a worn saffron robe, an acolyte leading him on each side until he was standing in front of us with his sightless eyes, his head tilted carefully to listen.

Soong Li-fei presented me to him, speaking in Chinese; then I interrupted her, asking her to send the two boys away. The priest didn't object, but they went only a short distance, out of earshot; they were obviously responsible for him. Li-fei led him gently to a corner of the garden where there were stone seats, then looked at me in the half-light.

"We need to know where to find Tung Kuo-feng," I told her quietly. Within a few minutes he realized that I was the questioner, not Li-fei, and he sat with his head turned toward me.

"What do you want with Tung Kuo-feng?"

"He is guilty of crimes," I told him through Li-fei. "He has caused men to murder."

She spoke for some time, answering questions without consulting me, except for a quick "He wants to know how we are sure of this." I suppose she was telling him her brother had killed for Tung, and that it was too late to save him now. In the deepening gloom the old man turned his head more to Li-fei than to me.

"What do you want with him?" she asked me, translating that same question again.

"I want to bring him to justice."

Death would be justice, for Tung Kuo-feng.

"Who are you?"

I waited a moment, aware of the two young acolytes not far away, and aware that if any of the Triad put questions later to Li-fei she might not be clever enough to keep her secrets. The priest moved his head slightly toward me, alert to my hesitation. In a moment I said: "I was responsible for the safety of the British secretary of state in Peking."

Li-fei told him, and he was silent for minutes, while the robed boys watched us from the shadows and the smell of incense came on the warm evening air from the temple doorway; and now I was aware that the future of *Jade One* rested here in this peaceful garden, and that one of the signals they were waiting for at the console in Whitehall, London, would have to come from the lips of this old man. Ferris had persuaded them to give me twenty-four hours, and there was no other way I could think of that would get me any kind of access to Tung Kuo-feng. Even if I could find, and stalk, and interrogate one of the Triad in Seoul, I'd learn nothing; they'd keep their silence whatever I did to them; they were fanatics.

Fat chance, in any case, of my capturing one of these people; they'd got on to me right from the start in London and they'd been crowding me ever since: I'd kept one step ahead of death in the last five days, and that was all. I could see Croder's point of view: The odds were too high, and the Triad was too strong. Perhaps unbreakable.

The old man had begun speaking, and I sat listening, but understood nothing. Li-fei didn't interrupt him, though there were silences where it seemed he'd finished. His head was lowered now and he was facing neither of us as the soft variant tones and unaspirated consonants fell and flew from his lips in a kind of dry music; and when at last he was finished, Li-fei let the silence go on for a little time before turning to me.

"He was speaking in parables," she said, "but I believe what he means is that he possesses some kind of knowledge that would lead to Tung Kuo-feng 'losing everything' if the police knew of it—I think he means death by execution, or life imprisonment. Some time ago he warned Tung that he would have to expose him, so that justice could be done and so that Tung could be freed of his earthly sins; but at that time Tung said that he was going to leave the Triad and devote the rest of his life to solitude and prayer as a means of atonement. This is what I think the priest means."

I glanced at the ancient man in the gloom, but couldn't get any kind of impression as to his personality; he sat in perfect stillness, his back bent only a little and his sightless eyes giving away nothing; he looked like one of the stone Buddhas that inhabited every shrine. "From what he says," I asked Li-fei, "do you think he's naïve? Does he really know what kind of man Tung Kuo-feng is?"

"He's very religious, but I don't think he's naïve; and he knows Tung: He called him a 'bad devil.' Of course there are good devils and bad—" She broke off, uncertain of how to put it. "In French we'd say, 'the devil himself,' or 'a disciple of the devil,' something like that."

"Does he know where I can find Tung Kuo-feng?"

"He hasn't said anything about that."

I took a breath. "Ask him."

She turned to the priest, and as she began speaking he lifted his head to listen; then for a while he was silent, and I had to wait, and not think of anything.

Then he spoke, and she turned to me again.

"Yes. He knows where Tung is now."

I suppose I didn't believe it, right away. It looked as if we'd got access for *Jade One,* after five days of running blind and drawing blank and trying to stay alive; for five days the Bureau had been shaking the whole of the international network for information, and as it had started coming in it was sealed forever in death—Sinclair's, Jason's, Spur's. But now the luck was breaking, and we stood a chance.

Second question.

"And will he tell me?"

Then I had to wait again while she asked him, while he listened and was silent, sitting with his head turned to me as if he were watching me, trying to sense what kind of man I was, and whether I could be trusted to follow the path he believed was good, according to his gods and his teachings.

When he spoke, it was only a word or two, and I turned to look at Li-fei.

She nodded to me. "Yes," she said, "he will tell you."

Access.

XV

SIGNALS

✿

In terms of driving time Kimpo Airport was about halfway between Karibong-ni and the British Embassy in Seoul, so as soon as we left the temple I asked Li-fei to stop at the nearest service station with a telephone; then I called the number Youngquist had given me in the subway this morning.

I recognized his voice when he came on the line, but we went through a double code-intro routine to make absolutely sure; then I told him I wanted a rendezvous with the director in the field, fully urgent, in the departure lobby on the third floor of Kimpo Airport half an hour from now. He didn't ask any questions and he wouldn't have got any answers if he had; nor was there any doubt that Ferris would be there on time: Apart from a few hundred other things your director in the field is required to make himself immediately available to you at whatever hour of the night or day; the executive is his sole charge and his sole responsibility.

I rang off and went back to the car.

Li-fei didn't say a word all the way to the airport; I think our meeting with the priest had brought the whole thing back to her: This was the time when the sleepless nights would begin, when she'd lie awake and wonder where things had gone wrong for her brother, and whether she could have tried harder to keep him out of trouble, away from Tung Kuo-feng's deadly influence. *Nothing would have stopped him,* she had told me, *and I shall never know why.*

She pulled up at the entrance to the terminal building and looked at me and asked: "Will you need me anymore?"

"No."

"You must be very careful."

"Yes," I said, "I'll be careful."

I was looking for Ferris, but couldn't see him.

"What will you do," Li-fei asked me, "when you find Tung?"

"I don't know."

"Will you arrest him?"

"Something like that."

"Or kill him?"

"I really don't know."

"Whatever you do to him," she said in a small cold voice, "let it be also for my brother."

I got out and she drove away and I watched the little Subaru heeling as she made the turn, with the bright overhead lamps throwing their light across the pale china-doll face at the driver's window; then I went through the main doors and took the stairs to the third floor, walking with my head down and turned slightly toward the walls, because they were out there somewhere and ready to try again the moment they picked up my trail.

You'd think my instinct to survive was adequate, but now there was something extra I wanted to live for: If they were going to finish me, let it not be yet, because now I'd got something to do; grant me, O Lord, at least the luck of a street dog, and let me endure.

Third floor, because there were fewer people up here and all of them going one way. Two stairwells, exit report gates, two shops, airlines VIP lounge, and toll waiting rooms. A group of five Japanese in light summer suits, all men and bowing to one another with punctilious regularity; two China Airlines flight attendants hobbling on high-heeled shoes; a black-uniformed chauffeur escorting a small European boy as far as Gate 3. There was no one else here: This was between flights. Through one of the windows I could see the wink of a beacon and the yellow glitter of the city to the northeast, and headlights along the highway.

Ferris late, discount, traffic problems, look at the gift-shop window, what lovely plastic Buddhas.

Are you sure? Ferris would ask.

The map was in my pocket.

I'll have to signal London.

Of course. Tell Croder. Cheer the bastard up.

What pretty Japanese fans.

Get here. For Christ's sake, just get here. All I ask.

A big jet came in with a thump and I saw lights flickering across the windows. It was 9:17 on the clock. But there is absolutely no point in watching the headlights. Youngquist understood the message, and the message was ultrapriority and he knew that: When you're operational and you use a telephone to your director or a contact, it doesn't matter which telephone you use, it's a hot line.

Two heads floated against the glass of the window, bobbing up from the stairwell behind me and moving across the pantomime masks, a man and a woman; I heard their voices, half-lost in the whistle of the jet as it came in toward the parking bay.

Others came, their heads appearing above the stairhead and turning, floating across the row of masks while I watched them, one of them not turning but growing larger and facing in my direction, pink and sandy and with glasses catching the light, bringing me back to a world where a future was possible again. "Bit of a jam," he was saying, "leaving the city."

I turned round and said: "I've got access."

He opened his mouth to say something, but thought better of it for some reason and just stood watching my face as if he were trying to see if I really meant it.

"Access to Tung Kuo-feng," I told him. "I know where he is."

He glanced around and asked me: "Why the airport?"

"It would have taken me another half-hour to get to the city."

"Is time critical?"

I didn't answer, and it took him a full second to get it all straight.

"Sorry."

"I should bloody well think so." It had taken me five days of murderous pressure to get here with what they wanted, and he'd wondered why there was suddenly such a rush.

"Are you sure enough," he asked me, "for me to let them know?"

"You can put through an interim signal, in case they've got to take up any slack in the system."

He nodded and we went down the stairs and he used one of the phones near the post office on the second floor, giving it cold to Youngquist or the embassy or whomever was near a radio: *The executive in the field has access.* Then he put me in the embassy car and took the slip road for the highway and turned northeast, slotting into the traffic stream.

"Did you catch that leak?" I asked him.

"Yes."

"We're going to the embassy?"

"Yes."

He smelled of soap.

"Who was it?"

He always smells of soap. He's always washing. They say he's guilty about something, and I can believe that: There's something in his voice like the echo of a distant shot.

"A Korean clerk, handling host-country PR."

"How did you get him?"

"Routine trap. We asked H.E. to say there was a suspected security problem and checked everyone on the staff below second attaché on their way home. This character had some papers on him, nothing classified but not his business."

A lot of the elation going, downswing now, but that was normal. "This man Tung," I said, "is just about everywhere."

"It might not have been Tung's man. In Asia there's a lot of intelligence mercs; they'll pass on whatever they can pick up, to whoever will pay most."

"There could be someone else," I said, "at the embassy."

"No. I've been working all day on that: Five trial rendez-vous with Youngquist and three contacts, half of them by open phone and half over various radios in open speech, three languages, and no one ever turned up to survey. Youngquist took the skin off his feet."

"That's a shame."

"I thought you'd like that."

When the lights of downtown started swinging overhead I told him about the priest and he listened for ten minutes without interrupting before he asked: "Is he sure?"

"Yes. I told him that lives depended on it, and he said he could believe that, because he knew what kind of man Tung was and he knew I was an agent opposing him."

"You told him that, did you?"

"I had to, for Christ's sake!"

"Just wanted to know," he said quietly.

"Look, he wouldn't have opened up if I hadn't told him that much. Christ, I could've been anyone, can't you see that?"

"Everything's perfectly all right," he said, and I sat back and started cooling in my own sweat. Nerves, that was all; paranoia; it'd been a rough five days.

"Bloody Ferris," I said. "You know what they say about you in the café? They say you strangle mice."

He gave that thin, rustling laugh of his, like a snake shedding its skin, and we pulled into the embassy yard in Chung-dong Street and got out of the car and went into the building and up the stairs to a room on the second floor, empty except for some garden furniture and a cardboard box of paper cups and a projection screen hanging at an angle against the wall.

Ferris shut the door and I got out the map.

"You mean there's no approach by road?"

"The nearest road is this one, twenty miles away. All you've got are mule tracks."

Ferris looked at the larger map he'd got from the night clerk. "He pinpointed the monastery here?"

"Yes."

"He was absolutely certain?"

"He said it was his home for fifteen years."

"We're depending," Ferris said, "on the word of one man. A blind man."

"He had his sight up till three years ago."

"How did he lose it?"

"I don't know. But I asked him. He said it was 'karma.' And I realized we'd have to depend on his word alone; that's why it took an hour and a half to get it all clear; and I'm satisfied. He knows the mountains, the terrain, and the layout of the monastery."

"You say it's in ruins now?"

"Partly. There was a rockfall, three years ago, and the monks had to leave."

"That was when he was blinded?"

"He told me it happened three years ago, that was all. The time could have been coincidental."

"You think Tung did it? Or had it done?"

"That was my impression. I'd say their paths had crossed."

There was a knock on the door and Ferris went over and unlocked it. The night clerk looked in.

"I've got the cook out of bed." He was a young chap with a long face and inquisitive eyes; or perhaps they hadn't looked so inquisitive before we'd come in here and asked for food and maps and a camp bed and absolute privacy. He didn't know who we were but he knew Ferris must be *persona grata* with H.E. His eyes were darting from our faces to the maps all over the floor. "Bacon and eggs and toast, was that right?"

"And coffee," Ferris said.

"Coming up."

That was at 11:25.

I'd slept for an hour by the time Ferris came back from the cipher room, his face perfectly expressionless, which was the only way I'd ever seen it. He told me they'd exchanged fifteen signals so far and that London was "open-minded." Two people from the Bureau had gone across to the Foreign Office to sit at the radio and ten minutes ago Croder had come on the air.

"Why doesn't he make up his mind?" I asked Ferris.

"He's in the process of doing that." Cool tone: rebuke. He was getting fed up with his executive needling Control all the time; I could see his point, so I shut up. "They want to know," he said in a moment, "what the chances are of putting a chopper down in that area."

"I asked the priest. He said the only place you can put down a chopper in that region is at the monastery itself; the surrounding terrain is nothing but peaks and crags."

He got onto the floor with the maps again. "We're going to assume that if Tung is using this place as a refuge, it's liable to be more like a fort than a monastery."

"Thank you. That'll give me a chance."

"You wouldn't want to try going in with a chopper?"

That was obviously an official question and for the record.

"No. There's only one way I'm prepared to go in, as I told you."

He sat there cross-legged like a thin, sandy Buddha. "Why did he go there? Why did he need refuge?"

Some of these questions were passed on from London; some were coming into his mind as the sessions progressed.

"The priest didn't say."

"But you asked him?"

"Yes."

"You think he didn't know?"

"I think he knew, but wasn't saying."

"What are your thoughts on that?"

"I'd say that Tung is under some kind of pressure; that he's running his operation by remote control, using a radio."

"A defensive operation?"

"I don't think there's anything defensive about assassinating a secretary of state and an ambassador."

"So what do you think?"

"He could be running his operation this way to avoid the danger of getting hit."

"You think if he got hit, personally, it would destroy the operation?"

"Yes. I think he's running a cell of out-and-out fanatics, totally loyal, totally obedient, riders of the divine wind. They're the type who break if the leader breaks."

He went on questioning, with intervals of meditative silence. I did the best I could, but it wasn't easy, because there weren't too many facts: I was bringing out feelings, recalling things that Li-fei had told me in the Chonju Hotel, and at her house, and in the car, and at the temple, when I'd listened half to the things she wasn't saying, and taken more notice of them than of the things she was. I had also listened to the silences of the priest, unconsciously measuring their length—knowing that the longer he was silent, the more he was troubled by the questions I'd asked him through Li-fei.

"You think the priest would like to see Tung dead?"

"What?" I had to think about that. "Yes. But not in the way we'd mean it, in the West. He'd feel personally relieved to see Tung cleansed of his earthly sins; that was a phrase he used, if Li-fei got the translation right. And the kind of sins he was talking about can only be atoned for by death."

"But not death as punishment?"

"Death as atonement."

Then there was a knock on the door again and the night
clerk put his long face in the gap. "Kirby wants you, sir."
Kirby was the cipher clerk and this was another signal.
It was 00:46 hours, and already morning.

"They're in contact," Ferris said, "with the CIA."
"Because of the American ambassador?"
He didn't answer that. "I just want you to know there's now
an American connection. Are you still prepared to go in
there?"
"To the monastery?"
"Yes."
"If it's my way, by a night drop."
Ferris was sitting on the floor again with the maps in front
of him. He slotted his long fingers together and didn't look
up as he told me: "Control says you can go in, on his terms."
Dead end. Sixteen signals, leading us to a dead end. Be-
cause I knew Croder. He wouldn't have made this proviso if
they were the kind of terms I could accept. Croder is God:
He giveth and he taketh away.
"What terms?"
"That you take someone with you as a guide."
I said no.

01:32
"I always work solo," I said. "You know that."
"This time it's too critical."
"Only the landing. After I'm down, I don't want anyone
with me. They'd get in my way."
"You won't even find your way, without a guide."
"Look, I did a night drop into the Sahara and there was no
problem. I was alone."
"This isn't the Sahara."
"Croder doesn't trust me, that's all. He never has."

Ferris began whistling quietly, which was like anyone else kicking the door down. "They're putting everything on this one venture. If you take a guide with you, it's going to decrease the risk of your getting lost. All the guide has to do is get you to the monastery—to within sight of it. Then you go in alone."

"It's the drop I'm worried about. Two chutes are more visible than one: You're doubling the risk, not decreasing it."

"You're dropping by night."

"By moonlight."

"Over completely unknown territory."

"With a compass."

"And magnetic rocks in the area. You won't know whether you're north or south of the target."

"If they can drop me reasonably close I'll be able to see the monastery; there can't be too many rectangular mountain peaks."

He began whistling softly again, and I waited.

Hear me: If ever I get out of this one alive I'll never work for Croder again. This is the second time and he hasn't changed.

"Your arguments," Ferris said, stopping his pacing and looking down at me, "have been presented to London. I foresaw most of them; the others won't be transmitted, because it won't be worth it—they'll say no."

"They're not doing the drop. I am."

"What you're doing," Ferris said, "is provoking Croder. You hate his guts and you want him to know it. But he knows it already, so you're wasting your time."

"Croder's not doing the drop." I got up and moved about, keeping out of Ferris's way.

"Do you think this is the first one he's ever set up?"

"What are my chances, Ferris? You thought about that? I'd put them at fifty-fifty, and that's optimistic. That's why you've got Youngquist out here, standing by. *Who the hell is Croder to make it tougher for me than it is already?"*

"Croder is our Control."

"That doesn't mean he's God."

"Yes, it does. And he's the only one we've got."

It stopped me, but I don't know why. He saw it, and came closer, and lowered his voice. "It's the only way we can ever work, isn't it? With someone in London who knows more than we do, and who can get us out of traps we can't even see because we're too close."

I didn't say anything. I'd used all the arguments I could think of and they hadn't worked.

"You'd do it for any other Control," Ferris said, "wouldn't you?"

In a moment I said: "Yes."

"So you'll do it for this one. Won't you?"

I turned away from him.

"Yes."

He moved toward the door. "I'll go and tell them."

"Do that."

It was 01:40, and to hell with them all. We were going in.

XVI

USAFB

✣

"Okay," Captain Newcomb said, "these are hard copies of some stuff we took from high altitude with vidicon cameras three or four months ago." He pushed the square-format pictures across the briefing table and leaned over them with a pointer. "The scale is 1:944,300, or approximately one inch to 15.6 miles, and the ground resolution is 200 feet/line, so we have a pretty clear image of the monastery. It's right here."

One of the lights on the telephone near the door had begun winking, but nobody took any notice.

"Halfway up the mountain," Ferris said.

"Maybe a bit closer to the peak. We lose definition lower down on this picture because of the trees and shadow. We estimate the altitude at a thousand feet. The—"

"The altitude of the monastery?" I asked him.

"Uh? Right. The monastery, not the peak. The peak's around two thousand, which tallies with local survey maps."

Lieutenant Lewes sat hunched over the table, chewing gum. He was the pilot. After Ferris had told London I was ready to go in on their terms there'd been a long delay, presumably because Croder had had to go through Washington or the

Pentagon to set up liaison with the U.S. Air Force and arrange the drop. We'd only arrived here fifteen minutes ago at ten in the morning but Ferris had got me through Security with no problem. This was the new air-force base to the southwest of the city: I'd passed the gates last night on the way to Karibong-ni.

"You'll be dropping an hour before dawn, so that you'll have time to release the chutes and stow them and get yourself set up for the ground approach." Newcomb glanced round as the door opened, but went on speaking. "The Met. tells me the estimated wind at the three- to five-thousand-foot level is not more than ten knots. It's more likely you'll be going down in virtually still-air conditions."

The girl slipped into the empty chair without saying anything. Ferris gave her a nod and went on listening to Captain Newcomb.

"The estimated mean air temperature at that altitude band is fifty-six degrees at the time you'll be dropping. There's one potential problem, and that's the likelihood of ground mist at this season, especially after the monsoon rains. There just isn't anything we can do to help you with that." He straightened up from the table. "Are there any questions so far?"

"What about—" I began, but Ferris stopped me.

"Hold it a moment, would you?" He pushed his chair back and got up. "Gentlemen, this is Miss de Haven of Geological Survey. She'll be going in as the guide."

The rest of us got up, though Lewes looked a bit uncertain; the girl was in green battle dress and he'd heard all about women's lib. "This is Captain Bob Newcomb," Ferris told her, "Lieutenant Al Lewes, and Mr. Clive West."

"Hi," Al said.

"For God's sake sit down," she told us. "I'm sorry I'm late: Your security people held me up."

"That's quite okay," Newcomb said, and we all sat down again, rather awkwardly. "I'll just recap what we've done so far."

We listened again to the briefing while the girl slung her

canvas shoulder bag round the chair and put her elbows on the table and studied the photographs. The light on the telephone was still winking and Lewes went across to it and pressed one of the buttons and came back.

"There's a certain amount of night flying by the military and civil freight lines between Seoul and Daegu," Newcomb told us, "which is a plus in terms of sound cover; the direct air lane between the two fields runs approximately twenty-five miles from the monastery at its closest point on a horizontal plane, so they're used to hearing air traffic not too far away."

He asked for questions again, and the de Haven girl got up and walked about, her arms folded and her gaze mostly on the briefing table. She was short, with chunky blond hair and steady eyes and a square chin; I thought I'd seen her before, but couldn't remember when; I didn't believe the "Geological Survey" tag: It was almost certainly a cover, because this was a high-risk drop and she must be in some kind of spook unit.

"What jump altitude are you thinking of?" She looked at me for the first time since the introductions.

"As low as we can make it. Say one thousand."

"That's too low." She was looking at the briefing table again. "Even with ground wind zero it's not going to be much fun in that terrain. Let's make it three."

I got up, too, and felt Ferris watching me, and ignored it. "I don't know what a calculator would give us, but during that extra two thousand feet we'll be in the air for something like two minutes longer."

"So?" She glanced up from the table.

"There'll be a three-quarter moon."

"Oh. You mean we'll be visible for that much longer?"

"Yes."

"Are they going to be watching for us?"

"We don't know," Ferris cut in.

"Can we find out?"

In the silence I thought: Either she's been underbriefed or she isn't thinking.

"No," Ferris said.

She switched her hard blue eyes onto me. "You've made drops like this before, Mr.—?"

"Clive."

"Mr. Clive?"

"Clive West."

"What? Oh. Fair enough. I'm Helen."

"I haven't made a drop over mountains. But I'd rather risk a broken ankle than hang there in the sky for two minutes longer. I'm going in from one thousand."

"We'll talk about it later. For the moment we—"

"I'd like it to go down now in the operational notes," I told her, "since this is the only briefing session we're going to get. We jump from one thousand feet."

Al Lewes got up and went over to the window and blew his nose rather noisily. Newcomb went on staring at the aerial photographs. De Haven turned her head to face Ferris; she had a very direct gaze, always moving her head instead of glancing with her eyes.

"This is only a two-crew operation, Mr. Ferris, but there's got to be one of us in command, the same as if we were flying a plane in. I was called in as an expert to plan the drop, and the only way I can do it is my way. Is that agreed?"

Ferris slid his long fingers together on the edge of the table. "You won't accept Mr. West's authority?" He said it pleasantly.

"It's not a question of accepting him." Her tone was perfectly cool. "If he knows as much as I do about dropping into that area and finding his way afterward, that's fine, and you don't need me. But if he doesn't—which I assume is why you called me in—then I've got to be in charge, not only because I want to protect my life, too, but because it'll lessen the risk for us both." She took her sling bag from the back of the chair and swung it across her shoulder.

Captain Newcomb picked up his pointer and aligned it carefully along the edge of the nearest photograph. Lewes was still standing at the window with his back to us. In a moment Ferris looked up at me.

"My instructions," he said, "are that if any question arises as to who's in charge of the drop, it's Miss de Haven."

She took the bag off her shoulder and slung it round the back of the chair again.

"Well, that's got that out of the way."

"Decaffeinated," I said.

"Anything with it?"

"No."

Three pilots came into the canteen, still in their flying gear. I'd watched these people throwing F5E's all over the sky most of the day; then I'd seen a film in the auditorium; and now I was in here trying to absorb the shock.

"Can I join you?"

Helen de Haven.

"Of course."

I turned the newspaper over as she sat down; there was a photograph.

"How are you feeling?"

She was in a blue T-shirt and jeans; I hadn't recognized her for a moment; she looked younger, more feminine.

"Feeling?"

"About the drop."

"Not very good. What can I get you?"

"Coffee. Not very good?"

I gave the order. "You came at the wrong time."

"That's easily dealt with." She got up and slung her shoulder bag.

"We've got to talk," I said, "in any case."

"I'm not sure I want to."

"Anything to eat, with the coffee?"

"What? I don't know. A bun, I suppose. What the hell's gone wrong?" She sat down again and looked at me with her steady hard-blue eyes.

The paper had been lying on the counter when I'd come in. I suppose that was luck, of a kind: I might not have seen it otherwise.

She met her death, it said on the front page, *in the same grim fashion*.

"I don't know yet," I told Helen de Haven, "what's gone wrong. But we'll keep you briefed."

Her eyes were narrowed slightly and her mouth was firm. "Is it this thing about the jump altitude?"

"No. Although I'd like to reach some sort of a compromise about that." The girl put two coffees on the counter and pushed the cream and sugar closer. "When you were briefed," I asked de Haven, "what were you told, exactly?"

"It was a secret briefing."

"Were you told, for instance, that we'll be going into what might be called hostile territory?"

"Something like that."

The same bizarre method, the paper said, *was a feature of both killings*. Otherwise, I suppose, it wouldn't have made the front page in a city of seven million people. I watched her again for a moment as the little Subaru made the turn outside the terminal building, with the bright overhead lamps throwing their light across the pale china-doll face at the driver's window. It was the last I would ever see of her.

Only hours before her death on the steps of the temple in Seoul, the newspaper had said, *Soong Li-fei had been the chief mourner at her brother's funeral*.

Outside the canteen an F5E went down the runway and lifted off with a reverberating rush of sound.

You must be very careful, Li-fei had told me. She knew Tung Kuo-feng, and the things he was capable of doing; but she had forgotten to be careful herself.

"Are you getting cold feet?" the de Haven girl asked me.

"What?"

"This 'hostile territory' thing. It's losing its appeal?"

"I don't know," I told her, "if it's still on."

"The drop?"

"Yes."

"Oh for God's sake, they called me down from the North, and I'm bloody busy."

I was trying to focus on the fresh English face with its unwavering gaze, but there was a kind of double exposure and I was also watching the soft cinnamon eyes of Soong Li-fei.

"What do you do," I asked de Haven, "in the North?" Not that I was interested, but there was a social obligation to keep the conversation going while I thought things out.

"I train parachutists for NATO. Why?"

"Then you're too valuable to lose. How did you get yourself into this mess?"

She put down her coffee with a little bang. "Clive, are you always like this?"

"Like what?"

"A bear with a sore arse. Look, if you've decided to back out of doing the drop, then just tell me. Frankly I couldn't care less, but, by God, I shall want expenses and compensation for wasted time."

Her anger was finally getting through to me, and the image of Soong Li-fei was fading. "Something's happened," I told her, "that might stop us going in. I've got to ask Ferris for his instructions; then we'll tell you the score."

"That's extremely kind of you. Exactly how long do I have to wait?"

"I'd say an hour or two, that's all." I put some money down and left her.

"Thank you for the coffee," she called after me.

At eight o'clock Ferris signaled London and told them what had happened; then we went on talking.

"You left Soong Li-fei at what time?" he asked me.

"About ten past nine last night."

"And she was found outside the temple about midnight. Three hours at most; half an hour at least. I mean she could have been killed half an hour after you left her—the time needed to drive from the airport to the vicinity of the temple."

What we had to decide was whether there had been time for Tung's men to interrogate her before they killed her off, and whether she had been forced to tell them I now knew how to find Tung. The ultimate question was very simple: If we made the drop before dawn tomorrow, would Tung be expecting us?

If he were expecting us, we wouldn't have a chance.

"From what you knew of her," Ferris asked me, "do you think she'd break?"

"I think Tung's men could break a sphinx."

Ferris paced the small room; these were my quarters, courtesy of the U.S. Air Force, complete with bathroom, two telephones, a TV set, and an internal-communications panel. The equipment for the drop was stacked in the corner: climbing boots and gloves, rope, rucksack, provisions, field glasses, first aid, and the rest of the stuff.

"What is Youngquist's present status?" I asked Ferris.

"He's still ready to take over as your replacement."

"Briefed right up to the minute?"

He didn't look at me. "Yes."

"Does that reflect your estimation of my chances? Or London's estimation?"

He looked at me now, a bit annoyed. "Our estimation's the same as yours. We're not keeping anything back from you. If you'd like to consider your record with the Bureau, you might realize they're not out to throw you on the scrap heap."

"Civil of them."

"We think you've got a good chance of getting through to Tung Kuo-feng, otherwise we wouldn't ask you to go. Croder's discussed a dozen other options, including a low-level bombing raid, but the best chance we've got is by putting one man in by stealth, a man with your proven capabilities."

"Then send me in alone."

"You mean without de Haven?"

"Yes."

"She'll be with you only until you sight the monastery from the ground, unless you need her help after the drop. She's led climbing expeditions right across this country and she speaks fluent Korean."

"How will she get out?"

"You'll be given a final joint briefing before takeoff."

I turned to stand with my back to the stuff in the corner; it was tempting me: I wanted to go in, despite the increased risk, because it was the only way open to me. "What can you do to find out if Li-fei was made to talk?"

"Almost nothing. I've got Youngquist working on it, with five or six agents in place; but all they can do is hope for luck in tracing her movements from the time she left you—finding people who might have seen her or talked to her during that blank time period."

"Who's going to make the final decision?"

"London. Providing you agree to go in if they ask you to."

"I shall agree."

"You may want time to think."

"No."

Because Tung would have to be stopped: He'd already gone too far. He had ordered six killings, and Li-fei's wouldn't be the last; and since I'd seen the photograph of the pretty Chinese girl in the newspaper I had wanted urgently to meet Tung Kuo-feng, the Diabolus whose hand had reached out from the mountains to guide the sword that had struck across that delicate porcelain neck.

"We're not looking for personal reasons," Ferris said. "We're not mounting a vendetta."

I suppose he sensed my mood; or maybe he thought that Soong Li-fei had meant more to me than she had. But how much does a girl have to mean to you before you're ready to destroy the man who took her head from her body?

"What reasons are you looking for?" I noticed that my tone wasn't all that pleasant.

"We're running a mission. We're asking you to carry out a technical operation, an exercise in logistics. It's the only way you'll get through."

"That's the trouble with London. You're not meant to have a soul. You're meant to be a bloody machine. But just for your information, when I go in it'll be for my own reasons, and there's nothing you can do about that. Nothing at all."

An orderly woke me at 2:00 A.M. and I reported to the control tower as instructed.

London must have decided. I couldn't ask Ferris, because he wasn't there. At 02:15 they put de Haven and me into a transport plane and we landed at Daegu fifty minutes later, a hundred and fifty miles southeast of Seoul. The night was clear and windless. Ferris was there.

The final joint briefing was summary; the main points had been gone over before. Ferris was perfectly calm, but that didn't mean a thing. Helen de Haven had withdrawn into herself; either she was feeling tension or she had dismissed me as a boor and had no inclination to talk. We left the briefing room at 03:46 by the clock on the wall and walked onto the tarmac, already strapped into our chutes.

"Hold it," Newcomb said, and we stopped. He went ahead of us to join Ferris and Lieutenant Lewes. It was almost dark in this area; they must have switched off the tarmac lights.

I said to de Haven: "Did they tell you what our chances are?"

She looked up at me in the faint light. "They didn't give me any actual figures."

"Did they tell you we might be dropping into gunfire?"

She was quiet for a moment. "They used the expression 'extremely hazardous.' Does that fit?"

"Yes. As long as you know."

"All I know is, you don't want me on this trip. But I'm hard to scare. Sorry."

A figure was moving across the tarmac to our right, toward the buildings. *"Put those goddamned lights out!"*

"The thing is," I told the girl beside me, "that the people I work for happen to use human beings as machines. They're not terribly concerned that in twenty minutes from now there could be two dead bodies hanging from parachutes over the Korean mountains. I just want to make sure they didn't sell you short."

The man was shouting again. This time someone called an answer.

"If there's a chance for you," she said, "there's a chance for me."

"It's not a big one; but I've got my reasons."

"And so have I."

Then the lights over the dispersal bay went out and we followed Newcomb's flashlight toward the plane.

XVII

DANCE

❄

Newcomb was using the omni stations at Seoul and Sogcho, and at 04:07 he came back from the flight deck as we felt the airspeed slackening off.

"Five minutes," he said. "Everything okay?"

"What's our altitude?" de Haven asked him.

"We're coming down from seven thousand now and we'll be running in at three-five." He crouched in the aisle between the seats, looking at us in turn. "The moon's at one o'clock, seventy degrees, so I'm going to put you down to the west of the target point by an estimated mile. That way, you won't show your silhouettes against the moon to anyone watching from the monastery. Is that okay?"

The pale blur of de Haven's face was turned toward me in the gloom; the interior lights were out, so that our eyes could accommodate for moonlight. "All right, Clive?"

"Except for the altitude."

"Except for the altitude," she said, "all right?"

I looked at Newcomb. "What's the estimated ground wind?"

"There isn't any. Up here we're in still air, and from our experience of local conditions it'll be the same on the ground."

I twisted over on the twin seats and looked down through the cabin window and saw only patches of dark and light: the mountains and the mist between them. "What's the actual terrain look like, a mile west of the monastery?"

"You're on the mountainside, but it's not a steep slope; the the land falls away in ridges, so you—"

"Terraces?" de Haven cut in.

"Uh? Right—terraces. Be some flat areas in narrow bands, but there'll be loose rock. Have to feel your way in." He straightened up and went forward to the flight deck.

We were gradually losing height, and the airframe sent panels creaking as it flexed. Newcomb had forgotten to shut the door to the flight deck and its low-key illumination was in our eyes. I got up to go forward just as he remembered.

"Sorry."

"That's all right."

The panel of light narrowed and went out.

"Did you see that cartoon?" de Haven asked me.

"Which one?"

"It was in a flight magazine at the base. A picture of a sky-diving team: They'd just linked hands together after free fall, in a nice neat circle, and one of them was talking to the man next to him, you know, in the caption. He was saying: 'You should have thought of that before we jumped!' Is that your kind of funny?"

"Yes." I laughed for her, but it sounded false. The only caption I'd seen at the base just gave the name under the photograph: Soong Li-fei.

If they had made her talk, there'd be a night watch mounted at the monastery and it wouldn't matter if we went down on the blind side of the moon or not.

A crack of light came, forward.

"Two minutes."

Still losing speed and altitude; it felt more like an approach. Lewes had told us we could cut the engine sound by almost half this way.

De Haven got to her feet, clumsy under the weight of the parachute. "The captain would like to thank you for traveling USAF, and we hope you'll join us again on your next trip."

"Not if you serve that chocolate mousse again. You know what I thought it really was?"

She gave a quick dry laugh and the door of the flight deck opened and I went first down the aisle.

"One minute."

We checked our harness, settling the webbing.

Slight pressure under our feet: Lewes was leveling out.

"Thanks for everything," de Haven said; her voice sounded forced, a fraction too loud.

"You're very welcome," I heard Newcomb say; then he swung the door lever and suddenly there was the empty night sky and I went out first as we'd agreed.

No sensation of falling, just the slam of the air and then the diminishing sound of the plane.

One.

The body turning. Moonlight against the retinas.

Two.

Turning and tilting now. Two dark shapes in the dome of night, the plane and a small blob, de Haven.

Three. And pull.

Pilot chute crackling, and the hiss of the lines.

In London I'd been three thousand miles away from Tung Kuo-feng, and in Seoul I'd been only a hundred, and now, if it were daylight and I used the field glasses, I'd be close enough to see him, to see his face.

Access.

Main canopy deploying, black nylon against the black sky and the harness tugging and the windrush easing off. Swinging through the dark. And even in the dark, if he used his field glasses, he would see me now, a cloud drifting against the wink of stars, no bigger than a man's hand.

He would have all the time he needed. Things would be easier for him than at a shooting gallery.

Li-fei, what did they ask you?

Everything slow now, and no wind. Night and silence, and the wink of moonlight on the metal grip of the toggle above me and to the left.

What did you tell them?

The cold pressed at my face. When I looked down I could see mist shrouding the mountains in white. A blind landing could be a killer, but we'd known that.

Anything?

Hanging in the sky, like something caught up on a web and helpless there without the power to move in any direction. Loss of identity: neither fish nor fowl, with arms but nothing to hold, no ground to tread. A target, perhaps, if you must have a name.

A white sea below, flooding from horizon to horizon, with dark islands of rock, and suddenly close. I reached up to the toggles, rehearsing, and at the same time watched the high faint star fields for any sign of the girl; she wasn't in sight; she must be almost directly above the black spread of my canopy.

The mist smelled wet, and had the bitter taint of woodsmoke in it. There were three villages below, on the periphery of our main target area. Even a low wind would take us to any one of them, but once on the ground it would take us days to reach it.

The mist rushed white, swirling as I turned, with the dark peaks thrusting upward and tearing the vapors into shreds along the valleys. I pulled the toggles and started a swinging action, turning slowly to face the moon and then looking down: If there were lights burning at the monastery I should see them by this time unless the mist was too thick; it was patchy now and breaking up, and I saw a mountain peak at eye level and watched its dark cone rising against the stars, blotting them out one by one.

At any second now I could hit rock.

Dropping through mist, under the milky light of the moon.

I spat twice, trying to find the wind's direction so that I could turn my back to it for the landing; but Newcomb had been right: There was no wind.

Falling fast now: I could see crags and a dark cliff face through a gap in the mist as it swirled around me and filled the canopy, spilling away in the moonlight; falling faster and faster but at the same speed: It was just that I could see more of the environment and could orientate visually. Turning slowly away from the moon's white haze, the moon itself hidden by the canopy, turning and swinging and looking downward now, watching for the ground, if there was any ground and not just a cliff or a crag or an outcrop waiting to break my back; falling, falling fast with the mist clouding white and then suddenly dissolving, clouding again, the ground rushing up, then a great rock face sliding against the sky and the lines trembling as the canopy caught against something, tugging and swinging me full circle and back again, dizzying, *look down, keep on looking down,* everything dark now, the mist gone and nothing below me but black rock, *look down,* then suddenly the sense of nearness to great mass, and I dragged on the lines to soften the impact and saw the rocky floor and doubled my legs and pitched forward and flung out my hands, kicking at the rubble and feeling a tug on the lines as the canopy dragged and caught and jerked me upright before it broke clear and I went pitching down again, sliding on all fours across the rocks until everything stopped.

Release harness.

Then I heard her cry out and saw the huge shape of her canopy billowing against the sky before it reached the cliff and spilled air and she spun and struck the rock face and bounced away again, swinging in a wild arc as the canopy broke free and dropped her small figure beyond the edge of a ridge. I began stumbling forward, pulling the radio from the kit strapped to my waist and hitting the transmit button.

"Eagle to Jade One. Eagle to Jade One."

I kept moving forward, checking the straps securing the rest of the equipment; if she were still alive she'd need first aid.

The set put out a rush of static, then cleared as I adjusted the squelch. *"Come in, Eagle."*

Ferris.

"Eagle to Jade One. Q down and safe. DH injured. Will report."

He acknowledged and I shut the thing off and started running, my boots sliding over loose gravel and sending it scattering. Even with the noise I was making I was aware of the great silence around me, and the weight of the mountains that sprawled here in the shadow of night. I crossed the ridge and fell twice, loosening rock and hearing it tumble as small stones sent their echoes crackling against the hard face of the cliff. Three or four times I called her name softly, but heard no answer. The light was better here; the moon had found a break in the mist and the rocks glittered like jet. I called again, but there was only the massive silence pressing down.

I let myself drop again, sliding through a crevice and finding flat ground at the edge of a dark pool that had no reflection; and the eye-brain interchange of data and association took an instant to inform me that the pool wasn't water but her black canopy.

"Hello, Clive."

She was on the ground, faceup, just lying there. I bent over her, freeing the buckles of the medical kit.

"What's the damage?"

"Broken leg. Don't touch it; it's beautifully numb."

"Are you bleeding?"

"Not much, I think. Don't worry. I thought I saw a light when I was coming down, over to the east—did you see it, too?"

"No." I was touching her suit lightly, feeling for damage and odd angles, and also letting her know that she wasn't alone; sometimes the voice isn't enough. Blood glinted along her left leg where the suit had been ripped away. "I'm going to clean you up a bit; it'll sting. Try to—"

"Clive," she said, "listen to me. And don't do anything. I think I saw a light from the direction of the monastery; then either it went out or the mist hid it again. You know what I'm saying. They might have seen us."

I soaked one of the cotton-wool pads in the ether. There was no blood pooling anywhere; it was just oozing from the surface capillaries of the abrasion. "We knew there was the risk," I told her.

"Okay. Clive, please listen, and do what I ask. Put that stuff away. It stinks." Her voice was light but emphatic, and I stopped what I was doing. "I've got a broken leg, and there is absolutely no way you can get me out of here: no way. When the pain starts, I'll need morphine—I'm no bloody hero; and that would mean carrying me across these mountains to a goat track, and finding a goatherd and asking him to fetch a horse and cart from the nearest village, and waiting till he did that; and there'd be the trip to the village, in a bumpy cart. Clive, do you know your paramedic stuff? Do you know what state my leg would be in by then? After two days, maybe three days?" She put her hand on my arm. "There's just one other little thing. When daylight comes, we'll be in sight of the monastery, or if we're not, we'd move into sight of it a dozen times on the trek to the goat track, unavoidably. Are you starting to get any kind of message?"

I began swabbing her leg and she hissed her breath in, gripping my wrist. "The sooner we start getting you out," I told her, "the more chance we'll have."

"Oh, Christ," she said, "I didn't know you were such a stupid bastard."

I finished swabbing and went for the roll of lint in the canvas bag. "Save your energy, Helen. Relax. Are you feeling thirsty yet?"

She closed her eyes and began laughing strangely, and the

sound went on until she could speak again. "Am I thirsty? Clive, I'm dying."

I stopped unrolling the bandage. "Of a broken leg?"

"Of a broken leg. And the mountains."

There was a gash on the side of her crash helmet: I'd noticed it when I'd been feeling for damage. Perhaps she'd struck her head on the rock face and the pain was making her irrational. But somewhere in my own mind there was a cold thought creeping: that she wasn't being irrational at all.

"Did you hit your head? Do you feel disoriented?"

She struggled to move a little, lifting her shoulders and propping herself on her elbows, watching me steadily in the moonlight.

"Clive, will you bloody well listen to me? I know you're acting according to your instincts, and I understand that. You think the first thing to do is to save life. But there isn't one to save—only yours." She spoke with slow clarity, as if she wanted to make absolutely sure I understood. "I'm not only talking about the sheer physical impossibility of getting me through those mountains with anything left of what I am now; and I'm not only talking about gangrene and pneumonia and no chance in hell of finding competent medical aid in the nearest village, though I'll just mention that morphine isn't totally effective with bone trauma and that I do *not* intend spending the next two or three days in screaming agony before they see us from the monastery and shoot us both. I'm also talking about why I took this job on, and what they told me when I was briefed, and what I agreed to do. I agreed to give you whatever assistance was necessary in making the drop and getting a fix on the monastery, and then to make my own way out while you proceeded with your mission; those were the actual words, in writing: *while you proceeded with your mission.* And that's what you've now got to do."

She went on watching me, giving me time to think over what she'd said.

"And leave you here?"

"And leave me here. I'll be all right. You're going to fix things for me."

"Fix things?"

"They shoot horses, don't they?"

"You're out of your mind."

"I've never been more rational in my life." Her voice was perfectly steady. "All you've got to do is cut a wrist. I'm an awful coward when it comes to self-inflicting anything. I can't even get a splinter out. We're all different, aren't we?"

I was aware of the bandage in my hand: Conscious thought was overlaying the desperate attempt to deny all she was saying, to believe it wasn't the simple and appalling truth.

"You're asking me to kill you?"

"Don't be so melodramatic, Clive. I'm asking you for your charity. I'm asking you to save me from unbearable pain, and the unbearable waiting for the time when they see us, and come for us. I'm going to be killed anyway; you'll be more gentle than they will."

I thought for a long time, or it seemed long, kneeling on the loose shale beside her with the lint bandage in my hand and nothing to do with it, while I relearned the lesson that had been brought home to me rarely in my life: that to be helpless is the most subtle of all agonies.

"What we're going to do," I said at last, "is to find our way out of here without being seen, and to assume quite confidently that the morphine's going to do its job for as long as—"

"Clive, you've got to face it. *You've just got to face it.*" Her small fingers were dug into my wrist. "If this were just a geological field trip I'd let you try getting me across those mountains before I went out of my mind, but it isn't like that. When they briefed me they told me enough about your operation to let me know it's important. I've worked for DI6 and I've worked for NATO Intelligence—which is why your people trusted me with this little trip—and I know the signs of a top secret mission when I see them; I know it's quite likely that if you reach your target you'll save lives, maybe a lot of lives, but certainly more than one—more than this one. You—"

"You're just making up your own weird scenario—"

"I haven't finished. The thing is, Clive, that my integrity is at stake; and if you think for one moment that you can monkey with that, you'll get a real surprise. Who the hell do you think I am? D'you think I'm the type to give my word to your people and sign the clearance form and then go back on it when the going gets rough? You know the kind of form I've signed—you've done it often enough yourself if you're in this game. Last bequests, next of kin, the whole bit. And listen to me, and understand what I'm saying: I agreed that whatever happened to me, I would do everything in my power to help you proceed with your mission. *Whatever happened.* And now something's happened; one of the many calculated risks we accepted has come up and hit me in the face; and you're asking me to go back on my word. By God, you've got a nerve!"

Her voice had begun shaking with anger because I wouldn't understand, because I wouldn't think it out, as she'd had time to think it out while I was looking for her. "And listen to this, Clive, and it's all I'm going to say. If you try to carry me out of here, I'm going to resist, every inch of the way. I'm going to fight you, every bloody inch and every bloody yard, till you realize it's not worth it, and drop me, and leave me to rot." Then the anger was suddenly spent, and she was speaking so softly that I could barely hear. "But if you've got any kindness in you, any humanity, you'll face what you know you've got to do, and be gentle with me, and save me from all those things we all hope never to die with: pain, and humiliation, and indignity."

I knelt there for a time, going over it all, while the shadows in the moonlight crept from rock to rock, lengthening as the night moved on toward the dawn. I don't know when it was that she spoke again, as softly as before.

"Face it, Clive. Bite the bullet."

And at last I knew there was no argument, and no choice.

"I wish there'd been time to know you," I said.

"I've told you quite a bit in the last few minutes. I'm some-one to be reckoned with. Are you going to help me?"

"Yes."

She gave a quick, shuddering laugh. "I finally got it into your thick skull."

"That's right."

"What made it so difficult? Because I'm a woman?"

"Probably."

"Then you're a male chauvinist pig. Listen, the monastery is east of here, the other side of that long ridge with the funny-looking rock at the end. Okay?"

"Okay."

"You knew that already, but I'm just cross-checking. To climb that ridge won't be easy, but there's no other way to go. It'll be easier, though, with some of the extra equipment you'll have: You can make hay with the pitons, using mine as well—you won't have to salvage any. And there'll be double the food and water ration. Did you see the terrain the other side of the ridge?"

"Not very clearly, in this light."

"You're not trained. You have to watch for the shadows, and know what they mean, how deep they are, and how high the object is that's throwing them. Listen, the terrain on the far side is almost flat, a narrow strip maybe a dozen yards wide and almost as long as the ridge itself. Are you listening?"

"Yes." But she knew that half my mind was still circling like a rat in a cage, looking for an escape, an escape for her that didn't demand her life.

"I'd say you'd be in full sight of the monastery anywhere on that ridge, with one exception. There was a long shadow crossing it at an angle, starting just north of the middle and going obliquely southeast—in other words, toward the monas-tery. One thing I can tell you for sure: The monastery is some-thing like five hundred feet above that ridge; six hundred at the most. Did you notice the ring formation?"

"Where?" The only escape was an escape for me: to leave

her, and let her keep her word to them in any way she wanted, and let her do it alone. There was no choice there either.

"The rings on the mountains here," she said. "Clive, you'd better listen—there's no time to think about anything else. The ridges go up the mountains here in a typical ring system, though it's been mostly obliterated by time. You might be able to reach the monastery by following the oblique cleft toward the southeast, out of sight from the ridge. Okay?"

I was rolling up the bandage. "Yes. I'll try that."

"If it doesn't work, then you'll have to climb straight up from the north or south. That's when you'll need the extra pitons—you'll save time not having to retrieve any. There's no sheer rock face anywhere, except that bit we hit when we came down. You've got something like forty-five minutes of darkness left to stow the chutes and conceal them." She looked away. "And me."

I put the roll of lint back into the bag and pulled the zip. One had to keep order.

"I'll remember what you've advised. I'll try the cleft."

"It could work. But don't try it while it's still dark; there's a nasty bit between here and where it begins; it's where the sheer rock goes down."

"I'll wait till daylight."

"That's about it, then." She turned her head and looked at me again. "Except that I've got a last request. I want you to make love to me."

I'd noticed a movement in the mist here, not long ago; there was a bluff of rock throwing its shadow across the ground where we were, and the shadow was creeping as the moon lowered toward the mountains in the west. I suppose a wind was getting up, though hardly what you'd call a wind: just a stirring of the air, its movement playing on the insubstantial vapors, giving them the life of ghosts. There'd been the hint of woodsmoke, too, before, coming from one of the villages, one of the villages that was so close that we could smell its fires, so far that she would never see it; now there

was the scent of pines on the air; or it had been here too, before, but overlayed by the bitterness of the smoke. Make love,
yes, a certain logic in that, the way she saw things; I was beginning to know her nature.

I'd been quiet for too long, because she said: "Of course I
might not be your type. I don't want you to think I'm—you
know—sort of soliciting." She tried a laugh, but it didn't
quite come off.

I told her quickly: "Certainly you're my type. You'd be anyone's. Newcomb could hardly keep his eyes on the navigation,
as you must have noticed."

"You were very well brought up."

"Last dance, is that it?"

"Last drink, or whatever. Last anything I can get. I'm not
one to go out with a whimper."

But I knew it was more than that: It was her sense of af-
firmation, of life at the death. It had been a good party, and
she wasn't going to leave until the music stopped.

"Can you smell the pines?" I asked her.

"Yes. I wondered if you'd noticed. Isn't it lovely?" She
was lifting her hand to me and I kissed her fingers; they were
deathly cold: There'd been a certain degree of shock, and I
thought anyone else would have passed out by now.

"We'll have to look out for your leg," I said.

"You bet. Forget the missionary position, but, thank God,
there are plenty of other ways." She was trying to reach for
one of the haversacks, and I got it for her. "Put it under my
head, Clive; there's no need to be uncomfy."

Then the tears began, as she let everything go. There was
no grief in this, I thought, and no self-pity, but just the gathering sense of loneliness that even she couldn't hold back; and
perhaps it was a sign that she could now trust me enough to
let me hear her cry, knowing I wouldn't think of it as weak-
ness. I remember being surprised, as I put my mouth on hers,
that her tears could feel so warm against the coldness of her
face, and so tender in someone so strong.

"Clive," she said in a moment, "we're strangers, but it doesn't mean we can't find some kind of love, just while it lasts. Do what you can."

Her blood was black in the moonlight, pooling among the stones. My hand was over her wrist, held loosely there, and I don't know why: to stop the rhythmic spurting from staining her flying suit—one must, yes, keep order; or to tempt me to deny all her arguments and grip with sudden force and reach with my other hand for the pressure point and then a tourniquet and somehow carry her through the mountains; or simply to ease the soreness for her, by the comfort of touching.

"I could have done a lot worse, Clive."

The strength was leaving her voice.

"A lot worse?"

"Than finding you, for the last dance."

Her cropped head turned sideways on the haversack, but she straightened it to look up at me, like someone falling asleep and then waking because the time wasn't right.

"I wouldn't have wanted anyone else to be here now," I told her. "It was a privilege."

"A privilege?" A little dry laugh came. "Oh, God, I'm in such a mess." Her lips could scarcely open now. "You must try the cleft in the ridge, Clive . . . the way I said . . ."

"Yes." Her head fell sideways again, but this time she let it stay there, and closed her eyes. "Sleep well," I said.

"Dizzy . . . Clive?"

"I'm here." I lay beside her, covering her as much as I could so that she'd know she wasn't alone. She felt like a child in my arms.

"Clive . . . good luck. . . ."

The sunrise was beautiful, a filling of the sky with saffron and then rose and then a flood of blinding light across the peaks to the east.

I had stowed the chute canopies and spread rocks over them, and sorted out what extra equipment I'd take along. Helen de Haven was over there, where the heaped stones were catching the first light of the day. I turned away and moved through the rocky terrain, keeping clear of the sheer face and the drop below it.

In an hour I had reached the bottom of the ridge where she had told me I should go, and rested for a moment against an outcrop; then I dropped flat as the shot came and splinters of stone cut through the air near my face.

XVIII
HUNT

✿

I didn't move.

The splinters of rock were still falling, one of them humming through the air with the loudness of a bee, its sharp edges spinning from the impact of the bullet until it struck ground and skittered across the shale.

Incoming data, item one: There was no echo to the shot.

He was in cover. There would have been an echo otherwise, from the sheer rock face between here and the ridge higher up. He was shooting from cover, but not from the monastery or anywhere near it: From here, the monastery was out of sight above the ridge and a thousand feet higher. He was shooting from a north vector: Without raising my head I could see the chipped rock, a few feet south of where I was lying prone.

Moving my eyes only, I looked for the bullet; if I could find it I could learn a lot more about him, and where he was.

At some time during the ritual of love she had said: *Don't pity me; I can't stand that; besides, this could be the last time for you, too.*

There were grasses higher toward the ridge, and I lay watching them; but their movement was so slight that I couldn't hope to tell the wind's direction. I took deeper breaths, alert for the smell of burnt powder, but as yet there was nothing; even if the wind were from the north he might be too far away for any scent to carry.

The sun was four diameters high, northeast by east and approaching the mountain; it would clear the peak in another hour, and I couldn't hope for shadow. The ground here was still moist from the receding mist and I began digging into the soil between the rocks, using one of the sharp splinters his bullet had chipped from the rock; no thanks to him for the convenience: That bullet had been meant for my brain.

As soon as I had enough loose soil I began caking it over the buckles of the haversacks and the binocular case to take away the shine; then I smeared my face and hands, taking my time: He wouldn't come close yet, in case I had a gun.

He was using a long-distance rifle; its sound had been a heavy cough rather than a bark, and the chip in the rock was larger than a watch face. He knew I was still alive; to have placed the shot that close he must have seen enough of me to notice how I'd gone down, dropping voluntarily for cover, not spinning or toppling with an arm flung out. He would have reloaded by now, waiting to see what I did.

There were no real options. He was waiting for me to show him any one of the four most dangerous aspects of a hunted man: movement, reflection, color, and human shape. But I couldn't stay here; he wouldn't wait beyond a certain time; there would be the moment when he'd believe I was wounded, and then he'd come slowly, using all available cover until he could see I was either unconscious or unarmed. I had to be gone by then.

I checked the time at 06:17 and took my watch off and put it into my pocket before I moved. There was a wall of rock extending a long way to my left, so I covered fifty yards at a low crouch, scuffling my boots into the shale and dragging their toes across grasses to leave them bent; then as the terrain became firm rock I turned at right angles and went for a cleft running south at an angle and providing cover for twenty yards before it finished in a slope of fallen boulders. I would have to climb there, or come back if I had to climb too high.

He might be using a scope sight; that would change things a great deal: It could mean he was farther away than it seemed, and knew there was no real cover here for me, none that could lead me clear; he'd be content to use me for sport, and watch me go from rock to rock like a rat in a maze. If he was shooting from a great distance it meant he must be on higher ground and could see beyond my immediate cover to flat terrain where he could finally bring me down.

He would try, in any case, to reach higher ground. That would take him toward the east, toward the ridge on the mountain; I must watch for him there.

Sound of a hammer blow and stone shards flew and I dropped flat. Close. That was close. He was higher than I'd thought, and could see more than I'd thought. I kept perfectly still, not knowing whether he was so high that he could still see me, whether he was now swinging the long barrel down and moving the cross hairs to center on the back of my head, moving his finger inside the trigger guard and starting to apply pressure to the spring. Time had slowed down, because I was at the frontier of existence and extinction, a place where, for all of us, man-made time loses its rhythm and real time does the reckoning; if the finger of the other creature out there moved by a further eighth of an inch, the complex and intricate computer inside my skull would become a mess of nerve tissue of interest only to a carrion crow.

The sweet scent of pinewood on the air, and the sound of a bird calling from the lower ground where there was scrub for its habitat.

Perhaps he wasn't absolutely sure that this shape was the right one among the kaleidoscope of rock and shadow; he was waiting for me to move before he contracted his finger.

I supposed he was one of the perimeter guards, patrolling the monastery's environment. Or he could have come down from there, from the ridge, to hunt me.

I think I saw a light from the direction of the monastery; then either it went out or the mist hid it again. You know what I'm saying. They might have seen us.

He wasn't simply a hunter out for game; he'd seen enough of me to know I was human, a biped.

Hammer blow and rock splinters fluting through the air and I moved now and very fast while he was reloading and taking aim again: It was the only chance because the bullet had tugged at my dark woolen helmet and I'd heard the whine of its passage and if I went on lying there he'd put the next one into the back of my head. Scuttling like a crab, looking for lower ground, the stones scattering from under my hands and knees and boots, my breathing desperate and my eyes darting for shadow as his gun coughed again and rock chipped close to my face and a splinter cut into my cheek: I was in his sights and if I lay still he'd steady the aim and make the kill so I kept moving, sliding across shale and dragging my own weight forward with hands like claws, hooking at the ground and tearing stones away and hooking again as fast as I could while he was reloading and taking aim and the gun coughed and my leg twitched to the tug of the bullet and I got up and ran low, dodging from cover to cover in the few seconds he'd need to reload, *now drop*, there's a chance here and there's shadow.

Sweat running on me. Lie still.

Time slowing.

My eyes were shut, because death is a kind of sleep and I'd composed myself; then after a while they opened again without my willing them; I was aware of the stones in front of my face, and a tuft of grass where a small green spider was clinging, and the bright copper bullet. It had ricocheted and fallen well ahead of me as I'd made my run, and I picked it up. It had mushroomed a little after hitting something soft, perhaps a tree bole, but it still had the look of a 6 or 7mm projectile, long in proportion to its diameter and designed for high velocity at long range, with enough mass to counteract wind bucking; it was still warm from the friction of its impact, and nestled comfortably in my fingers, more comfortably than it would have nestled in my brain.

He was a confident man, and trained; this bullet wasn't from a hunter's gun: He was a professional marksman, brought into the area by Tung as part of his entourage, a technician in death-dealing capable of placing one of these copper artifacts in the body of any man of Tung's choosing: a president, a general, an ambassador. Or me.

Blood on the stones from my ripped cheek, not black in the moonlight as hers had been, but crimson in the sun. I turned three of the stones over and picked up three more and went on, crawling toward a group of boulders where the sun threw shadow from the east as I noted incidentally that I was still alive, and must therefore be out of sight here. I left the three bloodied stones in my track and turned at right angles, moving for deeper shadow and at last turning to face the way I'd come, my back propped against a rock and my eyes narrowed to reduce their reflected light.

There was the mountain, and the encircling ridge, and a mass of rock below it where some ancient slide had tumbled it toward the foothills. I kept perfecty still now, moving only my eyes, because he should be there somewhere and I wanted to see him, or at least see the place where he was; I'd taken a risk in turning round to face him, and I wanted to profit. I was taking a risk now, even in keeping still, because if I could see him, or the place where he was, he could see me, or the shadow where I was sitting. But it was no good trying to run from him blindly through these rocks; I could run into his fire whenever I changed direction. I had to know where he was so that I could move accordingly, putting rock after rock across his line of vision until I was out of range and could wait for night.

"There isn't much of a choice," Ferris had told me in my

final briefing. "There's only one man we want, and we can send only one man in to get him. London's quite adamant about risking innocent life, and there could be fifty monks at the monastery who know nothing about him except that he's asked for shelter."

The shadows up there were longer, vertically, as the sun climbed on the far side. Two birds were circling, predators, toward the north, so he wouldn't be there; they wouldn't have liked the noise of his rifle. There was an area of low bush nearer the south, and I watched it carefully for minutes because a man can miss his footing on a loose rock and disturb foliage. I couldn't hope to pick up the glint of his scope sight, if he was using one; the only reflection would come from the sides of the gun, at obtuse angles, because the sun was somewhere behind him.

"What we want you to do," Ferris had told me in the air-conditioned room at the air-force base, "is to reach Tung and talk to him."

Through the slits in my lids I moved the pupils from left to right and back, left to right, covering the rocks below the ridge and moving down each time, from left to right. If he moved, I would see him at this distance; and he'd have no qualms about leaving cover: The most I'd have on me would be a revolver.

"We want to know Tung's motives in the two assassinations. We want to know if there are further killings planned, and who the victims are to be."

Something was moving among the shadows of the rocks, halfway up the slope to the ridge; the disturbance in the pattern of light and shade was so slight that I could detect it only at the periphery of my vision where the receptors sought only movement, not form. He was in that area somewhere, so it wouldn't be an animal: All wildlife would have left his environment, slinking or burrowing or flying up, long before now. I watched the movement, closing my eyes at intervals to rest them.

"We know Tung has a shortwave radio transceiver," Ferris had told me, "but we can't find his wavelength; otherwise we could have listened in. Any attempt to put a chopper down at the monastery would risk the lives of the crew, and that would only be acceptable if we asked for help from NATO. The assassination of the American ambassador has gained us certain facilities affordable to us by the U.S. Air Force, though not of combat status; we believe Tung Kuo-feng may have ordered the death of the ambassador and we'd like to stop him ordering further—possibly American—deaths."

The movement had stopped, but now I could detect form: the head and one shoulder of a man, with the glint of a reflection where the crook of his right arm would be; it looked more like a skull than a living head, and it took me a moment to realize that the dark eye sockets were in fact sunglasses; there was no reflection from them because the sun was behind him. He was facing in this direction, watching me as I was watching him. The distance was perhaps five hundred yards and he was some hundred feet higher than I was, dominating the environment with the muzzle of his gun.

But now I knew where he was, and what I would have to do.

"So the U.S. Air Force has agreed to overfly the monastery by night, and drop you and the guide. It's the only access we've got for you. Your objective is to reach Tung Kuo-feng and make him talk. London knows he has an overall plan, of which the two political assassinations were components. We want to know what that plan is."

The man with the sunglasses was still watching me with his rifle at rest; if I moved, he'd have ample time to bring it into the aim. I proved this as an exercise: I picked up a stone the size of a fist and lobbed it into the full sunlight, and within two seconds of its falling a bullet smashed into the rock just above it and dropped inert to the ground, smoking. It would be too hot to pick up, though I didn't need to examine it to know that the copper nose was flattened by the dead-angle impact, because of its force. Even a .22 can push a bullet a

mile away but at the end of its flight it has no more velocity
than a tossed pebble; the long-range rifle is designed to pro-
duce a very high remaining velocity, and that one over there
could put a projectile through a man's body at more than a
thousand yards.

I sat still again in the shadow, listening to the bird calling
in the scrub to the west of me, and watching the man lower
his gun.

"If you can get the better of Tung Kuo-feng, we'll send in
a chopper for you. Otherwise you must try making your own
way out. If possible, you should relay what information you
can get to the embassy on 5051 kHz, using Tung's radio, and
duplicate it on our own wavelength. Tung should be dispatched only if you're certain he won't talk or has nothing
more to tell you. I shall hold myself ready to interrogate him
at the monastery or wherever you can bring him; as you know,
my expertise has been proved effective."

Watching the man, I knew what to do now. If I moved to
the north or south I would move directly into his fire; if I
moved to the east I'd be going toward him; behind me, to
the west, there was a series of low rock ridges and then open
ground running two or three miles into the foothills of the
next mountain range, and if I moved that way he would pick
me off before I could reach cover. There was no way out in
any direction, and he knew that.

I watched him.

"Control realizes," Ferris had told me, "that the odds against
you are rather high; that was why he wanted you for *Jade
One*, and no one else. You can opt out at this stage, as you
know; but it wouldn't mean we'd then send Youngquist in,
simply because we don't think Youngquist could do it; we
think you can."

Bloody Control for you. Pat on the back and good luck,
lad, we know you can do it, never fear. Bloody London for
you. This was a last-ditch operation: Throw the executive in
and see what happens, never know your luck.

The man with the sunglasses hadn't moved. He knew where I was but he couldn't see me; more accurately, he could see me, but he couldn't tell rock from shadow, from this darker shadow that was his quarry.

Not strictly true of course: London knows what it's doing; it was just that I was lonely now, and scared; there was something almost acceptable about getting shot in the back of the head: One minute you were part of all this metaphysical extravaganza and the next minute you were a hunk of chemicals with no awareness of the transition. But if I sat here staring into his gun he might eventually define my shape, and fire, and in the final millisecond I might see the thing coming for me, much too fast to give me time to dodge it: a gleam of copper light in the sunshine, increasing in diameter until there it was, right in front of me, and moving at the speed of sound, its small mass warm from the detonation and the friction through the rifling of the barrel, its rate of spin slowing over the distance to a thousand feet per second and its initial degree of pitch damped out by gyroscopic action as it poised in timelessness an inch in front of my brow before it touched the skin and found the skull and broke the skull and found the brain and blew away the universe on this fine summer's day.

But I would have to stay facing him for a bit longer. And I would have to move, just a little, and with great care. I had to face him because I had to see when the gun came up, so that I could get the timing right; and I had to move, just a little, to get my flying jacket off. He wasn't using a scope sight, he was using his naked eye; if he'd had a scope sight I'd have seen him aiming the gun all the time, trying to find me. Even so, I must move with great care.

Nothing more awkward than getting out of sleeves.

He didn't move. I would see the glint along the barrel if he raised the gun, and have time to drop low and forward, decreasing the target profile. First sleeve.

He would be, I suppose, annoyed by now. They'd sent him down here to deal with me before I could get too close and do any damage, and even if I'd had a revolver on me there would have been no chance of a duel; he could stay out of range with that thing and make a remote kill. But I was still alive and he was aware of that: The stone I'd thrown had fooled him for two seconds—the time he'd needed to aim and fire—but he'd seen what it was immediately afterward. So he was probably annoyed, which was an advantage to me: You bring a flicker of emotion to the gunsight and you'll fire a foot wide. Second sleeve.

The timing was critical and I waited, drawing five deep breaths; then I raised the jacket and passed it slowly in front of me and to one side to let the shoulder catch the sunlight. A reflection sparked from his rifle as he brought it immediately into the aim and fired, and I had to wait through the next second while the bullet traveled the distance between us and tore the jacket from my left hand as I let it go, one sleeve flying out before it fell to the ground.

I dropped with it and kept still.

There was no second shot.

After a minute I crawled sideways to the shelter of deeper rock, dragging the jacket after me and leaving tracks. The leg wound was superficial and the blood had already started to congeal; I had to open it with my nails and wait for it to ooze before I could squeeze a trickle onto the stones. In an hour I made a dozen yards, taking my time and waiting for the blood to come, squeezing and moving on with the toes of my boots dragging at the shale. Above me now was a ledge some ten feet high with a sheer drop to the west, facing the buttress that hid me from his sight; it was the best that was offered.

There was antibiotic cream in the medical kit and I smeared it on the wound and bandaged it before I climbed to the ledge, pulling the jacket after me. My wristwatch was in my pocket and I fished for it and put it on again. It showed 06:49 as I settled facedown and began waiting for him.

XIX
VIGIL

✹

"Eagle to Jade One."
Playing bricks.
"Eagle to Jade One."
One on top of another.
He would take his time, of course. I might be armed.
"Eagle to Jade One."
A fourth stone, to bridge the lower three. Playing bricks
with the boulders, the small ones; but it didn't have to be too
fancy; it had to look natural.
Where the hell is Ferris?
07:12
"Eagle to Jade One."
In another hour the sun would clear the bluff to the east
of my position and I would no longer be in shade. But then
he wouldn't see me, because of the boulders. The set was live,
crackling. I wanted more than that, for God's sake. This thing
was a lifeline.
"Eagle to Jade One."
The peephole was too big: All I wanted was—

"Jade One to Eagle. You're very faint."

And very relieved.

"Eagle to Jade One. DH is dead. My present situation extremely hazardous. Will report if possible."

"Repeat that."

Did so. He acknowledged and we broke.

Within the next half-hour I completed the low rock wall; it was built on the assumption that he would pick up the tracks I'd left for him and follow them to the area immediately below the ledge where I was waiting; I could sight through the rocks in three places, and if he looked up, all he would see was my eye, and my eye would be in shadow, and it would be narrowed. If he was a cautious man he would circle the whole area first and climb to higher ground; in that case he would see me; but there was nothing I could do about that, except hide up in a foxhole and wait until he found me; there was no point.

Very faint because of the mountains. Up at the monastery, if I could reach it, the reception and transmission would be a lot better. It had been good to hear his voice, even faintly.

The executive signaled at 07:14 to say his situation was extremely hazardous. That was the last we heard of him.

Ignore. Too much bloody imagination. Eye on the ball.

07:46

09:51

He wasn't here yet.

He must be very close now.

The mountains were silent under the rising warmth of the morning; I would have expected more bird life here; the sound of birds is reassuring, reminding of spring, when the world is new again and nothing can go wrong.

There was open terrain below, where my jacket had gone jerking through the air; he could make his approach from that direction in almost a straight line without any risk, even if I were armed. Cautious bastard.

So cautious, perhaps, that he was making a wide detour and climbing to higher ground; then he would be close enough to put one straight into me with great force at close range.

Has there been any further signal from the executive?

No.

How long has it been?

Two and a half hours.

Do we write him off?

Not yet. Not yet. Give me a chance.

The scent of the pines was heavy on the air as the day grew warmer. *I wondered if you'd noticed it. Isn't it lovely?* Safe under her stones and unafraid.

Something snapped and I jerked my head and stared at the rocks to my left, heart thudding and breath held as I waited.

Nothing there. Tree bark cracking in the warmth, or dead timber splitting.

Perhaps I should have tried making a break to the west, clambering through the tumbled rock and making a run for it across the open ground beyond, dodging like a hare while he tried to keep me centered in the sights.

Trickle of sweat; it had sprung from the skin when the sharp sound had come a minute ago. I wiped it away from my eyes and manned the peephole again and saw him.

He was standing perfectly still, looking at the marks on the ground; then in a moment he raised his head, gazing across the wall I had built, across the hidden glint of my eye. He looked like a Korean, young and athletic in a striped track suit and running shoes; the long Remington was slung at the horizontal in both hands, ready to swing up and fire.

I narrowed my eye until the lids were almost together, and watched him as his head turned slowly to note the stones of my wall, studying them for a while and then passing on. The distance between us was some hundred feet. He began moving again, his head going down to follow my tracks, and when he turned to his left, toward the ledge where I was waiting, I brought my eye down to the third peephole and watched him from there.

He stopped again, lifting his head and turning it by degrees to look around him, glancing across my shadowed eye and surveying the heights at my back. It was five or six minutes before he was satisfied; then he moved on again with his head lowered, until he saw the dark blood spots I had left directly beneath the ledge; and now he stopped.

An hour ago I had brushed the ledge free of loose stones and measured the distance from the rock wall to the edge: It was the distance necessary to give momentum for the leap. The time estimated was three seconds, but if I controlled my breathing he would see me before he heard me, and that wouldn't give him long enough to swing the gun up and take aim; he shouldn't see me for at least half the total estimated time—for at least one second and a half—and he would need more than that. It was a long rifle and weighed ten or eleven pounds, and he'd have to swing it upward against the inertia.

Of course he might move faster than I'd reckoned, and make use of the final half-second before I was on him and blocking the swing of the gun. In that case I would drop straight against the muzzle and receive the shot at point-blank range. The issue was unpredictable.

His head was still lowered and I took a slow breath and whipped the muscles into movement, clearing the edge and dropping with my feet going first. He probably died before he hit the ground because I kicked downward with my right boot and felt its impact on the side of his neck: He was much slower than I'd estimated and had only got as far as turning his head to look upward as his peripheral vision had warned him of the changing light factor. I heard the snap of his neck and was briefly aware of sequential images: the shine of the rifle barrel swinging; the gold-rimmed sunglasses hitting the ground and for an instant showing the reflection of his face before the lenses shattered against the stones; his body meeting its shadow and blotting it out.

I spun full circle, breaking my fall with a shoulder roll and getting up as the two men on the track stopped dead and brought their revolvers into the aim.

XX

MARCH

❁

Dead weight.

The sun was much higher now, its heat throbbing in the air. I had begun making an effort not to look at my watch.

Dead weight on my back.

If he had started from the monastery at the time we had made our drop, it had taken him two hours to reach the area where he'd begun hunting me. It was going to take longer than that for him to return; much longer.

The sun beat down on the three of us. Four of us. One on my back.

Sometimes the two men spoke to each other, a few short words in low tones that I didn't understand; but the tone of the human voice is a language in itself, and universal, and I knew they were talking about the man on my back; there was grief in their voices for him, and hate for the man who had murdered him. I suppose they felt it was rough poetic justice, making me carry his body.

One of them walked ahead, springing easily across the un-even rock in his cushioned track shoes while I labored and

stumbled under my burden; the other man followed me, and
my back was already bruised from the prodding of the long
rifle. Sweat trickled on me, stinging my eyes so that they
watered all the time, making the flat gray rocks look like a
stream bed in the wavering light. I would have said we'd been
moving for three hours now, maybe rather less, because time
dragged under the dead weight.

They had tried mouth-to-mouth resuscitation for half an
hour; then one of them had raised his revolver to aim at the
center of my forehead and I'd looked down the barrel and
begun counting, for something to do; but the other man had
spoken to him sharply, with authority, and the gun had been
lowered. I was to be taken to the monastery, I suppose he had
said, and dealt with there. The tone of the man's voice had
sounded like an order, and it occurred to me that they might
be military personnel out of uniform, possibly North Koreans
whose uniform in the South would get them arrested.

I had tried them with English, French, German, and Russian as we'd started the march, but had got no reaction. We
had moved off as soon as they'd gestured to me to lift the dead
marksman and sling him across my back; they'd seen nothing
of the haversack, higher up on the ledge behind the wall I'd
built, and I hadn't tried to retrieve it; that radio would have
been embarrassing: It was U.S. Air Force issue and wouldn't
have suited the cover I was working out.

Staggering now across the uneven ground, the stones rip-
pling under the tears flooding my eyes.

The sun's heat rising toward noon.

Dead march.

One of his arms began swinging like a pendulum to the
measure of my pace, his hand brushing across and across my
chest as if he were trying to catch my attention; but he had
nothing more to say to me, and I had nothing to say to him;
we'd both been professionals and the match had been fairly
even; he'd come close to blowing my head off, so I'd broken
his neck, a good enough answer. But his arm was beginning

to irritate me and I grasped his hand, a little too late to show friendship.

The man ahead of me was following the oblique cleft toward the southeast, the way de Haven had told me I should go, the way I would have gone alone if these two hadn't heard the marksman's shots and come down to see if he needed help. Twice in the last hour I'd seen the glint of blue-gray tiles higher on the ridge; we must have climbed most of the thousand feet from the flat area below where my heavy friend had hunted me.

"What?" I asked them, and found the sun blinding in my eyes and their hands dragging me upright: I'd just gone straight out with exhaustion. They shoved the barrel of the long blue Remington into me, like poking a pig with a stick, until the pain overwhelmed the urge to go on lying there, freed of the dead-weight load. "Oh, shuddup," I told them, "don't be so fucking impatient." I suppose they didn't take it kindly that I'd dumped their friend so unceremoniously. Well that was tough luck, he shouldn't have put those bloody bullets quite so close to my head.

They humped him onto my back again and I stood there trying to adjust to the load while bright red spots dripped from me onto the stones; they'd broken the skin somewhere with that thing.

Off we go, then, yes, my friend and I, not much of a conversationalist, you can say that about him. One foot in front of the next through the throbbing heat of the day. And out of a job, by the way: It had been worrying me. They would have written me off by now, because I hadn't sent another signal.

Eagle to Jade One, my present situation extremely hazardous, will report if possible, so forth. Been no report, had there? It didn't look very jolly—one more ferret bitten the dust; it happens all the time. But I bet they don't send Youngquist in; he'd looked too intelligent to let London shove him into a shut-ended shambles like this one.

Stay on your feet.

On my feet, yes, but not your bloody business.

If you keep on falling down, they'll shoot you.

Shuddup. Sniveling little organism worried about dying, plain bloody suburban.

They're going to shoot you up there at the monastery.

Well, I didn't think they were going to offer me a franchise in a car wash, for Christ's sake.

Stones swimming. One foot in front of the other.

Gun at my back, prodding.

His arm was swinging again, the arm of my inert and unconversational friend. It was irritating; and after a mile or ten miles or fifty miles in this blinding heat I thought about grabbing his hand again to keep him still, and then I thought: Now wait a minute, this kind of pendulum motion might be an advantage, because every time his arm swings forward it helps me keep moving; very clever, yes, but every time it swings *back*, quite, not very clever, you're losing your nut, you know that? You're going stark raving bonkers.

A possibility, just a bare possibility, that if I could manage to center the psyche for a while and then fall down deliberately and land with him on top of me as a shield against the rifle and at the same time grab the ankles of the man in front and bring him down . . . you've got no energy left, you bloody fool. I know, but you've got to think about something.

Gun hit my spine.

Get on, yes.

Sound of my breathing, like sawing wood, sawing slowly through a huge tree trunk—in, out, in, out—while the muscles blazed, thirsting for more oxygen, more oxygen all the time, legs staggering with the knees locked, otherwise fall, fall down, ought not to do that, wouldn't take kindly, no.

Blinding sun and streaming stones and his swinging arm and the pain of the gun prodding, on and on, until there were roofs curving against the sky and a bell somewhere, tolling like a brainstorm in my skull, my legs lurching left and right, my feet shuffling like a cripple's, and the whole of my body burning under the weight of the man, the weight of the sun, the weight of the sky. Stop.

Several men, coming into the courtyard, one of them talking in Russian, asking what had happened.

Stood swaying, then no good, went down like an avalanche and hit the stones, man saying in Russian, *"Put him against a wall and shoot him."*

XXI

KI

❁

His eyes were dark stones.

A thin tendril of smoke climbed from the bowl of incense under the lamp, reminding me of the room where I'd met Spur.

What did they do to that snake? I wanted to ask him.

His eyes were so dark in the hollows of his face that they seemed to disappear sometimes, becoming shadows in the low light of the lamp; but I knew he was watching me all the time, with that reptilian ability to go on watching with such still-ness that you forget there's a brain behind these eyes, thinking about you.

He was sitting on his heels in the meditation position, his back erect and his thin yellow hands folded on his thighs. It might have been that he was trying to hypnotize me, and I took care to study him, noting everything I could to keep the conscious occupied: the intricate pattern of his kimono with its gold dragons and hieroglyphs, the wisp of white beard at the point of his chin and the sharp ears that had the bone-yellowness of ivory carving, the fine chiseling of the nose.

Tung Kuo-feng.

A Chinese, Spur had said, *scion of a family traceable to the early Ch'ing dynasty. Tung isn't a young man anymore; I'd put him at sixty. But extremely fit; lots of* ki, *you know, the real thing. If those bastards in London are putting you solo into the field with Tung Kuo-feng, you don't stand a chance. Not a chance in hell.*

A current of air met the tendril of smoke and twisted it into a spiral. From somewhere outside I could hear distant chanting to the sound of wooden clappers; it must be sundown. The man in front of me didn't speak; perhaps he was silently joining in the prayers.

What would he pray for? He should pray for the souls of the departed: This man had killed Sinclair; the British secretary of state; the American ambassador; Jason; Spur; Soong Yongshen and his sister, Soong Li-fei, their necks bared under the sword. Let him pray for them. And for himself, if I had a chance to close in.

We sat facing each other in the low light of the lamp. My back burned from the prodding of the gun; my legs were still trembling from the strain of the five-hour march with the man on my back. I was close enough now to Tung Kuo-feng, and I could probably move with at least half my normal speed; but he would have had reports of me from his team of hit men, and would be wary; he wouldn't allow me this close to him without some kind of protection, and his hands, lying so peacefully on the folds of the black and gold silk, probably concealed a ninja weapon. Or was he counting on the fact that out there in the courtyard he had saved my life?

I wasn't ready for him yet, in any case. *We want you to make him talk,* Ferris had said.

The chanting and the clack of the wooden clappers died away, and a gong boomed; then there was peace.

"Who are you?"

His voice was quiet, but the tone had an extraordinary harshness, sounding as if it weren't coming from a living body

but from a recorder that was distorting it, giving it a metallic
flatness.

"Colonel Clive West, British army, attached NATO defense
force, Asian theater."

The assumed rank of colonel came under routine instructions in the event of the executive's decision to use a military
cover; it was the only one I had: You don't do a night drop
with a black chute in the Korean mountains to look for geological specimens.

"You feel," he asked me, "that is the best you can do?"

"That's my true identity."

His English was correct and educated; when I'd been
sprawled on the big gray flagstones out there a few hours ago
he'd spoken Chinese and an interpreter had put it straight
into Russian; I'd understood only the Russian side, as Tung
had repeated with unyielding authority that I was not to be
killed until he had questioned me.

"What brought you to the mountains?"

"I was on a night exercise."

"With what objective?"

"Survival."

"I realize that your training as a secret agent requires you
to explain as little as possible, but we must not waste time.
I have to go through the formality of questioning you, since
those were the terms of your reprieve; I must therefore know
your cover story, so that I can prove later if necessary that I
have indeed questioned you. Let me at this point make it clear
that while I carry a certain degree of authority, the person
in ultimate command here is Colonel Sinitsin of the KGB,
whom you saw briefly, I think, when you arrived. In other
respects I am, like yourself, a prisoner."

The Russian connection.

I still hadn't got things worked out. I hadn't been fully
conscious when I'd arrived, and the incoming data had gone
into the memory in its raw state for later analysis, if I lived. I
had seen several Europeans looking down at me and at the

body of the Korean, two of them in gray formal suits and polo-necked sweaters; it was one of these who had told the Koreans to put me against a wall and shoot me, speaking in Russian to an interpreter. Other men had been there: Koreans again, wearing track suits with the insignia of the Olympiad; behind them there'd been the terraced roofs of the monastery, part of it in ruins, and the roof of a temple nearby, and two large shapes under camouflage nets, one of them with a rotor poking out; above one of the roofs there had been an omni-directional radio antenna.

I'd had time to do a rough analysis of all this data while I'd been recovering in the cell where they'd thrown me: origi-nally, I suppose, a monk's personal quarters, a narrow cubicle with a grilled window and a crude wooden bed. The most obvious thing was that Tung Kuo-feng hadn't sought refuge here, as the blind priest had thought; he was here to conduct or participate in what looked like a minor military operation. There were always several track-suited guards in sight, and from watching them I'd become more and more convinced that they were at least paramilitary and professionally trained.

"Where are your papers?" Tung asked me tonelessly.

"I lost track of them when I came down. It was a bad landing."

"Your flying suit was also lost?"

"I took it off when the sun came up; it was too hot."

"And 'lost track of it.' "

"That's right."

I sensed movement at the edge of my vision; there were two grilled apertures on one wall of the chamber, showing a lamp-lit arch beyond; I assumed someone was passing there, out-side, or had stopped to watch us, and listen.

"No one else here," Tung said, "understands English." I felt suddenly chilled; he was reading my mind. "It is important for you to know that when you and I converse, even in the company of others, it is in secret. What other languages do you speak?"

"A bit of army French."

He fell silent, waiting for me to say more. I didn't.

"You say you were on an exercise in survival. Who else was with you?"

"No one."

"You chose to be alone?"

"Yes. I was getting fed up sitting around with nothing to do. There's nothing here for a defense force to defend. So I asked permission to do a one-man survival course over the weekend. I've done it before, quite a few times, in England. Were you educated there? Your English is pretty good."

He said: "When will they begin searching for you?"

"They won't need to. I can use the radio here to tell them I'm okay." I left a slight pause, as he'd been doing, but he didn't ask what radio. "There'll be some trouble for those Koreans, though. That fellow was doing his damnedest to shoot me dead. I suppose you know that."

Two seconds, three. "I have told you we must not waste time. I know that you are an agent in the British Secret Service and that your assignment was to inquire into the death of your secretary of state in Peking. You have resisted efforts on the part of my own agents to eliminate you. You are here in the hope of eliminating me, since it is believed I was responsible for the two political assassinations in Peking, and might be in the process of ordering others, as indeed I am. For your information, TWA flight 232 from Peking sustained an accident on takeoff early this morning, killing more than fifty people including an American football team; they had been visiting the People's Republic of China on a goodwill mission with the aim of furthering the interests of international sport."

I think he wasn't quite finished, but I got up at that point and did a bit of walking about to ease the leg muscles. "Look, you ought not to be telling me things like that at this stage, before the trial. You've just made some pretty hefty confessions, and one day you'll have to answer for them."

His small gray head was turning to watch me. "As you know, the Americans are as fanatical about sport as the English. The object of the sabotage action was to further incense the Americans and strain their new relations with China."

"All I can say is, I've given you fair warning."

It was like having two conversations going on, but we both knew what we were doing, and we both knew that we knew. I kept on walking, five yards one way and five back, while he sat there like a carved Buddha. I didn't pass either of the two grilled apertures.

"You realize," he said evenly in his soft metallic voice, "that you have no chance of leaving here alive."

"Possibly not, but it's my duty to warn you that if I don't get a message to my unit by radio, then you'll have to suffer the consequences. They'll certainly start a search for me after forty-eight hours, because they know exactly where I came down and I told them I'd telephone them from the village to report progress."

"I am going to correct what I just told you. Your only chance of leaving here alive is to give me your confidence."

And blow my cover.

"That's what I'm doing."

His head turned again to follow me. "There will be a point in our conversation when you will realize that your cover is less important than the proposition I shall make. You might find yourself in a position to prevent the assassination of the next three people on the list. The dates of these events are already fixed, and the first is to take place in two days' time—unless you are prepared to cooperate."

I got impatient with him. "But surely you realize that the moment I rejoin my unit you'll be hunted down and arrested?"

He ignored that, as I knew he would; my remark was simply there for the record as part of my cover. It might not be true that he knew who I was, or that we were the only people here who understood English, or that he was a prisoner at the monastery; the chances were that there was someone on the other side of these apertures in the wall with a microphone, or that Tung had one concealed in his hand, for that matter.

But now I understood something about the Russian connection. Not all, but something. It concerned Chinese-American relations.

"I must tell you," he went on, "that the assassination of the British secretary of state was a mistake, and that I deeply regret it. The one responsible has already forfeited his life."

Soong Yongshen.

"That hardly helps the late British secretary of state, does it? You bloody terrorists don't care whom you wipe out. You know that man had a family?"

"I mention the incident so that you shall be conversant with the overall situation. And the situation is this. A short time ago I received a proposal from the Soviet KGB that I should assist them in a certain endeavor, the object of which would be the severance of diplomatic relations between the United States and China, and with it, the end of the so-called triangle diplomacy involving those two powers and Japan. The threat to the Soviet Union presented by the growing recognition of China is seen by the Kremlin as intolerable. The four thousand miles of frontier common to Russia and China, and the constant military skirmishes across it, are of deep concern to the Soviets; in addition, China is rapidly developing a nuclear missile with a range of eight thousand miles, capable of reaching Moscow.

"It is my personal opinion that the severance of relations between China and the United States may be a preliminary to a Soviet attack on China, with a view to preempting a nuclear-armed, American-supported attack by China against the Soviets. To you and to me, such fears on the part of the Russians may seem extreme; but you must remember these people are xenophobic to a dangerous degree."

I stopped walking about and sat down to listen, leaning my shoulders against the cool stone wall to ease the bruises. I

had fifty questions for him, but I didn't speak; I wanted to see
how far he would go in what he was telling me; but even at
this stage I was ready to take notice because he was answering a lot of the questions that had been on my mind before I'd
left Seoul.

He wasn't putting out an elaborate smoke screen, I knew
that. He wasn't even interested in my intelligence background;
if he'd wanted to get any information out of me, he would
have thrown me to the Koreans and told them to go to work,
and they would have enjoyed it after what I'd done to their
friend out there.

"I declined the Russians' proposal that I should assist
them." Tung hadn't moved since I'd come in here, but there
was nothing lifeless about him except his voice; I had the
feeling that if I made a wrong move he'd react with the speed
of a snake. "They offered me several million U.S. dollars to
help them—I forget how many; I was not interested. But they
persisted, saying that I was the only man who could success-
fully carry out the necessary tasks involved. I told them I was
no longer active internationally. They offered me political
power in the new government of China, but again I refused;
the power I have now is sufficient to me."

His ash-gray head was turning slightly, so that he faced me
directly in the low light of the lamp, and in the shadowed and
stone-dark eyes I saw an expression shimmering, like a reflection on black water.

"So they took away my son."

I felt a kind of pressure in the air, as if the edge of a storm
had passed across the mountains, leaving the chamber grave-
quiet and the flame of the lamp pointed and motionless in
this deathly calm.

"Tung Chuan, my son. He was studying the Buddhist faith,
and was to be a priest; but they seized him in North Korea
and accused him of spying, and now he has vanished."

The air seemed charged again with pressure, as if dark
lightning had struck, and I knew what it was now: It was an

expression of his psyche. His rage was so intense that it was producing an aura, and I was recording it, somewhere in the complex psychochemical organism that I identified as myself.

"I do not know where he is," he said. "My son, Tung Chuan."

It was a little while before I could get my senses back to normal.

"That's rough luck," I said. "The British secretary of state's family knows where he is. In a coffin, what few bits you left of him."

I think he could have killed me then, and I was ready for it. I think that at the back of my mind I was wanting to do something for Sinclair, and Jason, and the American, and the girl with the cinnamon eyes; I think I wanted to provoke this murderous bastard so that I could destroy him before he could destroy someone else.

Unprofessional conduct. I had business to do here. But it fitted the cover of a forthright army colonel shocked by the death of the British delegate.

In a moment Tung Kuo-feng said carefully: "My agents have been trying to find my son, and have failed; they report that he is known to be in South Korea, but that is all. It may be that the more powerful resources of the British Secret Service could discover more than that. Tung Chuan was seized by Russian agents, not Koreans; your service might have learned of it through its agents in Moscow, and be unaware of its significance. You should inform them. A great deal of trouble would be avoided if my son were set free."

"I'm afraid the British army hasn't any agents in Moscow, or anywhere else."

He said: "The moment my son was safe, I would halt my operations and you would have achieved your objective."

Cool stones against my back, and the stillness of the lamp's flame against my eyes; voices in the distance, coming through the grilled apertures, and farther away the sound of miniature bells as the goats were gathered in the mountain dusk. No real sense that we were ourselves held captive by guards armed

with submachine guns while two military helicopters stood
by; instead, a sense of karma, a feeling that what this man was
saying was true, and that I should trust him; and a premoni-
tion of enormous danger, not only for me but for many.

Fatigue, that was all.

"You could avert enormous danger"—the quiet monotone
came to me through the waves of silence—"for many people."
A spasm of nerves passed along my spine as I realized how
easily this man was reading my thoughts; I sat straighter
against the hardness of the wall at my back, trying to borrow
from its strength.

"Before the advent of Mao, the Chinese military was trained
by the Soviet Red Army, and it is still oriented toward the
Russians' tactics, strategies, and weapon systems. On the
political and ideological levels the two countries are opposed,
but there are several army generals still capable of wielding
great power, and they feel a natural brotherhood for their
Soviet mentors and would like to be training with them once
more. Lin Pao's attempted coup against Mao did not succeed;
but Mao is now dead, and a new power struggle has begun in
China. We are very close to seeing a general take command,
supported by high-ranking military advisers, all of them
friendly to the Soviets. I do not need to tell you what such a
volte-face would mean: the immediate destruction of the
American-Chinese-Japanese bloc and a massive Soviet-Chinese
threat to the West. The next two actions I shall undertake on
behalf of the Soviets will bring this about, within a matter of
days, unless you can prevent it."

The fatigue was leaving me, and I felt a singing in the blood
as the thought in my mind released adrenaline.

"You must find my son," he said.

His voice seemed to echo among the stone walls, as if he
had shouted the words from a long way off, as if they were
echoing among the mountains out there as well as in here,
where the lamplight sparked on the gold of his robe and darkened his eyes in shadow.

One thing, yes, to be done, and to be done at once. Without awareness that I was preparing myself I could sense nerve and muscle and sinew awakening and becoming a force, and so rapidly that the explosion was only instants away as my eyes measured, my hands tensed, my thought raced toward detonation.

I think I had begun moving, before his voice came.

"No. Not that way."

He sat perfectly still as the air became silent thunder, hurling me back against the wall.

XXII

SINITSIN

✣

Igor Sinitsin.

I had heard of him more than once along the bleak corridors of the Bureau in London.

I had heard of him because he was one of our opposite numbers in the field: He worked for V, the Executive Action Department, a special service of one of the three subdirectorates of the First Chief Directorate of the KGB.

Department V is the most secret arm of Soviet operations and responsible for *mokrie dela,* the "wet affairs" outside the USSR involving sabotage, kidnapping, political assassination, and similar bloodletting operations designed to create chaos in foreign governments at times of internal crisis, to paralyze communications, provoke hostility among noncommunist nations, and generally to render foreign soil fertile for the seeds of Marxist Leninism. V was once called the Thirteenth Department, or Line F, just as the Bureau was once designated Liaison 9 before it broke away from DI6.

It is said, along the bleak corridors in London, that Colonel Igor Sinitsin was in Paris when the chargé d'affaires of the

Persian Embassy was found on the top floor of an apartment house in the Place Pigalle with a steel knitting needle buried in his brain through the left eye and no trace of the *belle de nuit* who had lived and worked there for the last three years before striking up an acquaintance with a member of the visiting Ballet Russe.

It is said that Sinitsin was in Buenos Aires when one of our people got on his track and was found the next day in the wreck of an elevator in the Hotel Conquistador with his spine driven upward into his skull.

Tilson says that Sinitsin was involved in the assassinations of General Batista, President Sri Phouma, and Minister of State Hasan Kazan, and that he personally dispatched two gentleman acquaintances of Eva Peron in the hope of receiving her favors in their place.

"Not permitted," he said.

The small Korean interpreter, a cripple with thick glasses, put it straight into Chinese for Tung Kuo-feng.

Igor Sinitsin didn't look like the archetypal KGB officer; when I had come into the room with Tung five minutes ago I'd thought at first glance that he was a Scandinavian. Of middling height, he was quick-moving and rather graceful, striking poses to suit what he was saying: feet equally balanced when he was being firm, as he was now; one leg bent and arms folded pensively when he considered. His eyes were light blue and he had the attractively crumpled features of an experienced ladies' man, not unlike Philby's. He dressed casually and at some cost: a silk scarf tucked inside the open neck of a Cardin shirt, a gray alpaca suit from Savile Row, and a thin gold watch from Cartier's; this, anyway, was the impression they gave and the impression he wanted to create; for a ruthless KGB colonel, it amounted almost to a disguise.

"You will have to permit it," the interpreter said in Russian, turning from Tung to Sinitsin.

The tension in the room was increasing rapidly; it had begun when Tung had brought me in here to find Sinitsin and his two aides sitting near one of the big radio transceivers. They had all stood up, less out of courtesy, I think, than out of an unwillingness to be caught off their guard; whether Tung carried some kind of ninja weapon in the folds of his robe or not, they were uneasy in his presence, perhaps because they sensed the same powerful emanations of *ki* that had seemed to throw me against the wall not long ago.

Through the interpreter he had made the introductions: Mr. Clive West of British Intelligence, Colonel Igor Sinitsin of the KGB, and his aides, Major Petr Alyev and Captain Viktor Samoteykin. The aides looked more traditional, with flat Slav faces and badly fitting suits; their expressions hadn't changed during the introductions. Sinitsin had studied me with interest for a moment and then given me a brief energetic nod as from one professional to another; he hadn't bothered to hide the impression that as soon as possible he would have me shot dead. This wasn't only because I'd killed that marksman out there—in our trade the opposite numbers in the field don't bear each other any grudge, and there's even a certain degree of respect on an impersonal level—but the KGB have had their knife into me ever since I wiped out their Colonel Vader, right on his home ground in Dzerzhinsky Square; his own bloody fault, he shouldn't have tried to throw me into a political asylum, but it had really got them on the raw, and when I'd looked into Sinitsin's light blue eyes for the first time, I'd known his thoughts.

"You will have to permit it," I heard the interpreter saying in Russian, "because otherwise our operation will be increasingly endangered." This was from Tung Kuo-feng.

After Tung had used the force of his *ki* against me as a warning that I must not try to kill him, we'd talked for only a few minutes longer. "I am taking you to the operations room," he had said, "to meet the Soviet contingent. I have decided not to attempt persuading them into accepting your cover as a NATO officer. Instead I am going to use you against them, and for this your true identity is essential."

Then he had briefed me.

We were still standing, all of us; the light was brighter in here than it had been in Tung's private chamber; they'd set up two butane lamps, one on each side of the radio console, which was mounted on a wooden trestle; the light was bright and harsh, and shadows were sharp against the walls. This place wasn't an enclosed room but a kind of hall, with open arches at one end and massive double doors at the other, and iron sconces along the walls where the flames of oil lamps had left patches of soot on the ancient stones. In one corner a huge bench bore what looked like wooden printing blocks, carved with the letters of the Buddhist scriptures; along the main wall stood a hearth built of carved stone with a Buddha at each end, flanked by two faded tapestries.

The heat of the day was still in the building, and the night air was still; through the archways I could see two figures moving as the moonlight sent an occasional reflection from the weapons they were carrying: From this distance they looked like submachine guns. One of those men would be Yang.

He, too, was waiting to kill me.

Tung was talking again through the interpreter, whose accent I recognized as North Korean. "Since this agent arrived from London, my action group has come under increasing difficulties. I have been told that other members of his cell are now dangerously close to infiltrating our operation."

Sinitsin was listening carefully; the interpreter had run into trouble two or three times, hesitating while he looked for the right word, his dark head going down each time as if he were listening. He was good at his job: He knew what the situation was and he didn't try to alter the mood between Tung and Sinitsin by adding courtesies: When the Russian had said, "Not permitted," a moment ago, the interpreter had spoken what sounded like only one word to the Chinese; in the same way he'd told Sinitsin: "You will have to permit it," without any embroidery. The trouble he was running into was unavoid-

able even for an expert: the proximity of Korea and mainland
China has led, over the centuries, to a degree of lingual trans-
migration; but the Russian influence in communist North
Korea has added specialist terms, particularly in the intelligence field, and the young crippled interpreter had probably
had to change "Triad" to "action group" and come up with
the strictly specialist phrase "infiltrating our operation" for
Sinitsin's benefit.

The interpreter was also scared; not perhaps by the person-
alities of either man as such, but by the atmosphere of tension
that was affecting all of us. In the confrontation that Tung
Kuo-feng had started when he'd brought me in here, either he
or Sinitsin would finally have to back down, and I couldn't
imagine either of them doing that.

"If your operation is close to being infiltrated," the KGB
colonel said, "then you must take the necessary action." His
ice-blue eyes were leveled at Tung over his folded arms.

"Our operation" had become "your operation." Noted. The
Russian connection was telling the Chinese end that they expected the goods delivered, regardless of obstacles.

"British Intelligence," the interpreter said as he swung from
Tung to Sinitsin like a duelist, "has a high reputation for its
activities against the Soviets in the cold war, with notable
success."

"The high reputation of British Intelligence is going to need
a little adjusting if the Soviets keep up their notable success
in turning homosexuals among the knighthood into service-
able moles for Moscow."

Sinitsin glanced at me to catch any reactions. It was a waste
of time: I wasn't meant to understand Russian.

Tung left it alone. "My action group has reported to me
that our operation is in jeopardy. At this stage, when we are
halfway to success in our intentions, it would be invaluable
to use this agent for our purposes, and I am confident that
someone of your status in the intelligence field will recognize
the opportunity."

The twin reflections of the interpreter's glasses swung across the wall as he turned his head back and forth against the hard light of the gas lamps.

"This is why you asked me not to kill him?"

"Yes."

"What do you suggest he signal?"

"Disinformation."

"To the effect?"

"I would leave that to you, as someone skilled in such matters."

Light flashed again from the submachine gun of one of the men outside. Through the arches I could see the indigo haze of the mountains, with the moon's light silvering what looked like a waterfall several miles away, and the curving line of a pagoda roof in the foreground. One of those men would be Yang, because he never left me out of his sight: He would have been watching me through the grilled apertures of Tung's chamber ten minutes ago, though I hadn't seen him then. I'd heard his name earlier, when they'd ordered me out of my cell to go and see Tung Kuo-feng; he was the track-suited North Korean who had prodded my spine with the gun on our way out of the mountains, and when they had pushed me into the monk's cell this afternoon and slammed the heavy door shut he'd said something to me in Korean, a few short words with their sibilants spit out in my face with his eyes narrowed like a cat's. I appreciated his warning; he was under orders to leave me alone, but I knew now that he was waiting for me to make a too-sudden movement or break into a run, and give him an excuse to shoot me down. Perhaps the marks-man had been his brother.

"You should know," I heard Igor Sinitsin saying, "that this agent is very experienced."

"So my action group has reported."

"If we let him use the radio, he would certainly slip in what we call an 'ignore' signal, making it clear he was giving out disinformation."

The twin reflections swung across and across the wall.

"I finished my education at the University of Singapore," Tung said evenly, "and have a perfect understanding of the English language. I would instruct him to say precisely what you wish, and no more."

"Captain Samoteykin here understands a certain amount of English, you know."

Not true. If anyone among the Russian or Korean contingent understood a word of English, Sinitsin would have told him to be present when Tung talked to me in his chamber.

"So much the better," Tung said through the interpreter. "He'll be able to supervise the exchange of signals. In any case I shall make it clear to him that this is the only chance he has of saving his life, and that if he attempts any kind of deception I shall order him summarily shot."

"He'll be shot anyway, before we leave here."

"I shall not tell him that."

The KGB colonel had started moving about, his hands clasped neatly behind him and his gray suede shoes making a series of soft clicking sounds at precise intervals across the flagstones. He'd have liked to tell Tung Kuo-feng to press on with his operation and deal ruthlessly with any opposition, because he was a KGB officer and that was the way a KGB officer would think, with a million-strong organization behind him and almost limitless resources; in fact the only reason why Department V wasn't running this project directly was that if any mistakes were made, if there was the slightest risk of world exposure, the faces on the front page would have to be Asiatic, not Caucasian. The KGB had chosen Tung not only to carry out the operation but to take the blame if anything went wrong—or forfeit his son's life. But Tung now had him worried: Sinitsin would know from the radio reports that Tung's group was encountering opposition and that the murder of the British delegate had been a mistake; by now the KGB was walking on eggshells, because the one thing they feared was exposure: To have it known that the Soviets were behind the attempt to destroy Chinese-American relations would bring total diplomatic disaster.

If the operation failed, and failed because a British Intelligence cell had infiltrated it and blown it up, Colonel Igor Sinitsin's head would roll; and Tung was giving him a chance to avoid it.

For Tung the situation was different, and totally personal. He was fighting to save his son.

His own life was already lost, and he knew that. Whether the operation failed or succeeded, they would never let him live to expose the Kremlin.

"Ask him if he understands the situation," Sinitsin said, and came to a halt with his feet together.

"He already understands. He is ready to cooperate."

I saw anger behind Sinitsin's eyes; he was having to give in, and he wasn't used to that. "He is ready to do anything in his power to destroy us. To destroy us all. And to destroy our operation. If you use him, you'll be picking up a scorpion."

"A scorpion will hardly sting the hand that protects it."

Sinitsin held the silence, standing with his head tilted back as he considered, looking at no one; then he swung round and came toward me in three measured strides until I was looking into his cold blue stare.

"Do you understand any Russian?"

I looked blank.

"Tung," he said through the interpreter, "does this man understand Chinese?"

"No."

"Have you tried to trip him?"

"Yes."

The cold blue eyes watched mine. "I have decided not to permit him to send a signal. I have decided to have him taken out immediately and shot."

I went on looking blank as the interpreter translated.

Tung must have known the man was trying to trip me in Russian, but decided to play it straight. "That will lose us a valuable chance of saving the operation."

Sinitsin was silent, watching my eyes. He didn't worry me, but I thought I felt vibrations again from Tung Kuo-feng's direction; perhaps he expected a final show of resistance, and was developing his *ki* to combat it. The little Korean stood in the middle of us, his body leaning awkwardly away from his deformed leg.

"Tung Kuo-feng," the Russian said at last, "will you interpret for us?"

"I will."

The game began, and it was for four people, in three languages, while Sinitsin and I watched each other's eyes to catch any meaning that was lost on its way from Russian through Chinese to English; the KGB man was also watching for me to react to what he was saying in Russian, or to answer too fast once I'd got it in English, having had time to consider the question. I would have to be careful; after the grueling trek through the mountains I was still fatigued enough to miss a trick, and that would be fatal.

"You're prepared to send disinformation to your group?"

The interpreter took it and passed it to Tung while I stood waiting, watching Sinitsin. Sinitsin had said "signal" and "cell," but this was normal: Tung was a terrorist, not an intelligence officer.

"Yes," I said.

"*Yau.*"

"*Da.*"

"You're obviously not worried about your reputation."

Bounce.

Bounce, like a ball.

"I've got a reputation for surviving."

"You're ready to sell your country?"

The interpreter moved back a little, so that we formed a ring to make things easier: He didn't have to keep on turning his head now from Sinitsin to Tung and back.

"If the price is right," I said.

"Even if the price is only your neck?"

Going faster now, getting into our stride.

"All right, I'll have to live with my conscience, but that's more than a dead man can do."

"Are you all like that over there in the capitalist states, ready to sell your comrades?"

Sinitsin put a lot of contempt into his tone for my immediate benefit, knowing it would be lost in Tung's flat metallic voice.

"I've told you, I value my neck."

"I could never betray my comrades."

"Then you should get a more valuable neck."

He dismissed this with a raised eyebrow, and changed the subject. I don't think he'd been trying to trap me into saying something that would call the whole thing off; I think he was just showing his contempt for the decadent West and its perfidious agents, in front of Tung Kuo-feng. That was all right; it meant he wasn't thinking about anything else.

I wanted to get at that radio. It was the only chance.

"Do you trust Tung Kuo-feng?"

"With what?"

"Your life."

"I think he'll keep me alive as long as it's in his own interests."

"They are also my interests."

Wrong.

I said: "Then I've got a double chance."

"Your chance of remaining alive for more than a few hours is precisely nil." Ice in his eyes.

"I wouldn't say that. I'm your direct access to the opposition. You can funnel enough dope through me to knock them right out of the running."

Dismissed with a shrug. "Where is your safe-house in Seoul?"

"There isn't one."

"Then where will you send your signals, if I permit it?"

"To my director in the field."

"What is his name?"

"Murray."

"Where can he be reached?"

"At the British Embassy."

He swung away from me and paced for a while, probably to show Tung that he was in total control here and still hadn't decided whether to use me or not. Beyond him I saw one of the Koreans standing closer to the archways, looking in at us; when he saw I was watching him he brought up his submachine gun and aimed it at me and I thought, Yes, Sinitsin was probably right: My chances of remaining alive for more than a few hours were precisely nil.

We listened to the sound of the gray suede shoes across the flagstones, like the ticking of a clock. I was getting no emanations from Tung; when I looked away from the muzzle of the submachine gun I saw he had his eyes closed, perhaps in meditation.

The little interpreter shuffled a few steps away, perhaps needing movement to ease his leg; he wasn't wearing a track suit like the rest of them; I suppose he was just a civilian from one of the communist liaison groups in Pyongyang or the demilitarized zone.

I watched Sinitsin. If he said no, Tung would have to abide by it, and they'd have no further use for me; there'd be the wall and the rattle of shots, and the name of my replacement would go onto the board for *Jade One* in London.

If he said yes, my voice would vibrate the speaker in the embassy signals room and Ferris would look up in disbelief, and we could start work again, and use our one chance in hell of saving the mission.

Shoes on the flagstones, like the ticking of a clock.

Then Sinitsin stopped pacing.

"No," he said.

XXIII
SHOOT

❄

It was only a short walk.

Tung Kuo-feng didn't come with us, probably because this was Sinitsin's show and they didn't like each other.

Sinitsin himself led the way out of the flagstone hall, through one of the arches and along the narrow courtyard between the monastery and the ruined temple nearby. The two track-suited guards came forward and I recognized one of them as Yang; apparently he knew Russian, because Sinitsin spoke a few words to him directly, without the interpreter's help, just saying I was to be executed immediately.

Yang moved behind me and pushed the muzzle of his submachine gun into my spine. It wasn't necessary, because I couldn't run away; he was just expressing his feelings.

They took me to the middle of the long wall between the monastery and the little pagoda, opposite one of those carved stone Buddhas that were everywhere. Yang left me now, swinging the gun barrel round and moving back to where the others stood, about thirty feet away.

I didn't know what had changed Sinitsin's mind. I'd thought Tung had won his argument in there. Apparently not.

My eyes were getting used to the moonlight after the glare of the butane lamps in the hall where we'd been. The soft indigo haze across the mountains was lightening slowly, and the tiles of the pagoda's curving roof had begun shimmering. The air was perfectly still, with the scent of woodsmoke in it. You could say it was a fine night.

Those present: Colonel Igor Sinitsin, Major Alyev and Captain Samoteykin of the KGB, five North Koreans in Olympic suits, and the crippled interpreter. The three Koreans who had come up were probably members of the helicopter crews, invited to watch the show because they still felt bad about the man I'd killed. Tit for tat, so forth, *c'est la vie*. You can't have everything.

C'est la mort also, of course; you can have that.

Moira.

One single rose, for Moira.

Listen, they can't do this. They—

Shuddup. You've got to die like a brave ferret.

Records for *Jade One: Executive replaced July 16 following final signal reporting extreme hazard. As far as can be ascertained, first executive in the field deceased shortly afterward, remains never discovered.*

Sinitsin was coming toward me, his leather heels clicking across the stones.

The last I'd heard from Moira was that she was shooting some retakes near Paris. I supposed it would be some bloody little second assistant director stopping her as she left the set: Miss Sutherland, there's some flowers come for you in a box. *Flower,* you idiot, *one* flower, don't you understand, *one rose,* don't you know the difference? And don't let her think it's just from one of her fans, make her open it *now.*

No. Never let her open it. Throw it away somewhere.

There weren't any lamps out here in the courtyard; there was just the moonlight, gleaming on the curved tiles of the pagoda and the bell in the archway and Yang's gun.

They didn't need any more light than this. Yang was thirty feet away and he could blast me into Christendom with one sustained burst of fire, even if I tried running for my life. The only logical place to run would be straight into his gun, to get it over with.

What will she do with the rose? Will she clasp it tenderly in her slender hands, closing her amethyst eyes while the first hot tears begin falling softly? You don't know her, my friend. She'll just look at it and say, "Christ, he was always so bloody sentimental. I wish he'd sent a case of gin so I could get smashed out of my mind."

Throw it away. Don't let her know.

Executive deceased. Relevant records show—

Listen, there's time to run. You can't let them—

Shuddup, will you. Be brave, little man. You're dying for queen, country, a stack of piratical death duties, and the over-weening arrogance that made you think you could run this one solo, so stop sniveling and let that be your epitaph.

Colonel Sinitsin stopped in front of me with his gray suede shoes neatly together. "Tung spoke a certain amount of logic in there: You could have been valuable as a disinformer. But we know your record and we know you can't be trusted to behave intelligently when it's all over. You'd only try something stupid, and I'm not going to have that."

I stared him back, but didn't show any reaction. There was no point now in concealing the fact that I understood Russian but it's the kind of thing we've been trained to do, in whatever circumstances: Maintain the cover. Actually it's a bit like running around like a chicken with its head cut off, and I would much rather have told Sinitsin something to annoy him—Lenin was a silly shit, something simple enough for him to understand.

"So you can only blame yourself," he said, and gave a brief energetic nod, as he'd done earlier when I was introduced; then he turned his back on me and walked with his measured stride to where the others were standing, saying a word to Yang as he passed him. Yang was standing alone and slightly forward of the group, and I heard the interpreter catch the

word from Sinitsin and translate it for him. Sinitsin had been
walking with his back to me when he'd spoken, and I didn't
hear what he was actually saying; I suppose it was something
like "When you're ready."

They say that we go through three phases in the last few
moments of our life: We panic, then we get angry, then we
accept. I had got through the first phase—*Listen, there's time
to run,* so forth—and my thoughts about Moira must have
been part of the acceptance. I didn't feel any anger, because
in this branch of the trade you kill or get killed, and there's
nothing personal. I was still in the final phase, the acceptance
bit, because my mind was clear enough to wonder why Sinitsin
had bothered to come up and speak to me. He believed I didn't
understand Russian, or he wouldn't have wasted his time with
all that palaver in there, with the cripple and Tung translating.
Was it conscience then? Wanting to go through the motions
of addressing the condemned man, telling him he'd only himself to blame? A KGB colonel from Department V with a
conscience, yes, that would do all right if I wanted to go out
with a funny story.

I watched Yang bring the submachine gun into the aim.
There would be fifty rounds in that model, and the stuff would
be coming into me with the force of a pneumatic drill. If there
were any humanity in him he would start with the head and
work downward through a series of a dozen shots, so that the
brain would go first and not understand what was happening
afterward. But there wouldn't be any humanity in him; he'd
just stand there and spread me all over the wall and leave it
at that; or to put it another way, he might have some humanity in him but that marksman was either his brother or a
good friend and he was very upset about him and he'd get a
kick out of blowing me apart.

They were all standing very still now, watching me.

Physical reactions normal for the situation: sweat running
down my sides, the pulse accelerated, a tightness of the chest,
and a reluctance to breathe in case it disturbed the delicate

balance between a living body and a mess of disintegrating chemicals.

The muzzle of the gun was a small black hole and I watched it, and the squat blockish shape of the magazine beyond it. He should be pumping that thing by now.

Everything very still, and the sweat trickling on my skin; moonlight and indigo dark, and faces, and silence, and suddenly someone's voice, pitched in a shout.

"Come on then, you bastard! Shoot!"

My own voice, yes. Its echoes came back from the walls of the pagoda. Rather bad show of nerves, but too late now.

"Come on!"

Sweat pouring on my face; staring into the muzzle of the gun; breathing rapidly now and the heart thudding under the ribs: *If you're going to do it, do it; if you're going to do it, do it—*

"Shoot, damn your eyes!"

Shaking all over, the animal smell of fear, breath coming painfully, sawing in and out, only one thing to do, Mahomet, mountain, so forth, my legs weak as I began walking toward him, toward the gun, watching the small black hole where the flame would burst with its orange light puckering to the dark stitching shapes of the bullets—

"Shoot, fuck you! What are you waiting for?"

Walking into his gun.

Tung Kuo-feng was standing there in the shadows.

I had only just seen him.

And now I knew what they were waiting for. Page 97 of the KGB manual entitled *Treatment of Prisoners and Hostages.* The heading for chapter 4 reads: "Effectiveness of Fear Inducement."

This was Russian, and it was routine.

But the human body is a body, and as I walked right into that bloody thing he didn't lower it, and I stood there with the muzzle against my stomach and the sweat still running on me because *you can never be sure* . . . you can never be absolutely sure that you're right, that they're just pulling your psyche apart to soften you up, to make you afraid, to make you obey. Because prisoners and hostages get shot dead every day all over the world and you can't simply stand there and whistle just because you've read their bloody manual half a dozen times in the Behavior Under Stress class at Norfolk.

Yang must be military, and under tight discipline; otherwise it would have been too much for him: He would have pumped that thing at me like an orgasm he couldn't stop.

I looked up from the gun and into his dark burning eyes. He'd frightened me, and I felt the reaction developing inside me with the gathering force of an explosion and then I was working hard, my hands driving down against the barrel of the gun and smashing it away so fast that he could loose only a short burst before my half-fist went into his throat and he staggered back.

Hands grabbing me, dragging me away from him, that's all right, you frightened me, that's all, and I've got a rotten temper, not my bloody fault, I was born with it.

XXIV
MINEFIELD

❁

5051 Hz

Tung was on one side of me, Sinitsin on the other. Somewhere behind me were the two track-suited guards, one of them Yang. It hadn't been my intention to kill him, though I could have done that: I had been fast enough and there had been more than enough rage behind the half-fist strike to the larynx; but discipline hadn't been undermined even after what they'd done to me, and I had known that if I killed Yang there wouldn't be another mock execution: They would gun me down on the spot.

So he was behind me now, with a bruised throat and the submachine gun in his hands again, in case I tried to smash up the radio or said anything wrong. I hadn't increased my chances, of course, by going for him like that: He'd want even less an excuse now to shoot me out of hand; but without having to think about it I'd realized we had to do something about the fear they'd induced in me, about the wish to obey; we had to minimize the effects that were the object of the whole charade, and the rage and then the release of rage by going for Yang had done that. It had been a calculated reaction on the part of the psyche, bringing in the risk-benefit factor: The risk of death at the hands of Yang was now increased, but I would benefit from the fact that my fear of these people and my wish to obey them was much less than it would have been; and it a chance came of destroying them I was more ready to take it.

But everything is relative. As I sat in front of the illuminated console the nerves in my spine were crawling, because the smell of cordite was still on the air and I knew they were standing behind me with loaded guns in case I tried to smash the radio or use my bare hands on Tung or Sinitsin.

5051 Hz

"Eagle to Jade One. Eagle to Jade One."

I'd been trying for ten minutes or so, without getting anything more than a faint voice speaking what sounded like Korean; the interpreter said he couldn't understand what was being said. I was rather sorry for the interpreter: I was certain now that he wasn't military, even in a noncombatant capacity; he'd really thought they were going to shoot me out there, and when we were all coming back into the operations room he'd stayed outside and we'd heard him vomiting.

"Eagle to Jade One."

The Korean voice came again, and this time the interpreter said we were being received.

"Ask for Murray," Sinitsin told him, and the interpreter leaned over my shoulder while I held down the transmit lever.

They would know who Murray was in the embassy signals room: It was the giveaway name for Ferris, the one I'd given away to Sinitsin earlier tonight.

I was worried about the bad reception we'd been getting; it wasn't the mountains between here and Seoul: This was a Hammarlund HQ-105-TRS with a multiplier and BFO and an autoresponse circuit—they could raise Moscow with this. Maybe there was something wrong with the antenna rig, or we weren't getting the full 105 volts from the generator.

"He will find Murray," the interpreter told Sinitsin.

I felt a sudden surge of confidence. Physically I was less than a hundred percent after the march through the mountains, and the bullet wound in my cheek had swollen half my face in the healing process, bringing a fever and leaving a tenderness that kept the nerves bared; but the physical is infinitely less important than the psychological when the stress comes on, and I'd needed an antidote to the lingering fright induced by standing against that wall out there and staring at the muzzle of the gun. Sinitsin had compromised: He'd decided to accept Tung's logic and let me use the transceiver, but had first put me through page 97 to reduce the risk of my breaking out. To a certain degree he'd done that, but the thought that *Jade One* was still running and that I was resuming contact with the director in the field was almost heady.

The Korean voice sounded again but almost immediately faded, and the interpreter told Sinitsin he hadn't caught anything intelligible. We went on waiting.

The idea of smashing the radio kept recurring, but I hadn't got enough data to work on. If this was the only radio at the monastery I might do quite a bit of good by knocking it out and cutting their communications with Moscow, but it wouldn't cut off Tung from his action group: He could raise them with one of the helicopter sets, and they might well have a shortwave transceiver that could reach Moscow. I couldn't destroy their operation; I could only cause temporary confusion.

"Jade One to Eagle."

Something like a spark went through my nerves. It was the voice of Ferris, loud and clear: a voice I thought I'd never hear again.

"Eagle receiving."

I sensed Sinitsin closing in from my right side.

"You are in danger," he said, "but you have obtained information and may be able to obtain more."

I sat doing nothing while the interpreter put the Russian into Chinese for Tung Kuo-feng; then as Tung began speaking in English I hit the transmit lever.

"There is a Russian connection," he said. "The operation is being run from Moscow."

I gave it straight to Ferris, but had to use speech code because even among people who speak only their own language there are many who pick up foreign words: Most English people know *niet, parachik,* so forth. This applies particularly to the names of people and cities, and a KGB colonel would know the English for "Russian" and "Moscow," and if I hadn't used "bearish" and "Place Rouge," Sinitsin would have dragged me away from the radio and told Yang to wipe me out, this time for real.

It was like moving slowly through a minefield, and there was a lot to think about. Tung had opened up with a hot signal, and I'd had to control my reaction. The last thing the KGB wanted anyone to know was that there was a Russian connection, and as I sat here waiting for Sinitsin to give me the next item of *dezinformatsiya* I knew that I'd just dropped an intelligence bomb in the signals room of the British Embassy; depending on the turnaround facilities there, it could be known in London within minutes from now that Moscow was behind the assassinations in Peking.

I wiped sweat off my face as I waited.

Sinitsin spoke. "The Peking assassinations were designed to divert both world and intelligence attention from the actual operation Tung Kuo-feng is running."

I sat listening to the interpreter.

We'd passed the first hump in the minefield, but there would be so many others. Whenever Sinitsin spoke, I must remember not to react, but to wait for the translation. Whenever Tung spoke to me in English, I had to assess what he wanted Ferris to know, and if I didn't like it, I would have to try inserting an "ignore" key word by careful rephrasing, and that would be dangerous because he might realize what I was doing. I had to use speech code for any words Tung gave me that Sinitsin might understand, like "Russian" or "Moscow," and I must hope that Tung would know why I was doing it. I had to listen for any internationally known names or words— "Peking," "airport," so forth—spoken by Sinitsin, and put them faithfully into the final signal so that he would hear them, because he'd be listening for them; *and Tung would have to do the same.* At the same time, I had to insert an "ignore" key to cover them, because they'd stand out oddly in the message. If Tung didn't understand what I was doing, he couldn't ask me, because Sinitsin would want to know what we were talking about.

While I waited for the interpreter to finish I thought over what Sinitsin had just told me to send. *The Peking assassinations were designed to divert world and intelligence attention from the actual operation Tung Kuo-feng is running.* "Peking" and "Tung Kuo-feng" would have to go in.

When the interpreter had finished, Tung leaned over me. "The Peking only chance of stopping the operation is by finding and releasing Chuan, Tung Kuo-feng's abducted son."

He was on to what we had to do: He'd inserted "Peking" at the beginning and got his own name in the right place near the end, using exactly nineteen words, as Sinitsin had. If we could work together like this we had a chance, but it would need only one slip, and Sinitsin was listening hard.

I opened transmission. *"The Peking, really, only chance of stopping . . ."* It was the only "ignore" we had to insert.

We all waited.

"Message understood so far." Ferris.

He wouldn't be worried by the "ignore" key word "really." He would be cautious, but not worried. He was already wondering at the delay between my first and second transmissions, and would almost certainly realize I wasn't alone; he would be listening carefully to the tone of my voice, alert for any stress tones or background sounds; but he would know that the signal as a whole could be trusted and that I was sending what

I wanted to send, without duress; otherwise I would have thrown in a priority "discount" key right at the outset and the only reason he would have gone on listening would be to hear what kind of disinformation the opposition was trying to feed him, and to respond with formal acknowledgments to give the impression he accepted the signal.

When they'd led me to the radio I'd tried to angle my chair slightly so that I could press down the transmit lever without anyone seeing, so that Ferris would hear the Russian and Chinese in the background; but it hadn't been possible: Sinitsin and his aides had been watching for that.

I looked up at him now, wanting him to know that the transmission had been acknowledged. He began speaking again.

"The Tung operation is aimed at a mock overthrow of the Kim Sung presidency of North Korea, ostensibly by a South Korean terrorist group, followed by an immediate countercoup and a full military invasion of South Korea and the installation of a communist government."

The interpreter took it up and passed it to Tung Kuo-feng.

I sat waiting, conscious that Ferris, too, was waiting, and wondering at the delay; but he had some data to work on: He knew I spoke fluent Russian and that there was a Russian connection; he might assume I was concealing the fact that I spoke Russian, and was speaking through an interpreter; he would know I'd reached the monastery and made contact with Tung, because of the information I was sending; but he wouldn't know that the signal I was sending was totally different from the one Sinitsin was giving me, and that as a result I was having to insert sporadic "ignore" keys as I went along.

Tung began speaking. He'd remembered my use of "bearish" for "Russian" and used it now, putting his own name early in the phrasing and putting in the names of Kim Sung, North and South Korea, and communist. I'd been waiting for Sinitsin to pounce on something at any moment, but I should have realized that Tung, chief of a formidable Triad, would be capable of working out the game we had to play; and he knew that the better he played it the more chance he had of seeing his son again.

Minus the necessary repetition of the names Sinitsin was listening for, and minus the relevant "ignore" keys, Tung's transmission read: *Chuan Tung is held by Russian agents somewhere in South Korea. His location and release would bring the operation to an immediate stop, so you must do utmost. Tung ready to expose Russians' objective, which is to destroy Chinese-American relations.*

I lifted the transmit lever and waited on automatic receive. I'd had to use "subject" for the second "Tung," and "Red Indian" for "American," because "American," "States," "United States," "U.S.A.," "U.S.," "Uncle Sam," and "Yank," "Yanks," "Yankee" might be understandable to Sinitsin. For five or six seconds there was silence in the room except for the low hum of the transceiver.

"Message understood."

I didn't relax until the silence continued for another few seconds after Ferris acknowledged. Sinitsin would have jumped straight in with a question if he'd had one. Ferris himself was less of a worry: He knew he daren't ask any one of a dozen questions he was wanting to—my reasons for speech code and "ignore" keys, so forth; their presence alone warned him of danger.

"He doesn't sound very surprised," Sinitsin said.

I looked blank and turned to Tung Kuo-feng and waited for the translation to come through, at the same time thinking out the answer. When I was ready, I said through Tung and the Korean: "In our trade, colonel, there aren't many things left that can surprise us, don't you agree? And your transmission's being relayed to London, so he's not going to hold things up with any questions. Do you have more?"

"Yes."

He began on the next phase.

It was now midnight by the twenty-four-hour chronometer

on the lighted console, three o'clock in the afternoon in London. If the embassy in Seoul had immediate relay facilities, Croder would be channeling this transmission direct to half a dozen departments, alerting sleepers and agents-in-place throughout Southeast Asia, asking for an immediate two-week playback analysis from Asian Signals Coordinate to catch anything intercepted during the last fourteen days that sounded like a terrorist or political abduction, and directing emergency staffs into Soviet Department V Operations Monitor Section, Dossier File (Asia), Intelligence Support Stations (South Korea), and Active Signals Search.

Feedback would be reaching Seoul within minutes, and all of it would go to Ferris, but only for his information until someone picked up traces of the Tung Chuan abduction or made a lucky hit with one of the dozen radio direction-finding mobile units that would initiate roving missions even while the stuff was still coming in from London. This service offered the greatest hope: They could pinpoint an individual house if they were in the area at the right time; but high-speed transmitting would make it difficult, and if the Russian agents had an automatic player device it would make it impossible. But the signal I was now sending on this set was going to launch a massive intelligence search for Tung Chuan throughout South Korea: I wasn't just speaking to Ferris on an internal directive level.

Midnight plus ten.

We walked through the minefield together, a Russian, a Korean, a Chinese, and an Englishman, with the glow of the radio console on our faces and the hum of the transmitter bridging the silence between the babel of words and phrases.

Sinitsin threw in traps for me a dozen times, and when I looked up at Tung for the translation I warned him with my eyes and he stepped around the traps and I covered the transmission with insertions and "ignore" keys. Three times Tung missed an international name, one of them "Washington," and I put it into transmission as early as I could before Sinitsin noticed the omission. Several times Sinitsin threw in an inconsistency, and Tung questioned it, and I covered.

We walked through the minefield not as friends trying to guide each other to safety but as enemies trying to reach our different goals and reach them first. The terrain itself was innocent; the danger lay in our own conflicting objectives. If Sinitsin caught me in a deliberate mistake, or suspected for an instant that I was sending a different signal, he would turn to the guards and have me shot. If Tung Kuo-feng caught any hint that my transmissions were trying to compromise him or the rescue of his son, he would tell the KGB party that they were right: I was too dangerous to remain alive. And if I could see a way to do it, as I picked my way through the patterns of explosive phrases, I would destroy them both.

By 00:19 the transmission was completed. Sinitsin had ended his message with the implication that Ferris should ignore the events in Peking and turn his full attention to preventing the imminent coup in North Korea. I would send further signals when I had more information. This message did not go through. Tung ended his transmission with a warning that in two days' time the first of three further assassinations was due to take place, unless his son was located and brought to safety.

Ferris came back with a formal acknowledgment, and I shut the set down and sat for a moment with my eyes closed and the sweat drying on me and the strange feeling that inside the next two days we could achieve the objective and phase out the mission and let everyone go home. The Bureau had massive and effective facilities in the Asian theater, and Croder would press them into service to the limit, because, apart from anything else, his reputation was at stake: In the last eight days *Jade One* had been driven into the ground by the opposition, and now there was a chance.

A chance for the mission, but not for me. I wouldn't be going home. Even if Tung Chuan were found and released, the KGB contingent here wouldn't be threatened; they would simply go home like everyone else, after they'd shot Tung Kuo-feng to stop his exposing them, and after they'd shot me for destroying their operation.

I heard Sinitsin pacing now, his shoes clicking with precision over the flagstones. Tung Kuo-feng had left the console, and I could feel the release of tension in the air as the aura of his *ki* was withdrawn. Yang would still be behind me with the gun.

In a moment I heard Sinitsin say: "Take him to his cell."

The muzzle bit into my spine.

XXV

MOSCOW

✿

The fat crumpled face of a god.

A shadow passing.

Playing with bricks again.

The shadow belonged to Yang. It was his tour of duty.

These bricks had belonged to the monk, I suppose, who had lived in this cell; blocks, rather than bricks, smelling of ancient wood and with yellow dust in the carving, perhaps fibers from his saffron robe. I lined up the three fat gods in a row, putting the five thinner ones below them and adding the ram, the deer, and the eagle, giving the left hemisphere of my brain something to do while I ransacked the other one for ideas.

But there weren't any. It was the evening of the next day, and for seventeen hours I'd been stuck in here while Tung's Triad was carefully lining up the next shot in Seoul or Peking or Tokyo, the next step in the destruction of Chinese-American relations and Chinese-American-Japanese triangle diplomacy.

Tung was powerless to do anything, I knew that. The KGB never let him go near the radio console unless two interpreters were also there; he couldn't send a signal to his Triad, order-

ing them to postpone the three final assassinations in the hope
that the Bureau could find his son. I couldn't get near the
radios myself; and even if I could, Tung would be listening.
In any case I had nothing definite to tell Ferris: Two of the
three people on the death list were likely to be the U.S. chargé
d'affaires in Peking and the Japanese ambassador; the third
was certain to be the premier of the People's Republic of
China, though his death would have to suggest natural causes:
The Soviets wouldn't want China's ostensible responsibility
for these assassinations to extend to the killing off of her own
kind; but Tung's scenario of a pro-Russian general's assuming
power in China would obviously require the premier out of
the way.

It wasn't easy to play with my bricks while somewhere a
telescopic rifle was swinging into the aim with an innocent
man's head in the cross hairs.

Tung Kuo-feng, I'd written on a 10-*won* note, and on the
other side in English: *Urgent we talk again.* I'd waited until
Yang's relief had taken over the guard outside my cell and
I'd given the note to him, tapping my finger on Tung's name.
He'd gone off with it, but I doubted if Tung ever received it;
Yang had a particular hatred for me, but the others had the
look of the executioner on their faces whenever they came
into the cell; I'd killed one of their own and they were all
hoping I'd try running for it.

At noon they'd brought me some bean curd in a small black
iron cooking pot; it was still on the floor, empty—a lethal
weapon, except that they never came in without a submachine
gun leveled at my heart; and if I could ever close up on one of
them I knew better ways to do it than with a saucepan.

The bell was chiming again at the far end of the courtyard,
and in the narrow slit in the thick stone wall I could see a
powdering of the dusk darkening the leaves of the acacia
trees. The wooden clappers began soon afterward, and the
low monotone of chanting voices. When it was over, Yang
came on duty again, throwing open the big tumbler lock and
pushing the door inward with his gun and looking at me with

his black eyes narrowed as if in contemplation. I don't think he was just trying to play on my nerves; I think he wanted to look at me and go through in his imagination what he would finally do with me. The bruise on his throat had darkened, though not so much perhaps as the bruise on his pride: He should have been quicker out there in the courtyard last night.

He backed away until he was in the stone passage outside, then jerked his gun in a sign to me to go with him.

Colonel Igor Sinitsin was in the operations room with his aides, Tung Kuo-feng and the crippled interpreter.

"I want to know if your people have started to act on the disinformation you gave them last night."

While I waited for the translation I noted that Major Alyev and Captain Samoteykin had their right hands in the pockets of their sports coats, even though Yang was standing behind me with his submachine gun. I was close enough to Tung to reach him, and they'd seen what I'd done to Yang last night. Killing Tung was the only workable method of destroying their operation, and they knew that I knew that, though I wasn't so sure he needed their protection: I could still remember the impact of that subtle force that had thrown me against the wall of his private chamber.

He said: "Call your embassy. What sign can they give us if they find my son?"

This was why I'd tried to see him. Even if Ferris wanted to risk sending us a signal, he wouldn't be able to do it: One of these sets was kept open for transmissions direct from Moscow, and the other for the Triad to report on progress with their continuing operations.

"All right," I said, and pressed down the transmit lever. An English voice answered this time, and Ferris came to the embassy radio within fifteen seconds.

"Jade One."

"Eagle to Jade One. If you find the objective, get a USAF fighter to make a low-altitude pass over the monastery."

"Understood, but we've made no progress yet. This is a tough one."

I began using speech code. *"Keep talking, and put in the names Pyongyang and North Korea, also President Kim Sung, with a neutral background."*

After three sentences I turned to Tung. "Over to you."

He spoke to the interpreter and I heard the three names being spoken at roughly the same intervals used by Ferris. While I waited I tried to think how to slip in a warning to Ferris on the three next victims of Tung's operation, but there wasn't a chance, and in any case the deadline was up and the first one was probably on the ground by now with a hand outstretched and the security guards keeping the crowd back and the ambulance siren fading in, and nothing I could do about it except watch Tung Kuo-feng from the corner of my eye and try to work out a murderously fast attack that would take him down on top of me as a shield when they opened up with their guns.

But I would have to change my thinking on that. With this heavy a guard at the monastery I had *no* chance of getting away; the only chance for *Jade One* was to find Tung Chuan and try to free Kuo-feng and set him up in a world spotlight and have him expose the Soviets; in no other way could the damage to Chinese-American relations be repaired. Even if a chance came, I mustn't kill him now.

I heard Sinitsin saying: "Five members of the Japanese Red Army will assist in the mock overthrow of President Kim Sung, and a few of his guards will be shot for the sake of appearances. These men are now on their way from Tokyo by commercial airliner."

When Tung spoke, it seemed to me that he was using precisely similar cadences and intervals as in the original Russian, and I admired his skill; he used names and speech code, as he'd heard me do; but when his totally dissimilar message came, it carried a brute shock.

"The American chargé d'affaires has just been ambushed and shot dead in Peking. You must find my son. The next action is scheduled for noon tomorrow."

I pushed down the transmit lever, sickened, and gave the

message to Ferris. There were people above Croder in London, all the way up to the prime minister, though he could short-circuit them and reach her direct if he had to. And by now she'd be asking questions as the slaughter went on.

The British foreign secretary, the American ambassador, the passengers aboard that airliner, and now the American chargé d'affaires. Have you replaced the agent in the field?

No, ma'am. He's close to the opposition now.

How close?

Very close. Within reach of an act of sanction.

A pause on the line while she considered, watching the rain on the window. *Then what is holding him up?* The tone severe as she demanded that Croder, and Ferris, and the agent in the field do what they were paid to do, and do it now.

There are difficulties, ma'am. The agent's position is hazardous in the extreme.

He's alone?

Yes.

Can't you invoke assistance from others? From NATO forces in the area, for instance?

While the rain ran down the window and the red buses swayed through the streets and the pigeons huddled along the parapets as Big Ben chimed the hour, the agent "in the area" sat in his sweat at the radio console feeling as impotent and as incompetent as that clear and admonishing voice declared that he was.

"*Message understood.*"

Ferris.

We waited. In a moment Sinitsin said: "In addition to the assistance of the Japanese Red Army team, there will be—" He broke off as the other radio opened up with a signal, and our heads turned to watch the illuminated panel. The sender was speaking in Russian.

"*Zero-one-nine. Zero-one-nine to Action Five.*"

Major Alyev moved quickly to the transceiver and switched to transmit. "*Action Five to Zero-one-nine, receiving you.*"

Sinitsin took three precise paces and stood next to his aide. There were now only Captain Samoteykin and Yang behind me, but they were both armed and I knew that Yang had his finger inside the trigger guard of the machine gun, and I was already feeling that sinister vibration in the air as Tung Kuo-feng sensed my thoughts.

"Zero-one-nine to Action Five. Further to our transmission of 14:16 hours, the developing opposition activities in the vicinity of Sinch'on-ni necessitate the removal of Tung Chuan to a more secure environment. Acknowledge."

I looked away from the transceiver, but went on listening. This was Moscow.

Alyev touched the transmit lever. *"Action Five acknowledging."*

This is a tough one, Ferris had said a few minutes ago on the other radio; but London had launched a massive intelligence search in response to my signal of last night, and local agents had been sensitized to the area where Tung Chuan was being held, and the KGB unit had felt the trembling of the web. At some time while I was in my cell playing with bricks there must have been earlier transmissions, alerting Sinitsin, who in turn had reported to Moscow.

"Zero-one-nine to Action Five. Tung Chuan and our party will board Cathay Pacific flight 584 departing Kimpo Airport, Seoul, 03:55 tomorrow, destination Pyongyang, North Korea. Our party will signal you on arrival. Acknowledge and repeat."

Major Alyev responded.

I sat picking at the grime that had got under my nails since I'd dropped out of the sky two nights ago. I was listening to the death knell of *Jade One* and there was nothing I could do about it. When Alyev completed the exchange and switched to automatic receive he was going to put the light out over the board in London.

Croder had been getting warm: too warm.

"Zero-one-nine to Action Five. You will remain open to receive."

The KGB major acknowledged and left the receiver circuit open.

I had enough time. I would only need ten seconds to hit my own transmit lever and tell Ferris: *Tung Chuan is being flown from Seoul to Pyongyang at 03:55 tomorrow, Cathay Pacific flight 584. Get him.* But I hadn't been told to start transmitting again and the moment Sinitsin heard me he'd be suspicious; if he didn't stop me before I'd finished the signal he'd pick up "Tung Chuan," "Seoul," "Pyongyang," and "Cathay Pacific" and would realize I understood Russian and was passing on the message from Moscow. He would then do two things: He would have me taken outside and shot and he would signal Moscow and tell them the plans would have to be changed. And Ferris could send in a whole battalion of NATO troops to pick up Tung Chuan at the airport tomorrow morning, and draw a blank.

There was tension in the room again.

"If they move him to Pyongyang—" Captain Samoteykin began, but Sinitsin cut him short.

"Say nothing now."

Professional caution: He wasn't trusting the Korean interpreter, the only non-Russian here—as far as he knew—who could speak the language.

Tension from Tung Kuo-feng, too. He must have picked up the same names from the Russian, especially "Tung Chuan," and probably realized his son was being taken from Seoul to Pyongyang; he didn't know the flight number or the time of departure, but the move was probably imminent and he'd heard the name of the airline; if he signaled his Triad they would move in on Kimpo Airport and wait for Tung Chuan to arrive and try to get him out of the hands of his KGB guards.

But he couldn't transmit without instructions, any more than I could; if he made an attempt, the crippled interpreter would read his Chinese and warn Sinitsin before he'd finished transmitting.

Some of the tension in the room was my own. While Tung was learning that his son was to be moved out of our reach and into North Korea, I was learning the most bitter lesson of the executive in the field: that he can come critically close to bringing off a mission and still have to see it snatched away from him without a chance in hell of holding on.

I wanted only ten seconds with my director on this radio, but I couldn't have it, and the only signal I could send that would make any sense would be: *Ferris, we're finished.*

XXVI
MOON

✦

Tung Kuo-feng sat perfectly still.

"My son is precious to me," he said in his toneless English. "Our line stems from the Ch'ing dynasty, and he is my eldest."

The thing moved closer to him.

I said nothing.

"They knew that," he said with his night-dark eyes brooding on mine. "That is why they abducted him."

The thing had reached him now, or one end of it had; the rest of it lay across the flagstones like a heavy rope. I tried to warn him, but there was no sound.

"That is why it is so important for you to find my son. If I die, it is not important to me. If my son dies, the line will be finished. I will do anything you wish, if you can save him."

The narrow mottled head slipped gracefully between the arm and the body of Tung Kuo-feng, appearing on his other side and curving across the golden dragons on the front of his robe, curving again and winding, compressing the dark silk.

Tung Kuo-feng began smiling, as if he knew a secret. I had never seen him smile before.

"They must have put something in the rat. Inside the frozen rat. *Kori,* perhaps. Or something synthetic, like flarismine." His body was almost hidden now by the squeezing coils. "Something to send it into a frenzy."

Then it constricted in one powerful spasm of nerve and muscle, and Tung's face turned dark with blood; it constricted again and again like a tensed coil spring retracting, until Tung Kuo-feng was a bloodied effigy in the shape of a man, with the dragons writhing across the wet silk of his robe as the boa went on squeezing, squeezing, until it blocked my breath and I woke shivering with the taste of his blood in my mouth, sour and primitive.

I opened my eyes. The oblong gap of light was still there in the door, with shadows moving across the arched ceiling as the flames of the lanterns moved in a draft of air. Under me I could feel the soft resilience of the straw-filled hessian mattress.

I often dream about snakes.

The sound came again.

Figures on my watch face: 11:36.

That bloody thing in Seoul had upset me; I was going to dream about it for a long time, if there was a long time left to me. Highly unlikely.

Came again. So quiet that it could have just been in my mind; but I know my mind; it doesn't play tricks on me; it lets me know things; it lets me know the kinds of things I should very much know.

The shadows on the arched ceiling outside the door of my cell looked much as I'd seen them before; they were moving in the same rhythm, as the mountain air breathed softly through the labyrinthine passages and apertures of the monastery, pulling at the lantern flames. These people could have lit this place like a supermarket if they'd wanted to—they had a generator going for the transceivers; but it was probably visible at night to some of the villages on the far slopes of the foothills, or to the wagoners and goatherds along the mountain tracks. They'd put camouflage nets over the two helicopters out there, so they wanted things to look normal.

A very definite click. Immediate associations: gun, wooden box, lock. It was too quiet for the moving mechanism of a gun, and there wasn't a wooden box in this cell for anyone to open, and nobody could get in here without—

Lock, yes.

Turning.

Rotten taste in my mouth from that dream: the taste of fear.

It was a heavy door, solid oak and with huge wrought hinges. I'd seen the key when they'd first put me in here, an enormous thing, the kind of thing you'd only see in a flea market, genuine antique, so forth. They'd oiled the tumblers through the ages; monks run a tight ship, orderliness is godliness. But there's no way you can turn a lock this size without making at least a slight noise.

Tung.

For the last five hours he'd been shut in with his sense of impotence in the face of karma, hearing his son's name again and again in that heavy Russian accent. *I will do anything you wish, if you can save him.* That was only in a dream, yes, but dreams are ciphers for a reality we haven't got time to understand.

No, it couldn't be Tung outside my door. He didn't need to come along here in the dead of night to talk to me, because he didn't think I knew any more about the Moscow signal than he did; he didn't know I understood Russian. Besides, he'd have to knock out Yang or the other guard: One of them was always outside, and at this hour it would be Yang; I knew the shifts they worked. Yang wouldn't let him in here without permission from Sinitsin: The KGB was running this show, not Tung Kuo-feng.

Yang wouldn't let *anyone* in here.

I would have to think about that.

Other tiny sounds, from a different direction. Immediate associations: water rushing, fire crackling, both very far away;

distant rain. I turned my head a little to listen and the sounds were suddenly much louder; it was the straw in the loose mattress, close to my ear.

Mechanical sound again, of tumblers falling against the force of the spring, held back by the tines of the key. And I'd thought about it now. Yang wouldn't let anyone in here, so either he'd been called away from guard duty or someone had got at him. Unsatisfactory: These Koreans were military and they wouldn't take a guard away without relieving him; and no one could have got at him, because no one would want to, except Tung, and Tung was under house arrest and had guards watching him wherever he went.

Pride?

There was nothing over me; the night was too mild. My arms were free, and lying along the mattress. The mattress was on the stone floor. The only light in here was coming from the small oblong in the door, and its source was a good way off, near the second archway along the passage to the operations room; if I lifted my hand I would just about see it, but that was all.

Wounded pride.

Because I'd gone for him in front of the others, even though he'd had a submachine gun pointing at me. Whatever his reasons, this was Yang coming in here.

He took his time. I watched the thin strip of luminosity forming on the wall as the big door began swinging inward, and smelled the oil from the lamps out there, and the lingering sweetness of the incense that had filled the arched chamber where Tung Kuo-feng had talked to me last evening. The far voice of a night bird came from the mountain heights; it had been too faint to register through the narrow oblong in the door, and there was no window here.

Yang was moving with infinite patience. I could see his hand now, and his shoulder, a shadow against the shadows beyond, as the door swung inward. Its edge was three feet from the end of my mattress; when he had the door wide open he would be within reach of me if he leaped. But perhaps he wouldn't do that. Perhaps he'd just come to talk. Not seriously, no.

The far cry of the night bird.

Incense.

The door was wide open now, and he stopped moving. He was a shadow the shape of a man, and I watched him. He had left the big gun outside; it would make too much noise in the still of the mountain night.

He stood watching me. I lay watching him.

I suppose the instincts of his ancient race had been working in him over the hours while he'd been pacing outside my door, pacing like a tiger, soft-footed in his track shoes, ten steps to the left and then ten to the right, the gun in his arm and hate in his heart for me, the bruise pulsing in his throat and in his pride, his instincts begging revenge and so strongly that his military training was gradually overwhelmed, with the stealth of a creeping enemy.

He wanted my blood.

Not moving. He was not moving now.

But what would he tell them afterward? That someone else had come here and done this bloody deed? There'd be a lot of awkward questions: Who were they, and why did he let them pass? Perhaps he was going to do it in some subtle way that would leave no mark, no evidence, pricking my skin with a poisoned thorn or holding me still while I inhaled exotic and lethal fumes, so that it would look as if I'd died in my sleep, or of a poison that someone else had put in my food. It wasn't my concern, and I stopped thinking about it, because time must be short now.

I had only worked once before against Asiatics and that was in Bangkok, nine or ten missions ago; but I remembered that they killed readily. In the Curtain theater it seldom happens; there are hundreds of KGB agents in London and as many CIA and British Secret Service people in Moscow, but we leave each other alone unless we're really pressed: There's a tacit understanding that if once we decided to wipe each other out on our home ground there'd be no possibility of carrying on our trade anymore, and that would be dangerous in the extreme because cold-war espionage lowers the risk of a hot war breaking out. The Asiatics are different, and these people at the monastery were terrorists rather than spooks. It wasn't that life was cheap, but that death was expedient.

They'd tried to kill me four times, and the odds were growing short.

The organism was sensitized now: The appropriate chemicals had been poured from the glands into the cardiovascular and muscular systems; blood had receded from the surface and I was breathing deeply; my pupils were expanded to make full use of the available light. I was cocked like a gun.

He believed I was asleep. He couldn't see the glint of my eyes between the narrowed lids because I lay in shadow; he would also assume that if I were awake and had heard him come in here I'd be on my feet by now. But all I had to rely on was the advantage of surprise; in all other respects I was appallingly vulnerable here on the ground. From my viewpoint he looked tall, dominant and invincible, and I knew that when he came for me he'd come very fast, exploding against me, fired by the hate that burned in him; he wouldn't be human, but monstrous, and with a monster's demoniac strength. My quickest way out would be to underestimate him, I knew that.

He seemed to be moving now.

Or I thought he was moving, my imagination anticipating the event. I wasn't sure; I had to watch the soft edge of his shadow and the gap between it and the shadow of the door, but even then I couldn't tell if his movement was real. The saliva was thick in my mouth and I wanted to swallow, but that would trigger him: The sound would be loud in the infinite stillness of the little cell. Anything would trigger him, however slight, even the rustle of the straw under my body. He wanted to do it while I slept, forcing my brain from its slow delta waves into the terminal stillness of death.

Yes.

He was moving.

He was crouching over me, so slowly that even now there was no real indication of movement; his shadow form was simply becoming larger, and changing shape. I could hear his breathing now, and in it the trembling rhythm of the animal engaged in a matter of life and death. And now I caught a glint of light on something he was holding in one hand; it was very small.

My breathing became deeper, and my veins sang with their blood, its coursing loud in my ears.

What have you brought for me, Yang, in the dead of night? Nothing kindly.

By Christ he was fast and the thing was in my mouth before I could stop it because my jaws had opened in readiness for stress the instant he'd moved and he'd known that would happen and as I bit into his fingers a warning rang in my head not to bite the capsule because that's what it was and we've all held them in our mouths before to get an idea of the feel and the taste, biting his fingers, biting hard, my jaws locked and my teeth sharp and the blood coming as I broke through the flesh, and all the time the feel of the capsule lying at the side of my tongue with only the thickness of the glass between the cyanide and my nervous system, I've seen the stuff work, I saw that poor bastard Lazlö put one in his mouth in Parkis's office in London because we were going to throw him back across the frontier, gone down in five seconds with his skin turning blue and his fingers hooked and his teeth bared, so *this* was what Yang wanted them to think: that rather than wait for them to finish me off I'd done it my own way.

Monstrous strength, his other hand rising and thudding against the mattress with the force of an ax as I rolled my head clear and used a splay-hand into his eyes, their soft resilience against my fingertips as I drove them hard again and again as he jerked his head back but not fast enough, my teeth clamped and his blood running into my mouth until I swallowed and felt the capsule go with it into the safety of the alimentary canal, unbroken, the cyanide unreleased.

I won't have this. A sob came from him because of the pain of his eyes; he was blinded by now because he'd brought me to the edge of death and I'd had to work hard to get clear again. *I will not have this, do you understand, coming in here and trying to kill me, this is the fifth time you bastards have—* his hand tugging to get free of my teeth, his other hand slamming a sword edge for my throat and reaching it and producing great pain for an instant before I rolled half over and brought my knee into his groin and felt him rock back with his breath hissing. *I won't have it, it's too personal, too intimate, you're too fucking impudent to think you can come in here and splodge me out like a fly, it can't be done, I won't have it,* but great fear somewhere, too, fear for my life, its stimulus giving me the strength I would not have had without it, and now an end to this, my hand rising for his larynx and connecting easily because he was blind now and couldn't see its shadow in the shadows of the night, rising and driving against the cartilage and breaking it and going deeper as his head and body jackknifed and their dead weight came down on me and we lay like lovers, where no love ever was.

Sinitsin lit a cigarette.

"That won't be necessary. They won't send a new ambassador now; even the Americans have that much sense."

"But the Chinese premier," Major Alyev said with a certain deference, "will have to go?"

"Of course. But not by violence."

He was sitting in the only chair, a bamboo tripod with goatskin stretched across it; his two aides were on the long stone bench nearer the radio transceivers; the crippled interpreter was cross-legged on the floor, one foot sticking out at an odd angle and his head in a listening attitude. One of the

Korean guards was crouched on his haunches in the big arched entrance, facing away from the room with a submachine gun tucked under his right arm. There might have been other people there, but I couldn't be certain: This was as far as I could go along the flagstone passage without their seeing me.

The time was 11:54.

There had been a rough blanket in the cell, folded tightly and thrust into a niche in the wall, and I had spread it over the body on the mattress, leaving the head half-exposed; in the faint light it hadn't been possible to see where blood had stained the floor and the mattress; all I could do was increase the chances that if anyone shone a lamp through the oblong in the door they'd believe it was the Englishman lying there asleep.

The element of time was totally unpredictable. If anyone went along the passage to my cell they would see Yang was no longer there on guard, and would try to find him, sounding the alarm when they failed. That could happen within minutes from now, although the cell was at the end of a passage forming a cul-de-sac where only my guards would normally go. The latest deadline was an hour and six minutes from now, when Yang's relief took over the guard and saw he was absent. That would be at 01:00 hours tomorrow.

I stayed where I was for a few minutes longer, hoping to pick up evidence of anyone else's being in the room with the KGB party. Both transceivers were switched on, with their panels glowing: One would be waiting to receive Moscow; the other would be tuned to the Triad or the KGB group holding Tung Chuan. It was tempting to stay here in case a message came through, but time was already running out. Half an hour ago the chances of my taking any kind of action, even to save my own life, had been nil; but now that I was free to move through the monastery the situation was radically changed.

There were eleven men here, all of them armed. This was excluding Tung Kuo-feng. He was the key.

His quarters were at the far end of this passageway and across the courtyard where they'd taken me out and stood me against the wall. I went in that direction now, moving on my bare feet in total silence. Not far from the pagoda there was a small fountain in a basin carved from the solid rock, and I stopped to lean over the water's surface and plunge my face where the moon's reflection lay afloat, opening my mouth and cleansing his blood from it, drinking deeply and slaking my bruised skin with its cooling touch, my body hunched at the basin's rim like a beast at a waterhole, easing the ravages of the hunt before moving on.

There was a guard mounted outside Tung's quarters, the white stripes of his track suit showing up against the stones of the building; I could see the blunt shape of the submachine gun slung from his shoulder as he moved into full moonlight toward the parapet that overlooked the mountain slopes, tossing a cigarette butt across the wall and standing there for a moment and then moving on, stalking his own squat shadow, his track shoes making no sound. A patch of light shone from a grilled aperture in the building, catching the hammered brass of a gong against the wall inside. I couldn't see Tung Kuo-feng, but he would be there, because the guard was there.

I listened. From the reaches of the slopes an owl gave voice, and I could hear the faint ringing of bells as goats moved; but they were far away. Behind me the small fountain splashed, and I listened to that sound particularly: It was between where I was standing and the distant arches of the monastery where Sinitsin and his aides kept their vigil at the radios. If they were talking, their voices didn't carry this far. I stayed for minutes, because this was important, and as I listened I watched the Korean pacing between the parapet and the lighted aperture; sometimes he looked up at the moon and halted, staring as if he'd only just seen it there; his face was white and shadowless in the flat light, a clown's face.

There was no way of reaching him from where I watched, in the shadow of the stone Buddha. I waited until he turned his back to retrace his steps toward the parapet, then I moved nearer, crossing the open space and risking his turning and seeing me; at this stage, risks had to be taken, and they were not small; they had to be taken because Tung was the key.

I waited again, in shadow; when the guard turned and paced back toward me I drew fully into cover and watched the edge of his own shadow flowing in rhythmic patterns across the uneven flagstones as he came nearer. During the time I'd been watching him, he hadn't come as far as the corner of the building here, but he might do it now, and if he did, there wouldn't be time to reach deeper cover; I'd have to confront him, and there wouldn't be much chance: His hand was near the trigger of that bloody thing and he'd only have to swing it toward me and there'd be nothing I could do.

I watched his shadow as it neared; his movement was no longer soundless; I could hear the soft wincing of his rubber soles and the faint brushing of his legs as the inner seams of the track suit rubbed against each other. He was so close now that I could smell gun oil. If he came right to the corner here I wouldn't have time to jump him before he put out some shots, and even if he missed me the sound would bring the others.

Wincing of the rubber soles, smell of oil, and the thought that I shouldn't have taken a risk so big so soon, that being suddenly free had made me overconfident: It was a classical syndrome. His shadow came on, and when an owl called from the bell tower my scalp shrank and I drew a breath sharply, and then the barrel of the gun swung in a half-circle as he turned and his shadow moved away, flowing across the stones obliquely in front of him and becoming smaller.

I broke cover and stood there watching his back and judging the distance and the terrain and the state of its surface and its acoustic properties and the number of steps it would need for me to take him down at this precise point and in total silence without the heavy submachine gun hitting the stones and alerting the other guards. Then I moved back into cover because it was no go; the distance and the terrain and the acoustics were all in my favor, but I would have to go for him alone and I couldn't do that, because of the moon; I'd have to take my shadow with me and he'd see it before I was close enough and when I jumped him I'd be jumping straight into the gun. No go.

From here he looked smaller.

A minute ago the owl that had called earlier from the bell tower had lifted, beating its soft wings three times and then dropping in a long slow glide to the rocks below the parapet, uneasy about my presence.

The Korean looked smaller because from this height his body was foreshortened, twelve feet or so below where I crouched on the roof of the pagoda. It had taken me some time to reach here, climbing the thick flowering vine and testing each glazed tile of the roof before I put my weight on it. The time was now 12:06 and I was sweating uncomfortably because the gap was narrowing and there was so much to do, yet I mustn't hurry: To hurry would be dangerous.

To delay would also be dangerous.

The man below me paced with his gun. All the salient factors were the same now except one. The terrain was the same, and from this height I could take him down even more easily, and do it without the gun hitting the stones if I got the angle right; and now I could do it alone, before he saw my shadow—*if I could do it blind*. This was my worry now, and it was in the form of a linear pattern: At the precise place where I could most easily drop on him, the moon and my head and the flagstone immediately in front of him would be lined up, and he'd see my shadow. I would have to watch him nearing below me, then move back and wait, judging the time and then dropping at once and almost blind, seeing him only as I went down.

I didn't like that, and the sweat was prickling on me as the watch on my wrist pulsed indetectably. To hurry and to delay were both dangerous, and for the first time since I'd left London I wondered if I was losing my nerve. It can happen, during a chain-action mission when there's no time between phases to relax. Stress is cumulative, and these people had been hounding me from the minute I'd seen Sinclair fished out of the Thames eight days ago. Stress is also at its highest when there is frequent killing: The theory is that when we go into the field we know we're moving into hazard and we've done it before and we know how to cope and we're ready to kill if we have to, rather than not go home; but in practice it doesn't work like that: When they come at us and we get away with it there's no relief, just the feeling of *Christ, that was close,* while the stress builds up in the nerves and that bloody little pest somewhere deep in the organism starts sniveling, *We ought to go home now,* raising the small and trembling voice that we learn to loathe because we know it's the voice of cowardice. You can call it caution if you like, but we know better—if we had any sense of caution in our souls, we wouldn't be out here at all.

Night thoughts.

Ignore.

Death thoughts.

Let them come.

Let 'em come, my brave lads, let nothing you dismay, the bugle's sounding and the flag's a-flutter in the wind, so let 'em come, my boys . . . but it's not like that anymore and it's not like that when you're alone and the notes of the bugle fade and the colors of the flag grow dark in the shadows of night and all you can see is his squat foreshortened body and the barrel of the gun sticking out and the moon's light on his white clown's face as you wait and count off the time and then kick forward from the edge of the tiles—oh come on for Christ's sake it's quite simple *but I might have got it wrong* as I drop and go down and take my fear with me, ice in the gut, watching his gun, death on my breath, all the way down, all the way down.

XXVII
STORM

❖

Tung Kuo-feng sat perfectly still.

"My son is precious to me," he said in his toneless English. "Our line stems from the Ch'ing dynasty, and he is my eldest."

I said nothing.

"They knew that," he said with his night-dark eyes brooding on mine. "That is why they abducted him."

For an instant I saw a sinuous shadow moving toward him across the flagstones; then it was gone. This time it was not a dream.

The submachine gun lay in the corner of the small ornate room under a folded tapestry he'd taken down from the wall. The body of the Korean guard was among the rocks below the parapet; in the pocket of his track suit I'd found some book matches and a half-empty packet of cigarettes; they were all the tools I would need.

Tung had asked me nothing when I'd called his name a few minutes ago through the grilled aperture and said I must talk to him. Seeing the gun and the empty courtyard, he knew what must have happened. Now we sat facing each other in

the lotus position on the Thai silk carpet. I had asked him
how much he valued his son's life, and he'd answered me.

"There's a chance I can save him," I said now.

"Was there a message?"

He meant from Ferris, on the radio.

"There was a message," I said, "from Moscow."

"How do you know?"

He alone here spoke English, the only language he believed
I understood. Only he could have told me there'd been a message from Moscow.

"It was the message we listened to in there, last night. It
was about Tung Chuan, your son. Remember?"

He lifted his head, his back straightening slightly, and the
movement was almost startling: It was like a reptile moving,
after that total stillness. "You understand Russian?"

"Perfectly."

His eyes burned: He'd lost face; I'd deceived him.

"What did the message say?"

"That there's a chance I can save your son."

"What did it say, in words?"

I could feel the force in him, as I'd known I would. He was
going to fight me on this issue of the message. I attacked at
once.

"I'm not giving you the actual words, and if you try forcing
them out of me in any way you'll lose the last chance of saving
your son, because only I can do it, and only if I can work
extremely fast."

He was silent, watching me. I didn't envy him the decision
he had to make. If he could force me to give him the exact
message he could signal his Triad and repeat it, using a speech
code of his own, and they could go straight to Kimpo Airport
and wait for Tung Chuan to arrive. But how long would it
take to make me talk, if he could do it at all?"

"Why is time so important?" he asked me, his tone strident.

"At any minute they're going to find my cell unguarded.
They'll tear the whole place apart, looking for me. Before that
happens I must get away. Otherwise I can't save your son."

The air was trembling, and I wanted to close my eyes, but that would be dangerous: I mustn't give him ground.

"Where is my son?"

The air shuddered and I was appalled.

He'd made his decision: He would force me to talk, and he'd do it without wasting time.

"I don't know."

If his Triad could free his son, he would never have to do what I was here to make him do. *Jade One* had become a double mission: It wasn't enough to halt Tung's operation; the damage to Chinese-American relations was already too great. We had to make him expose the instigators: the Soviets. I was here to do a deal with him.

Reptilian stillness, his eyes on mine, dark, shimmering with an inner light, the sound of soundlessness shaking the air and drumming softly against my ears as the force in him rose like a storm.

"Where is my son?"

"They're going to—"

Christ alive, don't let him do this.

"They are going to what?"

His voice came through the drumming air like a shaft of thunder aimed at my head and I shook it away, dragging in breath, my own *prana,* my own *ki,* you're not the only one, damn you—

"You're not the only one!"

"What are you saying?"

The gong on the wall vibrating, pushing out rings of sound, waves of brass vibration that boomed in my head while I sat there staring into the dark shimmering eyes, *look away,* his terrible reptilian stillness at the heart of the storm, *look away—*

"Where is my son?"

His voice crashed over me like waves over a rock and the rock shuddered and I was afraid, crouching under the onslaught of the force he was gathering in him and hurling

against me, *look away,* yes, *look away,* the patterns on the
Thai silk carpet, a sea of leaves with white beasts leaping,
leaping but never moving, suddenly still, the air clearing,
you'll lose your—

"*Where is he?*"

Huge waves beating me back, beating me down under their
darkness. "You'll kill him like this! I'm the only one who can
save him, and you're trying to—"

"*Where is my son?*"

Crashed against me and flung me back and I hit the wall
and fell down and got up and fell down and got up and started
staggering, *where is he,* behind me, *don't let him,* I suppose
I was a bloody fool to shove that gun in the corner, I should
have kicked the fucking door down and shot him right between the fucking eyes, that would have shown him what
was—steady, we need to think, we need to stop waste, stop
wasting—

"*Time—you're wasting time.* Listen to me, damn you, I
can't save him if you waste my time like this. You're killing
him like this, don't you understand? *Because I'm not going
under,* I don't care what you—"

"*Where is he?*"

Wave crashed and I went under, black water rising, crashing again, but could swim all—

"*I can swim—listen to me, I'm not going under,*" dragging
in breath, not frightened now but very angry. "Tung Kuo-
feng," I said, and looked down at him, swaying and looking
down at him in the middle of the room, "you tried it and it
didn't work," head hammering like a brass gong but I knew
now, "it didn't work, you understand," knew I was all right
now and even the anger going because he looked so terribly
pale, trick of the light perhaps, white as anything, and terribly
still. "If you want your son to live, you've got to let me go
and see to it. Now, is that message loud and clear?"

Not swaying anymore, but rather weak—never mind, be
better in a minute, but by Christ I could have kicked his face

in because I had an operation to run and time was of the essence, very much of the essence, my watch said 12:29.

"Listen to me. *Do you want me to save Tung Chuan?*"

I noticed his face was running with sweat, and deathly pale.

"Yes." His voice was perfectly normal.

"I'm not sure I want to. You're giving me a lot of trouble. Are you going to give me any more trouble?"

"No."

"Well that'll be a nice change." I walked round the room a bit, finding my feet again, rotten headache but not surprising, covered in sweat, stinking with it, damn him, what did he want to go and do that for, bloody great brass gong, I wanted to kick it, bring it down off the wall with a bloody great *boom, boom, boom*, steady for Christ's sake, it's over now and we've got to get moving. "Listen," I said to him, "I've come here to do a deal. Tung Chuan's life for exposing the Soviets, and I can't give you long to think it over."

"I will do anything," he said.

I stopped walking about and looked down at him. He'd aged ten years in the last six minutes. I suppose it took an awful lot of effort to throw that much force around, served him bloody well right.

"It's going to be up to you," I told him. "You make one false move and Tung Chuan won't live. One false move. Just one. For Christ's sake get that into your head." I crouched on my haunches in front of him. "I'm getting out of this place now, or I'm going to try. You've got that submachine gun in the corner there, and there's another one behind the Buddha at the end of the passage where they had me in that cell, you know where that is?"

"Yes."

"If you need them, use them."

"Both?"

"What? One at a time, of course." Wild laughter ringing out, somewhere inside what he'd left of my head; long time since I'd heard a joke. "I don't want either of them, that's why I'm leaving them to you. I'm not going to try shooting my way out of here, because you might get killed by a stray bullet, and you're one end of the deal, remember. Besides, you can never do anything really useful with a gun."

I straightened up and tried to think, still a bit wobbly but managing well enough now. "It's your job to stay alive, you understand? That's the deal. They won't connect you with my getting out of here—you've been sitting here praying on your bloody mat all night and you never heard anything happening to the guard. As far as they're concerned, you're still in charge of the Triad and your operation's still going and you've got the next assassination set for noon tomorrow, or that's what you told me. All that's going to happen is that I'm going to get away, in order to save my own skin. Nothing to do with you."

What else? Something else. I wish I didn't feel so bloody tired, suppose I lack protein, bean curd's not the answer, you can stick it. Yes, "Listen, if we can get your son away from the KGB unit we'll keep him under guard till you've honored your part of the deal." Banner headlines, we're interrupting our scheduled program to bring you this flash, so forth, *Soviets Responsible for Peking Assassinations. World Shock at Terrorist's Exposure.* "Sometime before dawn," I told him, "we'll be sending in paratroopers to pull you out of here, understand? I can't take you with me, there's too much risk. Hide somewhere until they come, and use the guns on Sinitsin if you have to. *Stay alive.* That's the deal, understand?"

"Yes." He got up and stood facing me. "How will you escape?"

"None of your bloody business."

I left him, checking the courtyard and using shadow cover, my bare feet silent across the stones.

XXVIII

FIREBALL

✿

I stood in the jungle shadows, with the moon's light dappling the ground through the filigree pattern above my head. Then I went forward, stopping for a few seconds to listen.

The luminous digits of my watch cast a faint glow across the hairs on my wrist: 12:48. In twelve minutes they would relieve the guard on my cell, and see that Yang was gone.

I looked upward, and the moon's light burst against my eyes from the edge of the big black cross. I listened again, and then looked for a foothold, swinging upward with one hand on the grip. The fuel cap was now within reach and I unscrewed it, putting it in my pocket so that it shouldn't fall and make a noise. Then I opened my jacket and took the book matches and lit the cigarette.

There were two Russian Mil Mi2's standing side by side under a single camouflage net, with only a few feet of clearance between their rotor radii; I'd seen this much when they'd brought me in from the mountains. This was the biggest area of flat ground anywhere near the monastery, but it wasn't ideal: There wasn't room for one of these things to be pushed clear of the other in an emergency, because of the parapet walls.

When I had arranged the cigarette and the matches, I climbed down and made my way toward the second machine, pulling myself up and opening the door quietly. By the time I was sitting in the pilot's seat my watch showed 12:56. I'd left rather late, because that bastard Tung had decided to fight me for the information inside my head. The twelve minutes had narrowed to four.

I looked around the cabin. There were two seats forward and four behind, with the cyclic column and stick disposed for right-seat pilotage and the facia panel set centrally inside an antiglare hood. The general layout was much the same as the one we used for refresher training at Norfolk; the only differences would be in the operating requirements for the two GTD-350 turboshafts and the triple-bladed rotor.

A pair of string gloves was lying across the cyclic column: the pilot had sweaty hands. The navigational map was on the left seat, opened out and clipped to the board and showing South Korea. The radio display was central, with headsets hooked behind the seat squabs, and I found it tempting to switch the thing on and raise 5051 Hz and tell Ferris to alert the airport police at Kimpo and watch for Tung Chuan's party coming through; but the sound of my voice in the stillness could reach one of the guards, and if the embassy didn't answer immediately or if Ferris wasn't actually at the console I wouldn't have time to get the signal through before they came for me.

12:59

I thought I heard voices; perhaps I did; they probably came from the operations room where the two radios were: Twenty minutes ago when I'd crawled on my stomach below the parapet wall I'd heard Sinitsin talking in there. These weren't raised voices I was listening to.

The moonlight picked up silver crescents from the chrome rims of the reserve-fuel tank gauges; they should have been blacked over. Small sounds came as the landing-gear suspension shifted minutely under my weight, and I stopped moving and sat still and listened to the deep percussive rhythm of my heartbeat as the idea came to me that perhaps it wouldn't work; technically I was satisfied, but the psychological aspect was starting to worry me: I was resting the outcome of the whole mission on a single cigarette, and not because it was the best way but the only possible way; it wasn't that the odds were long, it was that the stakes were high.

Ignore.

01:00

Deadline.

Synchronize your watches, gentlemen, so forth: Maybe Yang's relief had his watch a bit slow.

The incandescent end of the cigarette should have reached the match heads by now.

Sweat. Sitting in my sweat.

Left it too late.

Ignore negative reactions and concentrate and look at the map. There wasn't enough light to see any of the figures, but I'd worked them out already from the data de Haven and I had been given at the U.S. Air Force base. Kimpo Airport, Seoul, was 224 kilometers from here and the max. cruise speed of this thing would be in the region of 200 kph and we'd need an hour and eight minutes to get there, giving us an ETA of 02:11 including a possible five-minute delay in getting this thing off the ground, which gave us a margin of seven minutes before Cathay Pacific flight 584 got the green from the tower and started rolling.

Seven minutes wasn't going to be long enough.

Thing is to keep control and remember that all we've got to do is get airborne and then raise the embassy and get Ferris to do the rest: He could put a NATO battalion into the field so long as communications with London held up.

Leave it to Ferris.

Look, do you really think you can just light a cigarette and sit back and—

Voices, and this time raised voices. It was 01:01; they'd missed Yang and now they'd start looking for him and they wouldn't take long to find him and then they'd start looking for me.

Running feet and more voices.

Give that bloody thing another two minutes to burn and then give it up and get out of here and take to the mountains and let them put the light out over the board for *Jade One* in London, but Jesus Christ I'd got close, I'd got bloody close.

Voices again, Sinitsin's among them now, *Where is he?,* so forth, he'd strip the hide off them for letting me get away.

01:02

Give it another minute. One more, and then if—

Fireball.

The camouflage net shivered as the chopper alongside rocked on its landing gear to the shock of the explosion as the tank went up and hurled flames into the night, their bright banners catching the net and firing it as I pushed open the cabin door and got ready to jump because if the whole lot went up I was getting out, stop panicking and shut that door and keep low before they see you, haven't you felt an explosion before, *get down.*

Voices again above the roar of the flames, and I dropped low behind the front seats because the pilots would be first here and there'd only be one thing they could try doing.

The night was orange now, with the flamelight flooding into the cabin and the net shaking as the men below started hacking at it with knives to free the rotor. Someone wrenched the door open and lunged in and dragged the extinguisher off its hook and threw it down to the others, shouting something in Korean. Then he swung out through the doorway and I saw the flash of a blade as he clambered onto the roof of the cabin; I could hear the tramping of his feet as he worked at the net, hacking it away from the rotor.

The night was full of cries, one of them shrilling as the flames caught a man. Black smoke was pouring from the chopper alongside and enveloping the cabin; two or three times I lifted my head but could see nothing but the darkness curdled with the light of the flames; the man on the roof was choking now in the thickening pall of smoke. Fire foam hit the Perspex window and a man shouted, quite close, words I didn't understand. Smoke began drifting into the cabin and I buried my face in my jacket and stayed absolutely still. Something smashed: I think the man had kicked the window in as he came dropping from the roof; I felt the machine lurch as he threw himself inside and slammed the door against the smoke; then the turbos began moaning.

The warm-up time for these things would be around three minutes but I didn't think we had that long; the fuel had sent a wash of flame across the ground and it was still spreading; there was the sickly smell of rubber on the air as the tires began burning. There was nothing much to think about as I crouched facedown in the dark: This was either going to work or it wasn't. There'd been a whole complex of unpredictable elements and it hadn't been possible to put them together and come up with any kind of certainty; it had just been the only thing I could do, short of putting Tung Kuo-feng at risk in a shoot-out. So I kept still and left it to karma, and listened to the rising moan of the turbos and then the sudden jerk as the rotor was cut in and began turning.

He wouldn't wait for all the needles to reach the green sectors—this wasn't standard takeoff procedure; but he'd need close to ninety percent rotor rpm and that was going to take another sixty seconds or more and there was nothing he could do about it except sit there with the flames washing under the wheels. Now that he was in the right-hand seat I could raise my head as far as the Perspex window, but couldn't see anything but figures darting through the smoke, their shadows thrown grotesquely against it by the livid orange of the flames. But the long blades of the rotor were getting up speed, and the smoke began surging lower in the downdraft until all I could see was the wash of flames beneath us; they were fanning out as the draft caught them, pulling them into a fiery disk and blowing the smoke clear of the area.

Through a gap between the seat and the cabin wall I could see through the undernose Perspex, where two men were dragging something blackened to the edge of the flames; then there was nothing but the flames themselves, flattening into a giant catherine wheel as the rotor picked up speed and the machine lurched as a tire burst, then steadied and began lifting with the bright disk of flame falling away below.

"Seoul," I told him, and dug my center knuckle hard into his spine at the fifth vertebra, jerking him forward and snapping his head back. "Kimpo Airport."

Most of his shock was at finding he wasn't alone, and his smoke-reddened eyes were wide as he moved his head to look at me. I bunched the knuckle again and drove it into the middle of his spine this time, sending a flash of pain through the central nerves.

"Kimpo Airport, Seoul."

Sweat shone on his face. The glow of the flames was dying away now, leaving the greenish illumination of the facia panel; when I looked into the windscreen I saw him watching my reflection, and shook my head slowly, meaning don't try anything; then he tapped the fuel gauge and looked up at me with a shrug, so I got the map on its clipboard and slammed it across his knees and jabbed a finger at Seoul and then hit the median nerve of his left arm enough to warn him because the fuel gauge was at half-full and that was ample for the run in to Kimpo and he knew it.

I got the headset off its hook behind the navigator's seat and started work on the radio panel, getting an answer in Korean from the embassy and then losing it two or three times because there was a hell of a lot of static from the rotors. We'd gained a thousand feet by now and he'd got the thing on an even keel but I wasn't trusting him: He was a fanatic and he wanted to put this machine down near the monastery again, even if it had to be on the roof, because Sinitsin and his group were now cut off.

Now 5051 Hz was answering again and the voice sounded English so I told them: *"Eagle to Jade One,"* and repeated it, but the static was appalling and I couldn't even tell whether it was Ferris responding or someone else.

The time was now 01:09 and I checked the airspeed indicator and gripped the pilot's fist, turning the throttle and telling him to stay at maximum speed, using words he didn't understand but a tone of voice that told him he had to do what I wanted. The floor shifted under my feet as the power came on, and I grabbed at the seat back and then tried to raise the embassy again. It was difficult to tell if they were getting my signal with any clarity, so I left the set open and kept on repeating what I wanted them to know.

"Eagle to Jade One. Hostage Tung Chuan and KGB captors due to board Cathay Pacific flight 584 from Seoul to Pyong-yang ETD 02:18. You must stop them and take Tung Chuan alive. This is ultrapriority, this is ultrapriority," my voice probably unintelligible, reaching them in an ocean of static, while the red light came up on the facia panel and the reflection of the smoke-blackened pilot's face watched me impassively from the windscreen, *"Eagle to Jade One, can you hear me?"*

I bent over the map and read the call sign for Kimpo tower and switched to that wavelength and tried to raise them with the call sign for the aircraft, but all I could get was slush, the red light beginning to worry me now so I looked at it and saw it wasn't on the facia panel, it was at the edge of the curving windscreen, the bastard had been turning full circle all the time and that was the fire down there, the one at the monastery—

"Turn this bloody—"

He'd been waiting for it and his bunched fist drove in at groin level and impacted on the thigh as I twisted in time and lost balance and hit the tubular metal along the back of the seats and found him rising against me with both his hands out and reaching for the throat. The deck was tilting badly and we both lurched sideways and the pilot's headset swung clear of its hook and struck my face, blinding me on one side before I could get my balance back and block him as he came in again while thunder broke out as the rotor tips went through the sound barrier and the whole machine started shuddering to the vibration.

Kaleidoscope of images in the glow from the facia lamps—his squat body frantic to get at me as the deck tilted again, tilted and swung down with the blades crackling and the seats shaking on their stanchions, his face suddenly looming as he got close with his hands hooking, catching my jacket and dragging me down across the cyclic column, and now the whole thing went wild as the deck came up and threw us both across the seat squabs with my shoulder crashing past the bulkhead and bouncing me the other way and straight into him, a chance in a thousand and I used a sword hand and found his neck and did it again and saw him pitch back into the Perspex window, did it again with the deck tilting me and lending me extra force till he wasn't there anymore but somewhere below me as the cabin began spinning slowly under the rotor and the deck came up and then sank and went on sinking as I tried to find the controls and couldn't manage it because of the angle, tried to get a grip on something, on anything, finally found the cyclic and brought it upward, twisting the throttle down a degree and feeling the sudden pause as the rotor steadied and the cabin stopped spinning and I slumped into the seat and trimmed the aircraft, locking the column on automatic and turning to see what had happened to the Korean.

He was watching me steadily, and I turned away and settled down in the pilot's seat, checking the compass and bringing the machine in a slow swing toward the northwest and then putting its nose down and going for maximum speed with the tips just this side of the barrier. After a minute the nerves in my spine began crawling, and I turned round and closed his eyelids and then faced forward again, concentrating on the compass and feeling with one hand for the headset and putting it on.

5051 Hz

"Eagle to Jade One."

Nothing but static when I switched to receive.

Time was 01:17—we'd lost eight minutes in turning back to the monastery and I doubted, I very much doubted now, that I could get this thing to Kimpo in time to do anything physically about the Cathay Pacific: I'd have to leave it to Ferris now, if I could raise him.

"Eagle to Jade One."

Nothing but static.

XXIX

5 8 4

❁

He came in at 02:12.

"Jade One to Eagle."

There was still some static, but the lights of Seoul were crowding against the undernose Perspex window and the distance was closing in toward zero.

I told him again: *Cathay Pacific 584.*

"It's too late," he said.

"Phone the airport," so forth.

His voice faded and came back. I suppose he meant it was too late to get there himself, from the embassy.

We had six minutes. I tried to think we still had a chance, but we didn't. The security people wouldn't move that fast: They'd want to know what authority he had; anyone can ring up an airport and start a panic.

I swung the Mi2 into the approach path, watching the cluster of lights moving into the nose window.

"Eagle to Jade One. Do what you can."

Then I checked the map and switched to the approach control channel at 121.3 MHz and gave them my call sign.

They came back immediately.

"HK-9192: You will turn southwest and hold clear of the field."

I throttled back and crab-flew for thirty seconds to see what the situation was on the runways, acknowledging and switching to Landing Control.

"HK-9192: You will make an immediate turn and keep clear of the field."

I didn't acknowledge yet.

Things didn't look normal down there. I could see a DC-10 moving toward the main runway, but along one of the intermediary paths. Security-control lights were flashing in half a dozen places as road vehicles crawled from the terminal toward the marker lights.

I tried the traffic channel and got voices.

". . . are ordered to keep their distance." A burst of static as I trimmed the rotor and settled at a hundred feet over the perimeter road, then it cleared again. *"Repeat, are ordered to keep their distance. This is a hijack situation."*

The jet was moving onto the runway and turning right, with the wind, its green-striped tail catching the light as one of the security vehicles closed in and then stopped at the edge of the runway.

Cathay Pacific.

The time was 02:27 and she was behind schedule—but then, the schedule had been wrecked anyway. I just began speaking, with no call sign.

"Is that flight 584 on the runway?"

Landing Control came back. *"Yes. This is a hijack situation."*

"Are the passengers on board?"

"No passengers. Only the crew and the hijackers." Then a break came and a different voice said: *"This is Security. Who are you? Please give your call sign."*

American accent. He said something else, but it wasn't to me: I could see a light aircraft toward the south, with its

strobe pricking the dark. Below me the DC-10 was turning
at the end of the runway, against the wind sock. Through the
side window I caught a line of flashing light as more security
vehicles moved into the airport from the city.

I kept the Mi2 hovering at a hundred feet between the
perimeter road and some hangars and watched the big DC-10
sitting at the end of the runway, facing into wind.

So Ferris had done something. I'd told him ultrapriority
and he'd known I'd meant it and he must have done the only
thing he could have done to get Airport Security onto the
KGB party coming through with their hostage: He'd gone
direct to NATO's Military Emergency Center with an alert
signal and then told them what he wanted.

But Airport Security had been too late.

It must have been one of the crew the KGB had taken as
their hostage. The captain. Or the whole crew, as they'd
walked out to the aircraft.

I hit the radio again and got voices.

"CP 584 to Tower: Do I have clearance for takeoff?"

There was a wailing noise in the background, covering
some of the speech. Sirens somewhere. I kept the machine
steady, watching the red flashes moving past the main terminal
as three vehicles cruised down past the fire station.

"CP to Tower: Do I have clearance?"

His voice was tight.

Another voice now, coming through the wail of the sirens,
Ukrainian accent: *"You will keep the runway clear. We are
taking off."*

"Jesus Christ," someone said, then the set crackled.

I watched the big jet with its green-striped tail starting to
roll as the brakes came off.

"You will keep the runway clear. We are taking off."

I counted five emergency vehicles standing along the edge
of the runway, none of them beginning to move. I looked up
and watched the tower, but couldn't see anything behind the
dark green glass. The telephones would be jammed in there,

with Traffic Control trying to get authority to stop the Cathay Pacific, and Airport Security trying to get an advisory from the metropolitan police.

I looked down again and watched the DC-10 gathering speed, the red splashes of light from the emergency vehicles staining its white fuselage.

I do not need to tell you, Tung Kuo-feng had said, *what such a* volte-face *would mean: the immediate destruction of the American-Chinese-Japanese bloc and a massive Soviet-Chinese threat to the West. The next two actions I shall under-take on behalf of the Soviets will bring this about within a matter of days, unless you can prevent it.*

The DC-10 was rolling faster.

They didn't have the background data in the tower. They saw this as nothing more than a hijack. Otherwise they'd block the runway, send every vehicle in, and stop the jet.

You could avert enormous danger, Tung Kuo-feng had told me as the tendril of smoke from the incense bowl had climbed past the face of the Buddha, *for many people.*

The wail of a siren came again above the steady chopping of the rotor above my head as another vehicle went swerving through the security gates and slowed toward the runway.

You must find my son, Tung Kuo-feng had said.

The emergency vehicle had stopped. They were all stopped, all of them, everywhere. The runway was clear, with the big jet rolling fast toward takeoff.

The dead man behind me fell forward and hit the back of the seat as I shifted the stick and put the machine into a fast emergency dive from a hundred feet across the roofs of the hangars and the line of flashing red lights and along the rubber-scarred strip of the runway until the long white fuse-lage of the DC-10 was sliding backward across the Perspex window below the nose and vanishing behind the Mi2 as I held it in the dive for another five seconds and then dragged the stick back and went for a dead-drop landing halfway down the runway and a hundred yards in front of the jet. The

cabin shuddered as the nose came up and the blades of the
rotor thrashed the air, and three red lights began winking on
the facia panel as I put the machine through a barrage of
stress it hadn't been designed for; then it was down and rolling
to a stop and I cut the turbo and sat watching the huge shape
of the DC-10 as it began closing in until its twin landing
lights came on and I had to jerk my head away from the glare.

I sat waiting, caught in a wash of frozen light and feeling
the panic flooding into me as the roar of reverse thrust came
slamming against the onslaught of sound, trapped in a drum
and hearing my own voice silenced as I went on shouting,
some kind of reason coming back as the panic spent its force
and I just sat watching the flood of dazzling light bringing
everything into knife-edge relief: the instrument panel and the
curved Perspex and the breakaway hinges of the door and the
dead arm lying across the other seat with its hand dangling
and its fingers pointing nowhere.

There hadn't been time to break out of here and run. I
could have run the wrong way, got blotted out like a beetle.
But I wanted something to do while I waited, and there was
nothing I could do except sit here and leave it to karma: It
will stop, or it will not stop; I will die, or I will not die.

Thunder in the night, and the blinding white of lightning.

The cabin shook, its Perspex tinged now with the red of
emergency lights as vehicles began moving in.

Uproar and dazzle, while the mind tried to stay calm. Then
fear, cold and shivering and primeval as I looked upward and
saw the huge shape of the thing towering against the night
sky while its bellowing shook the earth, and then I was working automatically, ripping the pins from the hinges and kicking the doors out and hunching low across the front seats with
my head in my hands as the impact came and its force
wrenched the machine sideways with the scream of metal on
metal as the jet's landing gear caught the tail of the Mi2 and
the main weight of the DC-10 passed on, veering toward a
group of hangers as I bounced off the wall of the cabin and

smashed through the jagged Perspex on the other side with one hand clinging and finding a grip and swinging me round before the edge of the Perspex came away and I went down, rolling through debris and finding my feet and beginning to run as the big jet ploughed across the grass median between the runway and the taxiing path, smashing away a radar dish and overturning a fire truck and hitting an earth bank and spinning slowly with its huge tail section crashing sideways against the steel doors of a hangar and breaking open the rear of the fuselage at right angles before it came to a halt.

I ran fast. Two emergency vehicles overtook me and a man shouted but I didn't hear what he said. The night was loud with sirens and bright with red as the lights moved in toward the jet. I kept on running. A man in police khaki tried to stop me as I neared the plane but I broke free and ran on, clambering up the sheared and twisted wreckage of the airframe and finding a way in. There was some gunfire forward and I saw the silhouette of a crew member knocking another man down in the center aisle. Much nearer me was a Caucasian with his neck broken, half-buried among shattered bottles and cups that had burst through the doors of the catering hatches. Then I saw the Chinese, getting off the floor with one shoulder bright with blood.

I steadied him. "Tung Chuan?" I asked him.

He was in shock, his young eyes staring into my face.

"Are you Tung Chuan?"

He went on staring, then nodded slowly.

"Tung Chuan," he said.

I began leading him out of the plane.